TILT

Creative Interventions in Global Politics

Series Editors:
shine choi, Cristina Masters,
Swati Parashar and Marysia Zalewski

The landscape of contemporary global politics is complex and oftentimes violent. Yet the urgency to provide solutions or immediate practical actions to this violence oftentimes leads to inadequate knowledge. This is despite the abundance of theoretical, conceptual and methodological tools available—much of this produced through conventional academic disciplines, notably International Relations, Political Theory and Philosophy. But the constraints imposed on these traditional disciplines profoundly limit their ability to incorporate and make effective use of more creative and innovative methodologies found in other disciplines and genres.

This series provides a unique opportunity to offer creative intellectual space to work with an eclectic and rich range of disciplines and approaches including performative methodologies, storytelling, narrative and auto-ethnography, embodied research methodologies, participant research, visual and film methodologies and arts-based methodologies.

Titles in the Series

TILT

A Novel on Intergenerational Trauma

MEGHANA V. NAYAK

ROWMAN & LITTLEFIELD
Lanham • Boulder • New York • London

Published by Rowman & Littlefield
An imprint of The Rowman & Littlefield Publishing Group, Inc.
4501 Forbes Boulevard, Suite 200, Lanham, Maryland 20706
www.rowman.com

86-90 Paul Street, London EC2A 4NE, United Kingdom

British Library Cataloguing in Publication Information Available

Library of Congress Cataloging-in-Publication Data

Names: Nayak, Meghana, author.
Title: Tilt : a novel on intergenerational trauma / Meghana V. Nayak.
Description: Lanham : Rowman & Littlefield, 2024. | Series: Creative
  interventions in global politics | Includes bibliographical references.
Identifiers: LCCN 2024025816 (print) | LCCN 2024025817 (ebook) | ISBN
  9781538187418 (cloth) | ISBN 9781538187425 (paperback) | ISBN
  9781538187432 (epub)
Subjects: LCSH: Generational trauma—Fiction. | LCGFT: Psychological
  fiction. | Novels.
Classification: LCC PS3614.A9357 T55 2024 (print) | LCC PS3614.A9357
  (ebook) | DDC 813/.6—dc23/eng/20240627
LC record available at https://lccn.loc.gov/2024025816
LC ebook record available at https://lccn.loc.gov/2024025817

CONTENTS

1

Autumn

TILT

Ranjeet grabbed Kavya's face from behind her and twisted it. He forced her to turn to him. "What is your problem?" he growled.

Kavya pleaded in a trembling voice, "Nothing, I swear."

His long fingers dug into her jaw and neck. "Look at you," he jeered. "Crying again! Are you made of tears or something?"

She wanted to soothe him out of his fury. She reached her palm to his face. It was watery and viscous. She immediately snatched back her hand and looked at it. Small strips of flesh stuck to her fingers. *What the hell?*

Before she could say a word, he pushed her into the closet. She heard the familiar click of the lock. *Stay quiet. Don't make him mad.* She picked the pieces of his skin off her fingers. *What is this?*

Then, she stumbled. As if the floor had buckled. She grabbed at the wall.

The floor started to tilt. Her stomach dropped. Her feet began to slide down the floor. *Oh God!* She looked down to see that the ground was perfectly still. But she could not stand. What had he done?

She opened her mouth to scream. No sound came out, no matter how hard she tried. *I'm going to run out of air. I can't get air. Help me!*

This time, he wasn't letting her out.

* * *

Kavya opened her eyes. Her entire body was tense. Her shirt was wet. Drenched in sweat, again. She quickly sat up, turned on the lamp, and blinked several times.

She reached for her cup of water waiting on the nightstand. *It was just a dream. I am safe now. He is gone. I will never see him again.* Another sip. *It was just a dream.* Sip by sip, her heart rate slowly returned to normal.

As was her routine for too many nights over the last several weeks, she stumbled into the bathroom to wash her face and pat her neck with a cool washcloth.

Back in her room, she changed into a new shirt and glanced at the clock.

3:45 a.m.

Fuck!

She knew how this went. The day after a nightmare was always filled with panic attacks or uncontrollable sobbing. Which would it be today? Should she cancel her plans?

Kavya was still tossing and turning under her blanket at 6 a.m. She slid to the other side of the bed. The light streamed through the blinds and made zebra patterns on her arm. She reached for the photo on the nightstand, one of the few professional shots of her family.

In the picture, her twin boys were a gangly eight years old, arms wrapped around Kavya's waist. Kabir looked right at the camera, confident and mischievous. His sleepy eyes, toothy smile, and dimpled chin made him a spitting image of Kavya. Samir, on the other hand, was the cherubic twin, with his round-tipped nose and chubby cheeks. He was gazing up at Kavya in the photo. Fitting, as he had always been the clingier of the two, still calling her Mama to this day.

This picture was from a decade ago, back when all three of them had lived with her best friend Janet in Texas. Now, her boys were almost-men away at college, hopefully unaware that their mother had turned into a madwoman.

* * *

A few hours later, Kavya took the R train to the F line to Prospect Park. As she made her way through the subway station, she scanned her body. Okay, so far. She could have a perfectly good day with her friend, just as she'd planned. She strummed the railing of a black metal fence as she emerged from the stairwell onto the street.

Without warning, her chest became unbearably tight, as if someone was pulling at the laces of a corset. She placed her hand on her sternum and took a deep, shaky breath.

She could see her friend Mingming at the park entrance looking intently at her phone, her sleek black hair tied neatly into a high ponytail.

Kavya's heart pumped harder as she waited at the intersection. She shifted from one leg to another, switching her purse to the other shoulder.

She looked at the couple next to her, trying to use the grounding exercises her therapist had taught her. *Find all the red items of clothing. Identify scents. Look at the details.*

Okay, here was a detail. This tall white man was picking his nose while pretending to just scratch it. He tossed whatever he dug out right in front of Kavya's feet. She stared up at him in disgust. The woman holding onto his arm was gorgeous, with dark brown skin, cascading black hair, and impeccable style. She turned and looked Kavya up and down with a slight scowl on her face, with that penetrating gaze South Asian folks sometimes gave each other instead of just trading familiar smiles.

Kavya raised her eyebrows. *What are you looking at? No one wants your ugly-ass man and his boogers.* Ha! Unsolicited petty thoughts totally meant she could have a regular day.

The light turned green. Kavya stepped off the curb and walked forward.

She was almost at the other side.

And then she swayed. Like she was suspended in air. That unnerving lightheaded sensation took hold of her again. The top of her scalp threatened to peel off and float away. *No, not now.*

Ahead, the light turned yellow. She stood still and held her arms out, trying to balance. *Don't fall!* A rush of air as a bicycle whizzed past her. Cars honked. She choked on the sob caught at the base of her throat, letting out a whimper as voices rang out.

"What are you doing?"

"Move!"

Slam! Something jolted her body, snapping her neck forward and back at the same time. A sharp object scraped roughly across her back. She tumbled. Her hands and knees landed hard against the road. A moped sped past her.

"Is she okay?"

Another car horn. She lifted one palm and examined it. It was bloody. Little pieces of gravel stuck out here and there.

"Kavya!" Mingming appeared next to her. She grabbed Kavya's arm, helped her up, and led her out of the street. "That moped driver hit you! He hit you! Are you okay?"

Kavya, stunned, let her friend take her to a bench. She gingerly sat down.

Mingming's face was etched with worry. Her deep black eyes bore into Kavya. "I'm taking you to urgent care," she commanded.

A string of thoughts unspooled as Kavya tried to stop shaking. She should have just taken Xanax before leaving the house. But sometimes the meds didn't kick in fast enough. Or made her too groggy. Sometimes she needed to prove to herself that she didn't need them. Her hands and knees stung. Was that blood soaking through her leggings? Her back was tender and pulsing.

What would happen next time?

Maybe a truck would plow into her. Or maybe she'd be at the subway station. Maybe she'd fall and get wedged in between the train and the platform. Her bones would crunch and splinter.

Mingming's frustrated groan interrupted her racing mind. "We have to *go*, Kavya. C'mon."

Kavya shook her head. "I've told you. My doctor already ruled out everything. It's just panic attacks." She pulled out hand sanitizer from her purse and exhaled through gritted teeth as she sprayed and cleaned her hands. She flicked tiny rocks from her palms.

"*Just* panic attacks? There's medication for that. What if the moped had been going faster, or you had fallen in front of a car? Huh?" Mingming's ponytail bounced indignantly.

Kavya opened her compact mirror. Her heavy-lidded eyes stared back blankly. Her wavy black hair going every which way, a few wiry gray hairs curled up along her ears. She looked sickly, her face wearing a greenish cast.

"I already have medication," Kavya finally answered. She snapped shut her compact. "I'm not going to keep adding drugs. No, thank you. I can barely go to work as it is."

Mingming pushed back. "What's causing the panic attacks then? It's been a while."

"I'm fully aware," Kavya retorted. "And I don't *know* what my problem is."

They sat in an uneasy silence and stared across the street at the movie theater they were supposed to go to. Kavya's face burned with the familiar sensation of shame. Here was Mingming on a precious Sunday afternoon—a time for rest from her torturous job at the law firm—babysitting her.

"Listen," Kavya said. "I'm sorry. Please go enjoy your day. I'm going to get a Lyft home."

"If you won't even take care of your injuries, then yeah, I'll take off." Mingming spoke quietly, with an edge of resignation or contempt, Kavya was not sure which. Her friend exhaled and then seemed to soften. "Please text me that you got home safe and then try to rest, yeah? Let me know if you need anything."

They stood up. Kavya suppressed a groan of pain. Mingming reached out to hug her and kissed her cheek instead.

When Kavya got home, she sent an apologetic text to Mingming. Peeling off her clothes, she climbed the stairs to the shower. She let the hot water beat down on her sore body. She cried as she scrubbed the dried blood off her knees.

After drying off and slathering antibacterial cream on her wounds, she slipped into a T-shirt and dragged herself downstairs to eat cold leftovers in front of the TV. She mindlessly watched and chewed as she sat, despondent. She was exhausted, as always after a panic attack. But she didn't want to go to bed only to be gripped by another nightmare.

Hours later, when she could no longer hold her eyes open, she finally went upstairs to sleep. She rested gingerly on her side, muscles throbbing, and stayed awake as long as she could.

At some point in the middle of the night, it happened again. Her brain held her hostage, taunting her dream-state with yet another terrifying scenario it had plucked from her life.

Ranjeet standing over her. The sensation of being smothered. Of struggling to breathe as something pressed down on her face.

Kavya opened her eyes, thrashing as she emerged from the dream.

She wanted to change her sweaty shirt, but all she could do was cry. Sharp pain traveled down her hips.

How was she supposed to teach today? This is what she got for thinking she could just hang out on a Sunday with Mingming like she used to. Before this hell began.

Mingming was her closest friend in New York, but it was Janet, still back in Texas, who held her heart. She stayed awake, breathing in and out as slowly as she could until it was a decent hour. Then she texted Janet, *I miss you. The panic attacks and nightmares are doing me in.*

Groaning, Kavya pushed herself out of bed. She walked to her window and peeked through the blinds, releasing a small cloud of dust as she did. She looked down from her second-story bedroom, watching the tops of people's heads as they walked to work, in straight lines, some even checking their phones or with headphones on.

She used to walk like that. At this time of year, she usually loved to step on the red and yellow leaves just as they were starting to curl up at the edges. And to take lazy strolls through Bay Ridge, her beloved Brooklyn neighborhood, to pick up knafeh from the Palestinian bakery. Along the way, she would run into her neighbors, like Erica, the effervescent and chatty yoga studio owner, or Camille, who knew everyone's business, or Naseem, the hardware store guy who talked her ear off about plumbing fixtures.

But pleasant walks were no longer hers. Sweet dreams and restful nights were no longer hers.

She massaged her neck. She could not fathom leaving the house without collapsing into tears. So, she grabbed her laptop and emailed her students to tell them that their International Relations class would be meeting online once again. She could barely hit send as the guilt overcame her.

Her phone rang. She picked it up and let out the breath she didn't know she was holding.

"Hey, you," Janet said in her perpetually raspy voice. "Tell me what's going on."

"Another nightmare about Ranjeet." Kavya's voice caught. "It's freaking 2022. We broke up in 2003! Why is this happening to me?"

"I know, it sucks," Janet said soothingly.

Kavya never told her about the other dreams about some of the other things that had happened to her, well before Ranjeet.

"So even when you're talking to me right now, you're having that kind of sideways feeling?" Janet asked.

"Not really. But I feel safe in my house. It's when I leave that all bets are off. I've cut back on hanging out with friends. Just Mingming." Even Mingming was going to get tired of her.

And then, in a small voice, Kavya added, "You know I've always had these anxiety problems. But this is something else. It's like I can't stay whole. And yesterday during a panic attack, I sort of got hit by a guy on a moped."

She continued quickly over Janet's gasp, as if trying to stay ahead of the frenzied thoughts flooding her brain, "What if I have to go on medical leave? What will happen to my career then? Academia is so cruel to disabled and ill people. I'm supposed to go up for tenure. Teaching is everything to me, and it's all screwed up now. Janet, I mean, shit, I feel alone."

"You are not alone," Janet replied, repeating what she had always said over the past thirty years of their friendship. Such a comforting phrase that would tenderly wrap itself around Kavya, while also cruelly reminding her that her own family was the reason Janet had to say it in the first place.

Skin

Kavya and Janet first met in 1993 as randomly assigned roommates their first semester at St. Edward's University in Austin, Texas. At first, Kavya wasn't sure they would even get along. But she soon discovered that Janet's severe bangs, pointed angry eyebrows, and hands-on-hips stance belied her gentleness and generous love.

They ate every meal together, giggled into the night, and attempted to study together but instead plotted prank wars against their suitemates. They went on road trips, like to Louisiana for a crawfish boil their friend's parents hosted over a long weekend, and to Houston for an outdoor Santana concert. They wrote coded messages to each other on the dry-erase board hanging outside of their dorm room.

But more than that, Janet was the first person to hear about Kavya's childhood. At least the details she could stand to share.

Even when it was Kavya's turn to soothe Janet's worries and to nurture her through break-ups with a string of girlfriends, Kavya saw her friend as one of those confident, witty sitcom stars. Beloved by all. Always in sweatpants, walking through the world casually and happily. You knew that her life would work out. She did not hide any darkness deep inside.

You knew she would be just fine if the weird sidekick friend was no longer around.

Janet's parents, Yumiko and Bob, and her younger brothers, Kenji and Bobby, also lived in Austin. Bob was an Episcopal priest who fought for more women to become priests and deacons. Yumiko managed not only to appear wherever needed in her community but also to run her own business as a tailor. They were *good* people. But most importantly, they delighted in their children and were abundant with their love. The whole family treated Kavya like she had been with them all along, while she fought the fear that she was their charity project.

Once, after one of many weekends the friends spent lounging at Yumiko and Bob's house, Yumiko dropped Janet and Kavya back off at the dorm with several containers of homemade gyoza and Japanese curry bread. The two friends watched a movie and then climbed onto their uncomfortable mattresses on wooden platforms atop cinder blocks.

In the safety of the dark, Kavya hesitated and then said, "This is going to sound creepy, but I swear I don't mean it that way."

Janet's voice came from the other side of the room. "Oh, well then, do tell!"

Kavya continued sheepishly, speaking to the shadows on the closet door in front of her, "I wish your family was my family."

"They *are* your family. You are not alone, Kav. I promise."

Janet's promise that night turned out to be genuine.

Three and a half years later, on a beautiful spring day to honor Janet and Kavya's college graduation, the two women walked into Yumiko and Bob's home for a celebratory brunch. Kavya's family was also invited.

Everyone sat around the formal dining table while Janet's brothers goofed around with a camcorder.

Kavya's aunt and uncle wore their sourpuss expressions the entire time. There sat Neela, with her Coke-bottle glasses and thinning, badly dyed hair tucked behind her ears, from which she hung cheap earrings from Target. And Pramod, with his uneven, too-small teeth, greasy face, and slicked back hair. She never thought of them as parents, even though they had adopted her when she was three years old. She was a burden for Pramod, a punching bag for Neela.

Kavya tried to ignore that terrible sensation that arose just from breathing the same air as Neela. She placed her hand on her stomach to settle that nauseating mixture of fright and disgust. *Forget them*, she told herself. Who needed them? They didn't deserve to celebrate her.

Her father, Mohan, could not come to the brunch because of work. The day before, Kavya had received flowers from him. She called to thank him. He didn't insult her like Neela and Pramod always managed to do, but he was disconnected as usual.

"You did a great job, Kavya," he had said on the phone, like he was trying to be sincere, like he was hoping she would find something tender in his generic words.

"Okay, thank you," she had responded, hoping that he would detect in her voice that she didn't think much of him. He was always hunched over, with perpetually droopy eyes. What right did he have to look so sad? He was the one who had abandoned her to his sister, Neela, too-soon after Kavya's mother died in a car crash. That man gave his own child to Neela like he was re-homing a dog.

And so, Kavya grew up with Neela and Pramod in a big, beautiful house atop the lush hills of Austin. A closet full of designer clothes. Violin lessons. Trips around the country and the world. But not one picture of her mother hanging anywhere in her well-appointed and perfectly coordinated pastel blue room. No commemoration of or even uttering a word about her mother.

Throughout her childhood, Mohan would come by every couple of months to silently drop off gifts or to join them for a meal. But they never spent any time together, just the two of them. Neela took up all the space with her thunderous thump-thump walk, her glasses magnifying her blazing, bloodshot eyes when she yelled. Kavya's father was only a shadowy figure at the edges of her life. Coward.

Bob clinked his fork against his glass, snapping Kavya out of her self-pity. His silver hair was brushed back, revealing an almost perfect peak on his forehead. His light brown eyes with their perpetually crinkled laugh lines beamed a loving light onto Janet.

"I want to toast these two beautiful young women," he started, in his deep, soporific voice. "As you know, I've accepted a call to ministry at a new church in Houston. And Janet's moving there, too. I'm grateful to God we will be together. But we are really going to miss Kavya. We think of Kavya, and you, Neela and Pramod, like family." He nodded to Kavya's aunt and uncle.

Neela gave him a wan smile. Pramod stared.

The heat of embarrassment surged through Kavya. Would it kill them to say something kind right now?

"And of course, congratulations to my sweetheart, Janet, for getting into a competitive master's program," Bob continued. "She will be the best graphic designer in the world."

"At least she is doing something worthwhile," Pramod interjected. "Kavya will be lucky to pay her bills. Gender studies!" He chuckled and looked around as if anyone would laugh along.

Bob stopped for a moment but quickly recovered. "Kavya is the college valedictorian, my friend. I fully expect her to take care of me and Yumiko in our retirement." He winked at Kavya. She tried to smile.

Bob subtly raised his eyebrows at Kenji and Bobby. Janet's brothers quickly turned on the camcorder and took turns pretending to have microphones in their hands.

"Where is our rock star going next?" Bobby asked.

Kavya gratefully leaned into the imaginary microphone. Tossing a withering look at Pramod, she gave her standard answer, "I'm getting my doctorate in Government at the University of Texas-Austin. I'm focusing on international relations, with additional coursework in gender studies. My research will be focused on these new gender guidelines that activists are proposing to facilitate the acceptance of asylum seekers escaping from gendered forms of persecution. That's because unlike race, nationality, religion, political opinion, and social group membership, gender isn't one of the accepted categories of persecution under international refugee law." She was sure to loudly enunciate "gender" each time she said it.

"What an important topic," Yumiko cheerily declared. She was almost as tall as Bob, and with her braided black-and-gray hair coiled around her head, her aquiline nose, and perpetual smile, Kavya thought she looked so regal. Like a kindhearted queen.

Bob patted Kavya's hand. "That's my girl," he said. "Cheers!"

She looked around the table and forced a small smile. Her aunt and uncle lifted their glasses when everyone else did but had nothing to add.

Kavya tried to wish away the hollowness that always appeared when she saw her uncle and aunt alongside Janet's gorgeous, overly attentive family.

Janet looked over at her and grinned. "I can't wait to see what's next for you, Kavya."

* * *

What was next was Ranjeet. They met during Kavya's third year of graduate school, when she had settled into a predictable albeit lonely existence without Janet and her family but at least with minimal contact with Mohan, Neela, and Pramod.

At first, Ranjeet seemed magical. His perfectly round, shiny black eyes looked like buttons on a teddy bear. His almost-pink full lips always in a smile. Even freshly shaven, bits of coarse stubble peeked through along his chin and jawline. He would rub his prickly face on her cheeks to make her giggle. When she confided in him about her father's abandonment and Neela's cruelty, telling him more than she had even told Janet, he listened and held her. He promised a new life. He was hurting too, still reeling from the death of his father. They would help each other.

But it was soon after they moved in together that things started to change. One day, Kavya mentioned in passing that she wanted to see a therapist for her ongoing struggles with claustrophobia. She was tired of taking the stairs instead of elevators.

Ranjeet smiled. "I know how to solve that."

He took her into the hallway closet as she tittered and picked at her nails nervously.

"What is this, silly?" she asked.

They stood inside together, with the door ajar.

And then he said playfully, "See how long you can last."

Before she could say anything, he left and closed the closet door, plunging her into darkness. Kavya was too shocked at first to react. But then she lunged at the door with her body, turning the knob and kicking at the thin crack of light underneath the door.

"Let me out!"

When there was no response, she banged on the door. The stupid light switch was on the outside of the closet. Her eyes slowly adjusted to the dark while she stretched out her arms to figure out what was in there. She accidentally hit a broom handle. She grabbed it, using it to whack the door.

"Let me out!" she screamed as loudly as she could. *No, no. He can't really be doing this.*

Eventually, the doorknob turned, and Ranjeet stood there, grinning.

"Three minutes!" he declared smugly. "See? They just do exposure activities like this in therapy. I'll help you get over it."

Kavya pushed him aside and walked quickly to the terrace to breathe in fresh air. She licked the salty sweat and tears off her lips. They didn't speak for the rest of the day.

The incident was so strange, so out of the blue, that she pretended it didn't happen. Until he locked her in the closet two more times, with an increasing undercurrent of hostility. Until he started screaming at her for not wringing out the dish sponge properly, for shrinking the shirts in the laundry, for anything. Once, he tossed a blanket over her head and held her against the wall and later said it was just a joke.

She went along, numb, trying to quickly contort herself at a moment's notice. He didn't know what he was doing, she reasoned. He was so very kind in the early months of their relationship. She just had to get him back to himself, the person who knew everything about her childhood and loved her anyways.

Ranjeet's mom, who lived nearby, then started to come over more frequently. She always appeared unannounced, wearing undersized kurtas stretched across her large chest, sweat dripping down her heavily made-up face. Ranjeet went on his usual tirades while his mother watched wordlessly, globs of mascara sitting in the corners of her eyes.

And she said all kinds of things to Kavya. "I can tell you didn't have a real mother, dear. That Neela couldn't teach anybody anything. But you're lucky that you have me to show you how to run a household and be a strong and poised woman. That's what you want too, right? How else will you be a good mother someday?"

In Kavya's graduate classes, her classmates and professors consistently praised her feminist analysis. "You make such great connections, Kavya!"

And then at home, that great feminist mind worked overtime to figure out what had gone so wrong in her life.

But despite it all, there was a familiarity to Ranjeet. The more he whispered humiliating insults at her, the more he tried to terrorize her, the more her life felt like the one she used to have with Neela. It felt like childhood. It felt like her skin.

RUN

The sound of brakes squealing on the street pulled Kavya out of her maddening time-traveling habit. Here she was in her own home, a college professor in New York City, far away from Texas, and she could still spend large parts of her days reliving scenes from years ago. She had long ago dubbed it the "slingshot feeling." As if released by a catapult, her memories would get dislodged and flung about, splattering all over the place. And then they dripped like paint down her insides, and she would be deep, deep within some scent or a dirty look or a bloodied face or a kiss. It was something her brain had done since she was a teenager.

But what was new was the disruption of her life. The unbearable episodes when everything—the floor, her mind, her body, her dreams, the world—started to tilt and let her know that something was horribly wrong with her. What if the dreams were premonitions? Was Ranjeet going to reappear? Or was she losing her mind?

Kavya looked out her window and saw the skid marks from where the car had stopped. She restlessly tapped her nails on the glass pane, realizing she still had some time before her online class started.

She headed downstairs to grab a family-size bag of popcorn from the kitchen pantry. Shuffling over to the wall facing her bookshelf, she sat down on the floor and mindlessly shoveled salty popcorn into her mouth until she emptied the entire bag. Her tongue was sore from the sharp crystallized edges of the sea salt. She tossed the bag aside, leaving a trail of popcorn dust and salt, and slumped down. Her neck and shoulders ached, but she didn't have the energy to correct her posture. Her whole body was battered and worn out.

Why was I with him? The thoughts ran their familiar tracts in Kavya's brain. *Don't be pathetic. Stop.* She propped herself up and rubbed her hands on her shirt. The large floor-to-ceiling bookcase across from her was jammed with books in all directions, every which way. *I should organize that.* She began to pull books off the shelves.

After making a little progress, she gulped down water until the salt burns on her tongue dulled. Upstairs, she washed her face and picked out a cobalt blue blouse she knew looked vibrant even on a computer screen, and a thick coiled necklace that laid beautifully across her collarbone. Sitting at her table in her room, she dotted and rubbed in concealer under her eyes. She chose a cheerful plum lipstick and plucked her eyebrows. She pulled her hair back and used spray to tame down the willful waves, some loose, some tightly coiled. Then she rubbed cream on her still aching, bruised knees and slid into fleece sweatpants.

She went back downstairs and looked at herself in the hallway mirror by the front door one more time before her class started. Waist up, no one would guess that she was anything but a put-together, well-rested professional woman.

She texted her sons, all part of the charade that she was perfectly fine. *Hi darlings. I'm about to teach. Just wanted to check in!*

Help me with my paper! Samir immediately responded. *The professor said my thesis statement was a mess. I thought I was good at writing!*

We can talk about it. But remember what I told you. Use the professor's office hours! I love you. Keep an eye on Kabir.

Kabir is getting straight As. Forget his smart ass.

Kavya had been so excited for her kids when they had left for Stony Brook University, just a couple of hours away. Even though she missed them, she devoured the stories they told her when they moved into the dorms. But after the panic attacks started, she could barely concentrate on what they said about their classes and new friends. She used up her energy to sound calm when she just wanted to howl and sob.

Kavya exhaled, fluttering her lips. Okay, time to get her mind right before teaching. She entered her office, a narrow room off the front door, across from the living room. She sat down, shook out her hands, and then clicked on the Zoom link she had sent out earlier.

As she waited, a jumble of names, pronouns, black screens, and videos rapidly filled the screen. Her students were unabashedly comfortable in their pajamas and bonnets, giggling with roommates. Others sat up straight, earbuds inserted, student union or library in the background.

Kavya turned on her video and waved. "Everyone, so good to see you, even though it's on Zoom. I appreciate the grace and patience you've shown me with my health issues."

Little heart emojis popped up. "We've got your back, Prof!" and other cheerful messages filled up the chat.

Kavya smiled, her first genuine smile in a while. There was something about being around her students, even on a screen. Teaching gave her a sense of stability that nothing else had ever been able to give her. She could create space for her students to figure out the roughest shit in the world yet still feel empowered to envision change, all within a tidy, predictable schedule.

But even so, after everything she had done to get this full-time job in New York, after all those years adjuncting and struggling to make ends meet, and the huge adjustment of moving her sons from Texas right before they started high school, maybe she was about to lose everything she had fought for.

* * *

Monday again. The previous week, out of three courses spread over four days, Kavya only went into school once. At some point, someone was going to complain about all the online classes.

She called her doctor to ask for a Xanax refill for the panic attacks. After bringing in the emptied trash cans from the curb, she saw a text message flash across her phone screen. *This is the last refill. Remember Xanax can be addictive. I'm sending a psychiatrist referral for a long-term solution. Dr. G.*

"Goddammit!" Kavya shouted. Just two weeks before, she had told this doctor that a psychiatrist was out of the question. She was already on an antidepressant for both depression and anxiety. She had started on it when the boys were very young. The one time she tried to wean herself off, she was not able to take the physical agony of the resulting brain zaps, stomachaches, and terrifying out-of-nowhere suicidal thoughts. No, she couldn't mess around with it ever again. Not to increase the dosage, not to add something else. It was too risky.

She had to somehow conquer her panic attacks with pure willpower. With a new therapist who knew what she was doing.

Later that day, Kavya rang the doorbell of her current therapist's house. She watched as people pushed carts stuffed with laundry bags and tiny children into the laundromat next door.

After a few minutes passed, she impatiently rang the doorbell again. She was tired of this woman.

Helen opened the door, straight gray hair pinned on one side, the ever-present smile taking over her wide, ruddy face. Wearing one of her flowy tops with gigantic bell sleeves, she swept one arm toward her office. "Come on in, Kavya."

Kavya entered her therapist's office and sank into the soft suede chair. She took in the scent of lavender. Every week, Helen infused the room with a different essential oil. With the aroma, the white noise machine, and the trickling water of the tabletop fountain on the grand oak desk on the other side of the room, Kavya was always lulled into passivity. Every week, she played with the fringes of the velvet purple throw on her chair, drip-feeding information to the exceedingly patient Helen.

Kavya had always been clear about why she had come to therapy in the first place. About four years earlier, she sat in this very chair, while Helen looked at her expectantly. Kavya described how she had moved her then-fourteen-year-old sons to New York from Texas for her first full-time job, and how they had been acting out ever since. Sweet, sensitive Samir was barking at her and covering for Kabir, who was skipping classes, sneaking out of the house at night, and having mood swings.

Kavya had told Helen that day that they would only talk about parenting, never about her childhood. Because the few times she tried speaking to former therapists about any of that, she would fall into a chilling emptiness and have a hard time getting out of bed for days afterward. Never again.

Over the years, she did eventually give Helen a very bare bones narrative about her family and Ranjeet, but her armor was something that even a gifted therapist could not break through. Though lately, Helen was trying to chip away at it, and today, Kavya had a message to deliver.

Helen settled into the chair across from her, chipper as always. That was Helen, her reddish complexion and bright green eyes giving her a perpetually sunny appearance.

Kavya spoke as firmly as she could. "I have really enjoyed working with you. You helped me so much when I first came to you."

"Are you breaking up with me?" Helen gave her a coy smile, the kind Kavya used to give her boys when they were little and trying to get away with some antic or another.

Kavya looked back, stony-faced. "This isn't funny. This is just not working for me anymore. I am worse off than when I first met you."

"You're worse off?" Helen's smile disappeared.

"Please don't take it personally." Kavya described what had happened at the park with Mingming, rubbing her neck just thinking about it. She ignored Helen's astonished reaction. "So, I'm just saying, I just think I'm the kind of person who . . ." She trailed off because she wasn't even sure how to finish the sentence.

"As I have always said, sure, I am happy to go at the pace that is best for you," Helen said gently. "But what just happened with the traffic accident is serious, and I wonder if maybe this whole therapy thing might

work a bit better for you if we could talk about your emotional pain aris-
ing from your childhood."

What was with this woman? Couldn't she respect anyone's boundaries?

Helen spoke slowly, advancing quietly, as if that would make Kavya
lower her guard. "If you don't feel that therapy is working for you, then we
need to address it. We would need to see if it's a problem we can solve, or
what our next steps would be."

"Okay." Kavya braced herself.

And then Helen threw the bomb. "But your panic attacks started
right after your father's visit. And I think we need to talk about that."

Kavya swallowed and balled up one of her fists. This woman!

* * *

Several weeks before, in late August, Kavya's father had called her out
of the blue, something about meeting up because he was in town to see
some clients and unexpectedly had some free time. Out of curiosity, she
had agreed.

She walked into the rundown café he had chosen near Times Square
and saw him immediately.

His deep-set eyes, pointing downward at the edges, had sunken even
deeper into his face, which was now mottled with unsightly black moles.
She was surprised at how much he had aged since she had last seen him,
right before she and the boys left Texas.

She sat down at the table after giving him a half hug and patting him
on the back.

Tourists paraded in and out. She had to duck forward whenever
another oblivious person squeezed past their table with large shopping
bags. Her nerves frayed from the screeching and squawking of the big
tour group sitting next to them.

"So, Kavya ..." Mohan drummed his fingers on the table. "So. It's
2022. Big year. Give me an analysis of the midterm elections."

"Dad, you know that's not the kind of political science I do. I am into
international politics and human rights, remember?"

They each picked at stale croissants. He shredded his napkin into bits.
She checked her phone.

He barely even asked anything about the kids—even though Kabir
and Samir had moved to Stony Brook a couple of weeks before his

trip—or about Janet and her family. Instead, he asked her if she ever wanted to become the president of her university. How many subway lines there were. Her favorite pizza place.

More silence.

They had never known how to be together.

* * *

Kavya pushed herself out of Helen's chair and grabbed her bag. "I'm sorry. It's my fault for telling you about my dad's visit in the first place. But thank you for everything."

"Wait!" Helen held her hands up. "You and I are both here, Kavya. You're not back there anymore."

Kavya paused and looked down at her therapist's kind face. In that little moment, she flashed back to being seven years old, when she had been at a restaurant with Neela and Pramod and unexpectedly saw her father in the parking lot. Of course. It was Austin, small enough for random encounters.

She had slapped her hand against the window, waving and yelling, "Daddy! Daddy!"

Mohan did not turn around, and Neela and Pramod did not do anything to get his attention either. Instead, they sat there, eating their food noisily, smacking their lips. Smack. Slurp. Crunch. Never mind the little girl calling for her father.

"No," Kavya said aloud, both to Helen and to what was surfacing.

But another memory appeared in her mind's eye. Seven years old, again. A few days after calling out to her father. Sitting across from Mohan at a diner. Her legs swinging as she sat on the metal chair. Drinking a thick, chocolate milkshake while he took the napkins and tore them into smaller and smaller pieces.

Despite standing in Helen's office, Kavya could vividly smell her father's distinct, stale body odor. She could hear his voice saying, "I just didn't see you that day in the restaurant. I wasn't ignoring you," and his incessant throat-clearing in the silence that followed. She could remember that she had desperately wanted her father to announce that she didn't have to live with Neela and Pramod anymore, and that he was going to be her dad again. Even though she barely knew him. Even though it was the one and only time they had been alone together. Even though she felt so uneasy she couldn't even finish the milkshake.

"Can you wait?" Helen's voice snapped her back into the present. Kavya could taste the bile in her mouth, and she could no longer stand there, with such miserable memories awakening.

"No." Kavya clutched her bag strap and turned toward the door.

Helen quickly stood up, her notebook falling to the floor, but Kavya rushed out of the office and the house, desperate to be anywhere but there. When she reached the bottom step, she turned and quickly walked to the subway station. How dare that woman mention her father. How dare she do that to her!

As she stomped down the subway stairs, she saw a man grab a woman's wrist and hiss something in her face.

Kavya stared at them, until the woman noticed and barked, "What the fuck is your problem?"

Kavya muttered, "I'm sorry," and hurried away. As she always did when she saw a scene like that, she counted her blessings that she had left Ranjeet and gone on to create a new life for herself. She was once so brave. What had happened to her?

GIFT BASKET

In the summer of 2003, Kavya moved to Houston to live with Janet right after she and Ranjeet had broken up. Meanwhile, other people in her graduate school cohort were getting ready to start new jobs. Kavya had nothing lined up because she had not even applied anywhere outside of Texas, since Ranjeet had said he would never leave his mother or make her move.

When Kavya arrived in Houston with PhD in hand and nothing to do, Janet and Yumiko hooked her up with work. She did shifts at Yumiko's newly opened fabric store and landed a tutoring gig to help rich high school kids write their college essays. She cut off Neela and Pramod after they took Ranjeet's side, and dove headfirst into a new life. She worked, went to parties, met Janet's friends, and enjoyed the serenity of her days.

"I feel like a new person. I'm leaving the bad shit in the past," Kavya declared to Janet over dinner one evening. "I'm going to look for places to teach part-time. And as soon as applications come out for full-time faculty positions, I'm going to apply around the whole damn world and *not* in Texas at all this time. I'm going to be a professor, goddammit." She beamed as she delivered her speech.

Janet pumped her fist in the air. "Yes! I'll miss you. But you deserve this. You deserve to have that life."

And for once, Kavya agreed.

And then one day, she went to Janet's room, crying. She kept her hands behind her back and leaned against the wall, feeling weak and nauseated. She looked around the small room, littered with bras, shorts, and crumpled paper.

Janet looked up from her bed, where she was reading. "What's wrong?"

Kavya sat on the bed. She brought her hand forward and revealed three positive pregnancy tests.

"Shit. Should I drive you to the clinic?" Janet put her book down.

"Yeah. We have to go." Kavya stared at the threads hanging from Janet's shorts. This wasn't happening. It couldn't be. She looked again at the tests she had taken hours earlier.

"Does . . ."

"The guy isn't going to be involved," Kavya said quietly.

"Even if he wanted to be, you could still get an abortion."

The tears streamed down Kavya's face. "I know. It's just even more incentive to get one." She added nervously, "It was that guy Vinay I met at that party. He didn't tell me he had a partner. I just called him, and he doesn't want her to know anything. I was so stupid."

Janet looked at her for a moment. "What a complete asshole."

But they didn't go to the clinic that day, or the next week, or the week after that.

At some point, Kavya announced to Janet, "I think I'm going to keep it. It's a bad decision. But I need to keep it."

Janet's mouth dropped open. "Are you sure? You're not getting all pro-life on me, are you?"

"No," Kavya said somberly. "But it's what I want to do."

They sat in silence for what seemed like forever.

"Okay, listen," Janet said. "Stay here with me. Have your kid here. I'll help you."

"Are you crazy? I'm not going to do that to you," Kavya said emphatically. "I'm already thinking about where I could live for cheap. People do this all the time."

Janet snickered. "Lady, you have no idea. You're staying with me."

"No, that's ridiculous. I don't need anyone's pity."

"Kavya! Why do you always act like this? Did you ever think that it makes *me* feel good to have you around? You even know how much I love children. Aren't we always talking about chosen family?"

Kavya was chastened as she saw the hurt in her friend's face. "I'm sorry. I'll think about it, okay? And you think about it, too, and what you're agreeing to. Just let's not tell anyone yet."

Janet stared at her for a while. "But first, I want to make sure. You absolutely want to have a child?"

Kavya didn't know how to explain that maybe this was her only chance to make her own family, to be for a child what her own mother never got the chance to be for her.

* * *

When Kavya's five-month pregnant belly popped out and she could no longer pretend she had gained weight, Janet and Kavya decided to come clean when Janet's parents invited them over for dinner.

Janet broke the news as only as she could. "Well, guys and gals. Our girl's preggo. With twins! Look at her!"

Kavya immediately looked down at her stomach and said shyly, "I might as well tell you that it was this guy I only hung out with once. And then I found out he was in a relationship. He doesn't want to know anything about it."

She waited for Bob and Yumiko to be scandalized. To berate her for being so careless. To wring their hands and say, *You're not getting married?*

Instead, they cheered and whooped and praised God.

A month later, Yumiko drove over with a carload of baby items from their church's clothing and furniture swap group.

Kavya stood at the back of her room, in disbelief as someone else's mother gently folded tiny clothes. She had known Yumiko for so long, but everything still felt too intimate. She so desperately wanted to accept Janet's insistence that Yumiko saw her as a "bonus" daughter. But she didn't want to be an extra daughter. She wanted to be her mother and father's daughter. She wanted that crater-like emptiness in her soul to be filled.

Yumiko stopped folding and walked over to Kavya. She lifted Kavya's chin and looked her in the eyes. "What's wrong, darling?"

"I don't know. I'm freaking out." Kavya burst into tears.

Yumiko laughed her bouncy, singing bird laugh, pulling her in for a hug. "You will be fine."

Kavya rested her head uneasily on Yumiko's shoulder. "I haven't even told my father."

"You can tell him whenever you're ready."

"What am I doing?" Kavya sniffled and took in the gardenia scent in Yumiko's hair.

Yumiko pulled away to look at her. "Oh, my sweet girl. Trust God's plans. And I'm thankful for that one-night stand. You're bringing babies into our lives!"

"You didn't just say one-night stand."

Yumiko giggled. "I did! I'm not so old that I don't know what that is. That's what everyone does after a bad break-up, so I hear."

Kavya hugged her. This time, she let herself relax into the embrace. Just to see what it was like to be held by a mother.

* * *

Kavya's sweaty thighs rubbed up against each other, one of the babies' heads a bowling ball threatening to pop right out of her. Her doctor said she was already dilated two centimeters and would deliver soon. She kept up her daily walks to hasten labor.

Even though it was not yet officially summer, the unbearably hot sidewalks radiated steam. Kavya's discomfort increased with each step. She turned back toward Yumiko's fabric store. She looked around at the complex as she waddled along. Brick buildings with steepled roofs lined the evenly paved sidewalks, adorned with carefully manicured plants.

She reached the store and welcomed the blast of cold air. Janet pulled out the donut cushion from behind the counter for Kavya to sit on. Coralynn, Kavya's temporary replacement at the store, walked by. She bent down with her face level with Kavya's large taut belly and said, "Any day now!" as she did every single day, multiple times. She pranced off with her clipboard.

Kavya moaned and buried her face in her hands as Yumiko rushed over. "Everything okay?"

"I didn't realize it would be like this in the last weeks."

Yumiko laughed. "Oh, don't I know it. I went through it three times. It gets easier after the first."

"I'm done!" Kavya exclaimed. "Two for one. I'm good!"

Four days and an emergency C-section later, Yumiko and Janet sat next to Kavya and two bassinets in a tiny hospital room. Janet was spending the nights on the spare cot in the room, and it was Yumiko's first visit to meet the babies.

A rotation of nurses was coming in at all hours to check Kavya's blood pressure and stitches—a brownish-pink line that itched furiously. The nurses, all too casually if you asked Kavya, also kept peeking inside her extra-large, blue stretchy underwear.

"Why am I bleeding so much if it wasn't a vaginal delivery?" she asked at one point. The on-duty nurse laughed and ignored her question.

After the nurse left, Yumiko leaned over. "It's typical, sweetheart. Whatever kind of delivery you have, the uterus sheds its lining."

Kavya nodded and winced as she tried to adjust herself in the bed, holding Samir to her breast while Kabir snoozed in his bassinet and emitted bird-like squeaks.

Yumiko helped rearrange the pillows, as Janet moved over to Kabir's bassinet and drowsily stroked his cheek.

Janet yawned. "Being around sleeping babies makes me sleepy."

"No, getting no sleep makes you sleepy," Kavya replied dryly.

"No more full night's sleep, like ever, right?"

"Nope! Never again!" Yumiko giggled and winked at Kavya, who was sinking deeper into an exhaustion that wrapped cozy layers around her body.

Kavya fed Samir for several more minutes, and then remembered saying, "Take Samir," before she entered a gorgeous, pitch-black nothingness.

She woke up when the same nurse who had laughed at her came in with a gigantic basket with a bow.

"Look at what you got!"

The basket came with a typed note that said *Congratulations! From, Dad.* Tissue paper surrounded a wide assortment of sausages and cheeses.

Yumiko said gently, "Oh, that's sweet. It was a nice idea to let him know after all, Kavya."

"I'll die from hypertension if I eat all this salty food," Kavya tried to joke. But she was so angry about being woken up. Distraught that it was surely time to breastfeed one or both babies. Ashamed of her resentful thoughts about Janet's mom inviting herself here. *You can't make up for what I don't have, so don't even try, Yumiko. Go help one of the other lost souls out there.*

And she could feel the sting of this generic basket of food. That was her dad. The kind of guy who offered money to help with his new grandchildren and then had his assistant order a bunch of crappy food and write a pithy note.

Don't cry, don't cry, don't cry. She pulled close Kabir's bassinet and gently lifted him out.

Janet was digging through the basket, removing blocks of cheese, while Yumiko held and rocked Samir.

Kavya looked down at Kabir. He was not forming the kind of latch the nurse had said he should. She was already supplementing with formula, but maybe she would have to formula feed both babies full time. The nurse had admonished her, "Try as hard as you can to breastfeed. It's what is best for the babies. Plus think of all the money you will save."

Kavya pulled Kabir's chin down a bit to try to get a better latch. His mouth reflexively widened, revealing her butchered, chewed-up nipple. How did a five-pound human do that? She stared at the long black hair framing his head and the downy wisps on his arms and legs and back.

She wanted to scream. She wanted to ask Yumiko and Janet to take the boys and raise them, and then she could run away, far from Texas, and have an exciting career.

She immediately cringed, her body shuddering at the thoughts invading her. Kabir was moving his tiny jaw, his gums grinding away at her nipple, grunting because he could not drink no matter how much he tried. Kavya finally let the tears fall. *I'm sorry, little baby. Please let me be brave. Please let me be a good mommy to you.*

BETRAY

Kavya returned to Helen's office of her own accord. Three days after running out of Helen's office—three days of obsessively reliving her past, more nightmares and panic attacks, maybe too much Xanax—she sheepishly called Helen to ask if she had any cancelations.

When Helen opened the door, she didn't smile as usual. Instead, she carefully touched Kavya's arm. "I'm glad you're here."

Kavya walked in with her head lowered. She plonked herself down into the chair and splayed the fringe of Helen's throw onto her lap. This time, a sandalwood scent filled the room.

"I'm sorry about last time," Kavya said.

Helen grinned at last. "It won't be the last time someone's run out of here."

Kavya nodded. Couldn't someone else explain her story? Or maybe she could somehow put her memories into chronological order, jumbled and chaotic as they always were, and present a neat little flipbook to Helen. She wrapped one of the fringes around her finger.

"You said on the phone that you couldn't understand the relentlessness of the anxiety," Helen said slowly.

"Yeah." Kavya unwrapped the fringe and moved her hands to the arms of the chair.

"We could sit in silence for a while, if you want to."

"I don't know." Kavya spoke in a low voice. "I feel like I need answers. Like, why can't I let go of the Ranjeet stuff, to the point of these ongoing nightmares? He was a complete loser. He got me to fall in love and then betrayed me."

Matching Kavya's tone, Helen asked softly, "Did your father also betray you?"

Kavya winced, keeping her feet planted so that she wouldn't race out of there again. "I don't know. I don't even know why I've kept my father in our lives." Her chin quivered.

"You told me that your father's summer visit was the only time you were alone together, well, as an adult. I wonder if the panic attacks and scary dreams started after that because you started to face your dad's failure to be there for you and maybe even protect you from the bad things in life." Helen paused. "Like the relationship with Ranjeet. Or what you always describe as a tough childhood with your aunt and uncle."

Heat rose through Kavya's throat and into her jaw. *No, no. Watch out. Something terrible is about to happen!*

"I know I need to feel better, but I can't sit here and dissect my dad with you. You don't have to psychoanalyze the whole thing like that." Kavya nervously rubbed her hands against the chair.

"I understand that it feels terrifying to talk about your family." Helen leaned forward and tucked her hair behind her ears. "I wouldn't usually push you so much, but you got hit in traffic, Kavya. And besides that, you're really suffering right now. I think we need to do a bit of this work and sort of go for it, okay?"

Kavya's hands were starting to feel numb, while her face burned. Everything in her body was telling her to leave this room, right now. If she wasn't careful, she might spin out to a point of no return. She might share something she shouldn't.

"Let's talk a bit about trauma," Helen continued, shifting into a more clinical tone. "Trauma is our nervous system's response when something dangerous, or perceived to be dangerous, happens. That something could be war, or it could be something like your mother's death and your father's abandonment, or anything that is way too much for someone to handle. I recommend we read some book excerpts together, specifically from van der Kolk's *The Body Keeps the Score* and Menakem's *My Grandmother's Hands*. They both show that unprocessed trauma stays in us and changes us, even our brains. Our body keeps that trauma alive. That's what these nightmares and panic attacks are."

What was being kept alive? Kavya didn't want to know. She was sick of her mind and body turning on her. She squirmed in her seat and kneaded her fingers, as they started to prickle and sting back to life. Her head was now on fire, and she tried to breathe out all the suffocating fright. She exhaled sharply.

And then, without warning, she was swept back into the memory of her father's New York visit. At the very end of the conversation, her father had leaned over and said, "This was nice. We can do it again. Maybe someday, you will even decide to speak to your aunt again. I bet Neela would like that."

And that rage she always stuffed down, deep inside, started pulsing. It pushed up inside of her and created a painful pressure right below her heart, right in the middle of Helen's office.

Kavya couldn't stop herself. She blurted out, "Neela was so horrible after the boys were born just because I told my father and not her, and I had said something like, 'Why would I tell you? He's their only grandparent.' And she needled me, like, 'Oh, only grandparent? Really?' Like, challenging me. Fuck off with that." She spit out the last words.

"I'm sorry, I don't follow. Challenging you on what?" Helen asked.

Kavya was so upset that she had forgotten where she was. She nervously crossed her legs. She could hear sirens in the distance. She wasn't sure how to change the topic.

She quickly clarified, "I mean, my aunt thought of herself and my uncle as being grandparents because they adopted me. So, that's all. Whatever." She uncrossed her legs. "So, umm, yeah. Long time ago, I stopped calling her and Pramod by their aunt and uncle titles. At the end of the day, they loved Ranjeet and hated me. They don't mean anything to me."

Kavya played with her bracelet, hoping Helen would talk about something else. See? She was already losing control, bringing up Neela like that.

"Their lack of support must have been very painful." Helen tapped her fingers together and furrowed her brow, as she momentarily paused. "You know, speaking of grandparents, you have mentioned a couple of times a grandmother in India whom you visited every summer, before she died, right? She seemed like a *positive* part of your childhood?"

"Yes, my paternal grandmother. My Ajji. Such a funny, clever woman." Kavya smiled wistfully. She missed Ajji. She yearned to feel her grandmother's soft cotton sari against her skin, to cuddle up together and read a book like they used to.

Helen keenly observed her.

"Oh, yeah, also . . ." Kavya sat quietly while she thought. Then she rattled off a few facts like she was giving a book report. "When Ajji's husband, my Ajja, was alive, he had started a printing press. This was after India's independence, maybe just a few years after. Then Ajja died, and his dad, my great-grandfather, took over the printing press and taught my grandmother how to run it because he was having some medical issues. Ajji had to take in her father-in-law after her husband died, because she was a widow, and women couldn't live alone and blah blah blah. But still, a widow running a printing press in 1950s India is pretty wild." She tried to smile. "Hey, maybe that's where I get my feminism from."

Helen nodded approvingly. "I bet. Your grandmother's achievement was amazing." She sat there, grinning, as Kavya glanced at her watch, wondering when this excruciating session would end.

But Helen wasn't done. "You know, some of my South Asian patients tell me stories about their families during that partition and after independence. Did your grandmother ever talk about that time?" She tapped her mouth, deep in thought.

Kavya shook her head. "I don't know." She imagined Ajji at the printing press. And her father-in-law, Kavya's great-grandfather, running the household. Yes, with an array of maids, drivers, nannies, and whatnot. But still. He was the one who was ultimately responsible for Neela turning into a wretched woman, and Mohan becoming an emotionally stunted asshole who threw away his only child. Great-Grandfather. The man who started it all.

Oh no. Helen was rubbing her chin. She always did that when she was about to share some deep, psychological insight. "We haven't yet talked about intergenerational trauma, which is when any unaddressed trauma that someone experiences then gets passed down through families, like through the people who raise us or even through how our genes function. Or through historic trauma, which is collective psychological harm from an event that's part of a community's cultural memory, like what you see with descendants of survivors of the Holocaust, slavery, wars, and the Nakba, as a Palestinian patient told me just the other day. Does any of this resonate at all with you?"

Okay, now Kavya wanted to keep her grandmother out of wherever this conversation was going to go. Since when did Helen talk about politics and history? Maybe this was a trick. She should be careful.

Helen kept looking at her.

Kavya finally offered, "I guess internalized colonialism affected everybody. Ajji told me a few times that my great-grandfather was utterly obsessed with skin tone and was very vicious to Neela for being too 'dark.' As in, he would always comment on it and be cruel and hit her and stuff. Neela was fixated on skin tone, too." She coughed and shifted in her chair. *Why did I bring up Neela? I can't think about this.* She quickly added, "But colorism is also just a thing in communities of color. It's not specific to my family."

Helen nodded, motioning for her to go on.

Kavya gripped the chair arms again. Her mind cycled through brief moments from decades ago. Neela wearing long sleeves on the beach. Neela hiding skin-bleaching cream in the makeup drawer that Kavya always rifled through. Neela chucking a hairbrush at Pramod when he cracked some joke about her light-skinned friend being prettier.

Thinking of Neela in this way—the split second of considering what must have happened to her aunt, the way Neela's grandfather and probably the entire goddamn community insulted her for being too dark—brought a wave of despair. Kavya swallowed hard as she tried to focus.

Helen leaned forward. "Kavya? How are you doing? Should we take a minute?"

Buried somewhere deep in the nooks and crannies of Kavya's brain were snippets of conversations she was not supposed to have heard. When friends and relatives at parties and get-togethers in India or the U.S. had not realized that little ears were listening.

Mohan is like that only. Always very frail, even as a kid. He never got over his father's death. And then living with that horrible man.

Neela is the strong one, no? Always arguing with someone.

No, Neela is the crazy one. She scares me.

She is lucky to have married Pramod. He lets her do any stupid thing she wants.

Who knows why his parents agreed to let him marry such a dark girl.

Pramod has problems, obviously. No girl's family wanted him.

Best that Neela couldn't have children. You can pass that kind of lunacy on.

Kavya was aware of Helen's steady gaze, but she couldn't speak. She slumped back in her chair, her face hot again. She put her hands over her face and pushed her fingers into her eyelids until she saw blotches of color.

"I have to stop talking about this," she finally muttered.

"Stay with me, Kavya. Just let's breathe together, okay?"

They each took a breath in.

1-2-3-4. Hold for four breaths. 1-2-3-4. Breathe out. 1-2-3-4. Repeat.

After a few rounds, Helen declared, "Wonderful job, and Kavya, I would love to meet twice a week for now, if you're okay with that. Let's switch to Monday mornings and Wednesday afternoons?"

Kavya nodded, breathing in and out as slowly as she could.

"But before we end for today, listen, how is it speaking about this to me, a white woman?" Helen narrowed her eyes. "Talking about colonialism, colorism, and that sort of thing? Maybe I was being presumptuous by bringing up other South Asian clients."

"I don't know." Kavya faltered. "I just need you to stop me from losing control. You have to stop me from turning into Neela." *I haven't even told you what she did to me.*

"I don't know too much about your aunt at all. But you're you. I see you, and you are your own, whole person."

They sat in silence, the water fountain's trickle the only sound, until Helen gently said, "I'll see you next time."

Kavya left Helen's office without a solution to her panic attacks. Or to the dread that had lived inside of her for as long as she could remember.

ANCHOR

Kavya spent the weekend alternating between stillness and distressing anxiety. As usual, she had her weekend call with her sons. As usual, she did her best to hide her crisis from them, focusing instead on "mom" stuff, like how they were eating, sleeping, and studying.

By Sunday night, she realized she was relieved to finally have a name—intergenerational trauma—for that lifelong foreboding sense that the scary thing that lived inside of her, that wasn't from her, that Neela had infected her with, would someday destroy her. Maybe Helen could help her get rid of whatever that scary thing was.

On Monday morning, she went to therapy. This time, she walked into the unmistakable scent of lemongrass. They read together a book excerpt describing family trauma but also the possibility of healing. They spoke tenderly and lovingly about Kavya's relationships with her sons and Janet.

"Feel anchored in the security of their love," Helen told her.

Kavya went to her class that afternoon and brightened at how well it went.

On Tuesday, Kavya was excited to teach in person again, hoping to have two good days in a row. She walked back and forth at the front of the classroom, listening in as the students discussed in small groups the readings for her International Law class. She stopped and stood tall, her body solid like a tree trunk.

"Alright, let's begin," she said. And that's when it hit. Right then. The floor started to tilt and sway. "Oh, actually, I have to check something in my notes, hold on." Two minutes, then almost five minutes passed. She pretended to write. But really, she was curling her toes, trying to feel the ground.

The sickening wave finally passed. She looked up and asked a question about the readings. But then, just as the students got into an animated discussion, it came over her again. She couldn't feel the ground. Her vision blurred. She gripped the lectern, telling herself, *Stop it. Just keep talking. Nothing is happening!* She would not be able to stay upright for much longer.

And then, by divine intervention, the fire alarm rang. She fled the classroom without waiting for her students. She almost tumbled down the stairs. The whole rest of the university gathered in the front, but she unsteadily crept off to the side to sit on the stairs facing the Brooklyn Bridge. She frantically gulped in the fresh air, despite the smell of the rotting garbage a few feet away.

* * *

That night, she woke up at 4 a.m., soaking wet and sniveling. Something had scared her in her dreams. Like maybe someone was chasing or choking her. *None of that is happening now. This is real life. I'm alone here.*

She usually felt overheated after a nightmare, but right now, she wanted something soft and heavy to encase her. When her ex-boyfriend Freddy had been here, he had taken up the entire half of the bed. His large arms held her as they talked late into the night. She always joked that he was her personal weighted blanket.

Kavya was so grateful she had ended things with Freddy. What would he have done with her disrupting everything with her night terrors? What would *she* have done, unraveling in front of him like that?

After all, their entire time together was playful and light. Holding hands at concerts. Inside jokes for days. Samir, especially, adored Freddy. Those two could sit in a coffeeshop discussing photography and literature for hours.

Even though Freddy was pretty much a fixture at her house during their year and a half together, even traveling with her and the boys, he wanted more. He asked to move in. He said he wanted to know everything about her, even more than the brief contours of her life she had shared with him. That was too much. Saying no to living together only made it easier to then end the relationship when the pandemic hit soon after, when the filmmaking company laid him off and he ended up leaving town to freelance all over the country.

Kavya walked into her bathroom. No, Freddy couldn't find out the truth about her. Not then, not ever. That's why, in the years since breaking up, she had always ignored his texts asking to meet up during his stints in Brooklyn.

She turned on the water and soaked a washcloth.

As she patted her face and neck, she looked in the mirror. No matter how much she missed Freddy and his tender smile, no matter how much he thought he loved cool, fun Kavya, this was who she really was. A mother who took away a beautiful person from her sons' lives because of the what-ifs that never left her. A haggard, shell of a woman too terrified to live her life.

She pressed her face into a dry towel. Then she went back to her room, lay down, and let the tears fall.

* * *

A couple of hours later, when she couldn't fall back asleep, she rolled out of bed.

She whispered encouraging phrases to herself as she showered, put on her favorite red shift dress, and left for work.

When she walked into her Wednesday Gender and Politics class, the students were chatting and laughing with each other. She stood up in front of the class and looked out at the full classroom. Then her stomach plunged.

She knew she should start class. Eight minutes late already. But she could not open her mouth. Her chest burned. The tears were finding their way from that very hot place, deep inside her body. *You are made of tears.*

She occupied herself with marking attendance. She stepped behind the computer desk at the front so they couldn't see her body. Leaning against it, she dug her nails into her arm and scratched hard until a droplet of blood formed. She exhaled. Some of the pressure building up inside of her slowly released.

Then she pretended to drop her pen so she could pop a Xanax from her pocket while crouched down behind the desk. Okay, maybe she could get through the entire class like this and then go straight to her appointment with Helen. Steady, steady.

"See you all next time." She tried to sound casual when class ended. She thought maybe the Xanax was working. She couldn't tell.

As the students filed out, one stopped in front of her to say, "I'm changing my major to political science. Who signs my form?"

Kavya looked up from packing her bag, being careful to hide her left arm where welts were forming. "Oh, the department chair does it. But I'm glad you're joining us!"

"Yep," he said. "My father was, like, really upset when I told him I'm not doing business anymore."

One of her top students, Yandelis, hurried over. "My mom is so mad at me too! Professor Joshi, I just finalized the switch from economics to a double major in political science and gender studies. And I told my mom that you're a political science professor and also teach some of the gender studies courses and how your work is as important as what economists do. I told her everything I want to do, but she's all, 'Why did I sacrifice so much in this country for you to do these stupid things?'"

"They legit want us to sell our souls," the first student declared.

They both looked expectantly at Kavya, especially Yandelis, her comically large plastic glasses accentuating huge black eyes that blinked rapidly in anticipation of some sage advice.

This was such a common scene.

Students with a barely veiled hunger for approval.

When will my family be proud of me? When will they take me seriously? When will they see me?

"Yeah, it's so hard," Kavya mumbled. "We should talk about it in depth another time. Gotta run. See ya!" As she hurried out of the classroom, she could feel Yandelis's blinking eyes on her back.

* * *

Later that afternoon, Kavya told Helen what had happened in class.

"Helen, I just can't keep doing this. This isn't a life. All I do is try to make it through my classes and come here. I'm still feeling weird from the meds. Just say whatever you have to say while I'm feeling numbed out, okay?"

Helen nodded vigorously. "Let's do it." She leaned back and clasped her hands. "Kavya, you seem very connected with your students."

Kavya sensed a trap but was also too exhausted to protest. "Yes. I absolutely love teaching and being with students."

"Imagine that a student told you, as I'm sure they have, that they have a very difficult relationship with their family, and they don't know how to move forward with their own decisions and lives. What would you say?"

"I guess you want me to say that my students should work through what hurts them and that's how they can heal and live happy lives. And that I should work through what hurts me as well?"

"You don't sound so sure."

"No," Kavya said, in a slight daze. "Because I have it very easy, relatively speaking. I really do. But this country has made it very clear to me since I can remember that I don't belong here. And your family should never make you feel the same way, especially when this country makes them feel like that too. It's hard to get past it when your own family makes you feel like you don't belong to *them*."

A thought lurked somewhere in her head, something about her aunt trying to kill her, but it slowly disintegrated.

Helen smiled approvingly. "Wonderful insights. I think that you and I can connect some dots between your anxiety, your family's story, and what happened with Ranjeet. I want you to process and live alongside this trauma and eventually reach a sense of peace within."

A sense of inner peace? Kavya almost laughed at the prospect. Peace was something she had never allowed herself to want. That was asking too much.

She let out a long, deep sigh. She so desperately wanted therapy to be a soothing balm for all the shattered pieces inside of her. But it wasn't.

She wondered whether maybe she was just ungrateful and immature. She thought about the hiking pictures Kabir had sent her just this morning of his sweet life with his friends. Kabir and Samir, the most beautiful creatures, more than made up for anything that had ever happened in her past. People had been through far worse, actual trauma, and managed to have happy lives. And here she was, spiraling, spiraling.

No one was going to be able to save her. No one ever had been.

REMEMBER

Pramod and Neela were at Kavya's kitchen counter, eating with their hands. Their bodies were grotesque and distorted, like they were standing in front of fun-house mirrors at a carnival. How could this be happening?

Neela asked, "Why haven't you come to see me?" The words twisted and broke apart, as if blades were slicing through her voice.

"Baby, come here."

Kavya turned around as Ranjeet pulled her to him. *He found me!* He was breathing heavily. She scratched at his face, pushed him away, and fled the room, only for Neela to follow her.

Kavya escaped into her office and stumbled right into the filing cabinet. Her face hit the edge as she fell, and she touched her bloody lips that were already swelling. The entire floor started to tilt. She frantically grabbed at the cabinet to pull herself up. It crashed on top of her. Even having a heavy piece of furniture on top of her didn't stop her from sliding down the floor.

She heaved and grunted under the weight of the cabinet. She saw the walls ripple. Her eyes turned cloudy, and she could barely see, as if a thin film was stuck on them. *Please God, no!*

"I don't want to be here anymore," Kavya cried out. "I don't want to be with any of you."

* * *

Kavya rolled over to her side, pulling herself out of the dream. She opened her eyes, the sleep still in them, blurring her vision. She dug into her eyes, clearing away the crusty bits, and blinked to make sure she could see properly.

She stayed curled up on her bed in the dark and let the tears fall freely down her face. Her fingers traced the tears' wayward routes down her cheeks and into her ears, and she let her hand drop down to her shoulder. She gripped her perpetually tight muscles, made worse since the moped accident. Freddy had always tried to massage the knots out and would eventually give up.

As she dug into the layers of tough, sedimented muscle, she thought about how the women on her father's side had the same bodies, with prominent broad shoulders. They all looked like swimmers. Her grandmother, her Ajji, was extremely short, less than five feet tall, but with very wide shoulders, so that even when she had to peer up at everyone, she always seemed so powerful.

Kavya thought about Helen's question about what it might have been like for Ajji in India's nascent days. She pulled her blanket up to her chin. And she could hear her grandmother's voice telling a story, one from long ago.

Ajji had been laughing. "Oh, Kavya, my child, did I tell you that my father-in-law, your great-grandfather, had the worst temper. He was so mad once because I made a bad mistake at the printing press with the

35

accounting. It cost us a lot, and we had so much pressure to make money. He slammed me into the floor." Her grandmother pointed to the ground near the dining table in her apartment.

"I dislocated my shoulder and couldn't work for weeks. It was the best revenge." Ajji chuckled. "I could not move my whole arm, and the maid served me homemade kulfi and lychees. Oh, I just enjoyed sitting around listening to the radio. It was like what your white women get to live." Kavya watched in horror as Ajji cackled, her chin vibrating.

And then there was another time when her grandmother had cried when they were going through old photographs. "Oh child, that man was a tyrant. God curse him and the day I visited his house," Ajji said, sobbing. "I lost that pregnancy. I lost that baby because of him. And your Ajja died before I could get pregnant again." Kavya, only about ten years old, held on to her grandmother, touching the soft skin bulging out from under her sari blouse. She was too afraid to ask why Ajji had gone to Great-Grandfather's house and what he could have possibly done to destroy a pregnancy.

Kavya sat up quickly in her bed. She wanted to scream at the memories flooding her brain. *Stop! Fucking stop!*

She turned on the lamp and looked around. She spotted the thick diary she kept next to her bed. When the boys were little, fueled by the heartache of watching her "mom friends" regularly talk with their own mothers, she started to write to her mother to document her children's milestones. Kavya opened the book and saw that she had last written over a year before.

Tonight, she told her mother about her dreams.

Amma, these nightmares are so real, and I keep reliving everything. I'm remembering everything. Except I don't remember how you felt or smelled. I don't know anything about you or any of our family. No one is here to tell me about any of you. What did my great-grandfather do? He cursed this entire family. I am losing my mind. Sometimes, everything feels surreal, like I'm going to disappear, or I was never here.

She paused, pen hovering in the air. Writing to her mother was not releasing her from her misery. She turned the page and started again.

My Fucked-Up Family Tree:

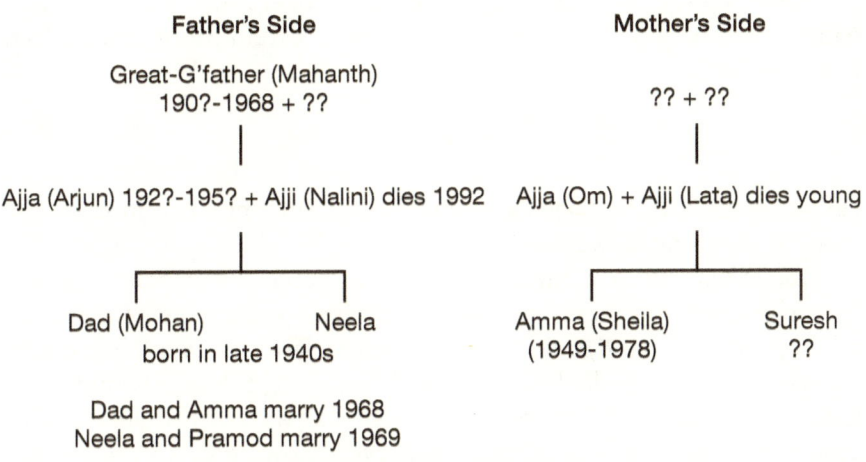

Father's Side

Great-G'father (Mahanth)
190?-1968 + ??

Ajja (Arjun) 192?-195? + Ajji (Nalini) dies 1992

Dad (Mohan)   Neela
born in late 1940s

Mother's Side

?? + ??

Ajja (Om) + Ajji (Lata) dies young

Amma (Sheila)   Suresh
(1949-1978)   ??

Dad and Amma marry 1968
Neela and Pramod marry 1969

Dad, Neela, spouses move to the U.S. 1971

She looked at the dates again.

She had never stopped to consider how her own family's history intertwined with colonialism, Partition, and independence. Did they ever talk about any of it? Was it scary? Also, her Amma's side was such a mystery. She had met them a few times but didn't know where they were now. How were they, and Amma, impacted by these events?

She closed the diary and walked carefully down the dark staircase to her office nook. She opened her laptop and searched for her teaching folder about British colonialism. Scrolling through the various articles and notes revealed an overwhelming amount of information, replete with all kinds of possibilities for why her great-grandfather was the way he was.

Kavya remembered that Ajji used to talk about Great-Grandfather's pride in working for the British railways. And that he had been asked not to return because of his infamous temper. What did he think about colonialism? Did the backdrop of colonialism even matter? Maybe he was just a horrible person who abused everyone.

And then she found a document from October 2018, during her first semester teaching in New York. It was labeled, "List of Stories for Project: Partition."

* * *

Fall semester 2018 had been a doozy. During those first two months, she thought the students would eat her alive.

The Introduction to International Relations course, in particular, was unraveling from the start. The students brazenly walked out of the classroom, phones in hand, only returning when class was over. They loudly whispered and giggled while she talked. Some slept. Kavya would come home and plead with her sons not to act that way with their teachers, only to find out later that Kabir wasn't even showing up to some of his classes.

One day, after a complex lecture analyzing U.S. foreign policy and Israel, three white male students stayed after class to question her.

"You do have your PhD, right?"

"Are you anti-American or antisemitic, or both?"

"Didn't you get any training to teach?"

The next week, those same three students snuck glances at each other the entire time she spoke. It distracted her, and she stumbled over her words.

Kavya tried so very hard to be deserving of this tenure-track job that had been so long in the making. She wore the kind of pressed linen suits and smart wedge heels that she saw the full-time faculty wear back when she was an adjunct in Houston. She delivered thoroughly researched presentations and name-dropped as many scholars as she could. But it wasn't going to work with this crowd.

One night after her sons went to bed, as she struggled with lesson plans and wondered why she thought she could be a career academic, she finally decided she had to be herself instead of the stodgy, lecturing "real" professor she was trying to be. She knew two things about teaching: be authentic; give students something to do with the emotions provoked by the topics they studied.

She knew what she had to do.

Kavya walked into the class the next day and handed a stapled set of papers to a student in the first row.

"Hi, everyone," she began. "I gave Stephen a list of readings with descriptions for our next unit on border politics. Our case study is the partitioning of British colonial India and its aftermath. We're going to do something different!"

They just sat there, lethargic as usual.

"Umm, okay," she continued, undeterred, moving to the door so no one could leave. "Pick one reading from this list of stories and put your name next to it. It's non-academic stuff, like fiction and graphic novels."

A couple of the students perked up, only slightly, but enough to encourage her. She added, "Then, you'll use the stories, our class readings, and your own research as inspiration for an assignment that I'm calling the letter project. You will write a letter to someone, in any time period, who was in some way responsible for or a witness to Partition and its legacies. That includes silence and complicity as well."

One person raised her hand. "Are we being tested on this, or what?"

Kavya smiled. "You're not being tested. You're being *invited* to help me create an interesting class instead of the boring and disconnected one we've had so far, right? And my students back in Texas *loved* this assignment. You will too!"

She realized she was moving her hands animatedly, and she could hear the cloying excitement in her voice. Okay, nothing was worth becoming this obnoxious.

Quickly regrouping, she offered the first thing that came into her mind, "Look, I'm going to write a letter and share it with you. You'll only do yours if you like mine and think, hey, I want to try that. What do you think?"

Nothing.

"Do I need to beg?" she asked playfully. "I mean, I know I'm Texan, but how much do I need to humiliate myself here with you Yankees?" A few of the students chuckled, which loosened them all up just enough so that, one by one, they started signing up for their stories.

As they did, someone asked Kavya if she missed Texas. Without missing a beat, she said, "Only the superior barbeque, the regular-sized rats, and the people who do this super weird thing where they *smile back* if you smile at them." A few more students laughed, and it was all still super awkward, but at least no one left.

One week later, after the students read analyses about the end of British colonialism in India and studied maps of the region, she passed out copies of her letter. She asked them to follow along as she read.

Dear Cyril Radcliffe,
You died at the age of 78, two years after I was born. In your last days, did you think about what you did? You were the British lawyer who spent about five weeks hastily drawing the boundaries of two new independent states, India and Pakistan. You were tasked with carving out where the Muslims would go, and where the Hindus and Sikhs would go. You had never been to India before this job, and the mighty men of the British Empire thought this lack of direct knowledge would insure your neutrality. But you got confused easily about demographics, history, and more, not even realizing Kashmir existed until you got back home. You were too scared of the heat to do proper field research and thus relied on outdated information.

You, a bumbling idiot, are the reason we have the Radcliffe Line that divides India and Pakistan. That divided Pakistan into west and east, with India in the middle, which of course led to bloody turmoil before the independence of Bangladesh. Okay, maybe it's not all your fault. But you made the final call on all the controversial decisions.

You gave the maps to the last viceroy of India, Lord Mountbatten, before August 15, 1947, the date of the transfer of power. But he waited until he could enjoy the celebrations of India's and Pakistan's independence and only released the maps afterward! Can you imagine how that only magnified the terror people were already feeling about being on the "wrong side" of your lines? But what did you care. You burned your notes and left India as soon as you could, petrified that the people would be angry at you and kill you. When I read about you, I thought, wow, mediocre white men really have been ruining the world for a while.

Kavya paused as she heard waves of nervous giggles.

I want to know whether you died peacefully. There was no peace for the one to two million people who died during the mass migrations of Partition. They were burned alive on trains trying to get to the "right" country. Pregnant women were chopped into pieces. And what about those who didn't die? Do you know how many stories I read about women whose families rejected them for being abducted and raped and thus "dishonored" by "enemies"? The violence intentionally inflicted on children? Families forever separated? The grandparents, silenced by the line you drew through their lives, who now struggle to talk with their loved ones who ask, but what happened back then? You got off easy. You got to go back to your wife. You had no children, but what about the descendants of your buddies, those British cowards? Look at the stories they write today about us South Asians. You completely shook our world! But they still say, "Look at those violent, backward people. Look at how they treat each other. Such savages. So many problems over there. Such a pity." But those British descendants don't get the last word, and neither do you.

Kavya stopped and looked up. "See how I get to insert myself, and say, hey, this is on you, look at what you did." She scanned the room. Every single student was listening, truly listening. That pleasant buzz she used to get while teaching finally hit her. Finally!

And that project turned everything around. While the students discussed with each other the stories that they had chosen, compiled lists of their research, and worked on their letters, Kavya added more to her own letter, bragging to Radcliffe about cross-border family reunions, the stunning corpus of Partition literature, people's resilience, and more.

The three white male students still smirked their way through the next few classes. But one of them, Jeff, created a provocative project, writing a letter about secrets to the researchers who recovered oral testimonies of Partition survivors.

Kavya pulled him aside and said, "Your research was so solid. But more than that, you are a gifted writer. I'm so proud of you."

He blushed. "Writing has always been a part of my life." He paused before continuing slowly, "I was in foster care for a few years and got moved around to a lot of schools. My social worker told me that writing would be a good constant in my life. So, you know, thank you so much for giving me a chance to write in this class."

And then they both stood and took each other in, each transforming into something beyond what the other had imagined. They nodded at each other, a silent agreement that maybe a tiny bit of trust now existed in the space between them.

Tell Me a Story

Kavya rubbed her eyes and looked around her home office, lit only by the computer screen. She stared at the screensaver of the boys that she had put up when they left for Stony Brook. She yearned to be smushed in between them for a group hug.

She let out a loud yawn.

Four years before, she had written that letter to Radcliffe. It was a simple little class assignment that shifted something for her and her students, even if just a bit.

Now, something was brewing inside of her.

She closed her laptop and made her way back into bed. 4:27 a.m. She closed her eyes and sank into a heavy, dreamless sleep.

When Kavya woke up, a sense of elation came upon her. She had fallen back asleep, even after a nightmare!

Even though it was Saturday, she didn't lounge around in her bedroom. She immediately made herself breakfast and settled in front of her computer.

She began to reread the letters her students had submitted since 2018. How strange. She had given this assignment every single semester for at least one unit in her International Relations course. Maybe she had underestimated exactly what this project could mean.

She leaned back as she ate another spoonful of granola and berries. She was enthralled as she read through countless papers. Sarcastic missives, heartrending pleas, enraged demands.

After a couple of hours, she stood up to stretch. She opened her window and took in the cool air and musky-sweet smell of the leaves all over the sidewalks. *Whoosh-whoosh.* Someone was kicking their way through the pile she had swept up in front of her house.

She sat back down and came across the letters from a class that had studied the writings of indentured workers' descendants. She remembered how those students couldn't quite wrap their minds around the idea that the British Empire shipped people around the world to work on plantations after the end of slavery. Yes, the empires specialized in human cargo.

Her cursor hovered over one student's paper about the agony of seeing one's family in pain yet not knowing what exactly caused the suffering. That student had quoted the eloquent writer Gaiutra Bahadur's struggles with tracing her great-grandmother's journey from India to a sugar plantation in Guyana:

If I draw an imaginary line from moment to moment on the ships, from glimpse to glimpse of women abroad, will her shape emerge, constellation-like? Could the wrong shape emerge, if I connect the wrong moments to one another? How do I know which are right? Will her constellation give off light?

Kavya was stunned. Yes, that was exactly what it was like to figure out what the hell had happened in her own family. She never had any answers, only dotted lines from memory to memory. Look at her brilliant students. Look at how they discovered the plot twists and holes that were a part of storytelling, that made it so confounding to comprehend one's own family history.

And Bahadur didn't give up. Instead, she conducted research about women *like* her great-grandmother, transmuting the gaps in her family's story and the silenced histories of indentured women into a revelatory, lush book, *Coolie Woman*.

Kavya could do the same, on a much smaller scale. Drawing out her own family tree had been intriguing, like she was trying to solve a mystery. No need to wail and beat her chest dramatically as she wondered about her family's past. No point in feeding her anxiety by trying to "process" all her feelings with Helen.

It was a simple matter of investigation into the stories of other families who had also witnessed India's post-independence years. Maybe she would discover some insight, even if in the "wrong shape," that would loosen the grip her past had on her. She could write a letter just for herself about families' experiences with colonialism and Partition. Oh, wait. The letter should be about who was responsible for historic, intergenerational trauma! If she pulled this off, maybe the dread that followed her everywhere might even dissipate.

A tiny voice nagged her. *I can't be so naïve. I'm no Gaiutra Bahadur. She is probably a strong, together person who can deal with her family's traumas. I am not.* But she ignored it, instead allowing herself to flirt with the idea of moving through the world with delicious ease, not the usual gnawing apprehension.

She closed her computer and the window and set out to enjoy her day. She rode her bike along the water all the way to the Verrazzano Bridge and back, enjoying the crisp air, the wind howling in her ears, the joy of being able to balance, something she thought she had lost. Then she walked her bike through Owl's Head Park, chatting with some neighbors along the way.

At some point, she pulled out her phone to text with her sons in their group chat. *Kabir, I was remembering my first year teaching here and your first year of high school, and how miserable I was at first with the students' disrespect, and then a month later, I had to drag you into the principal's office for acting up. But we survived it all, right?*

A response came immediately from Kabir. *Do you remember how you made me write a long research paper about adolescent rebellion and healthy outlets of expression?!!*

Samir added, *Big deal. Mama threatened to embarrass me in front of the whole school if I didn't rat you out the second you skipped class again.*

Kavya giggled as she leaned against a tree. *That's right! I was never actually going to do anything, but I did think about spreading a hilarious nickname. It was either going to be SAMosa or SAMsquatch. Or Pap Samir if you guys really pushed me. Get it??*

Oh, Mom, that's not the cutting-edge humor you think it is. Kabir shut her down cold, as usual.

Still laughing after they stopped texting, she did one more loop on her bike around the park.

When she came back home, sweaty and energized, she stood aimlessly in her living room. She almost cried with relief that little bits of "before" were reentering her life. *Thank you, God. Thank you.* The chants of gratitude continued as she showered and changed. She looked at herself in the mirror, trying on a bright smile and even flipping her hair, which was looking shiny and bouncy again. *Thank you.*

She ended up going right back to her computer to read more students' projects, this time seeking out the ones on Partition. As she read, she realized that she had completely forgotten how Ajji regularly talked about the tragedy of India and Pakistan being enemies. Ajji once said that she so badly wanted to visit the Shah Jahan Mosque in Pakistan's Sindh province to admire the tiles but knew she could never go as an Indian citizen.

By the time she finished reading, her grandmother had filled up her entire mind. Too many memories had been unleashed in therapy. They were tumbling out, groaning from being cramped up and hidden away for so long.

Time for a break. Kavya closed her computer, grabbed her purse and jacket, and left her house. She walked to the pub on the corner, always teeming with an odd mix of hipsters and cranky, old Italian men. She sat down at the far end of the bar, where she knew that her favorite bartender would quickly get her usual sparkling wine.

After catching the bartender's eye and nodding, she rested her head against the wall. *Ajji, Ajji.* She sighed, waiting impatiently for her drink, needing something to dull her longing for her grandmother.

As she sat, she watched two couples in the corner. Two women were holding hands under the table, while another woman was laughing as a man draped his arm around her and wore a sly expression.

Once upon a time, she had been a part of that exact scene.

She and Freddy had been laughing endlessly over drinks and hot wings, while Janet swooned over her girlfriend Fiona, whom she had brought up with her to New York to introduce to Kavya.

Kavya and Freddy kicked each other under the table every time Janet touched Fiona and said, "babe."

At one point, Janet pressed her hand onto Fiona's thigh, slowly inching up under her dress.

"Janet!" Fiona exclaimed while giggling.

Janet moved her hand to her girlfriend's arm instead. "I'll wait until tonight, babe."

Freddy bent his head to whisper to Kavya, "See, I told you we couldn't do a drinking game about this. We'd be in the hospital, *babe.*" And Kavya had laughed, the kind of loud body laugh you did when you were utterly relaxed, when you felt comfortable enough to even let out some snorts.

A few months after that night, Kavya, Freddy, and the boys were at Janet and Fiona's backyard wedding. Kavya and her sons taught Fiona's little girl how to line dance. Everyone bounced around and laughed, while

Janet's permanently angry eyebrows relaxed for once, and she cupped Fiona's delicate, pale freckled face in her hands in absolute adoration. At the end of the night, Kavya slow danced with Freddy as he kissed the sweat off her neck.

Kavya was startled out of her daydreaming when the sparkling wine appeared before her. Sipping, she looked at the laughing woman with the man. A wave of loneliness swept over her, surprising her with its force. She tested her balance by quickly looking from left to right, and back. *I'm okay. Everything is okay.*

She shifted her focus to the bar napkins in front of her. Her stomach growled as she caught a whiff of melted cheese. She pulled out a pen from her purse to doodle while she drank, but Ajji loomed large.

Ajji had died of a heart attack when Kavya was seventeen. After the funeral in India, at the stifling hot airport waiting for the plane to Germany and then Texas, she hovered around the edges of the small circle Mohan, Neela, and Pramod had formed at a table.

Pramod wiped his forehead with a handkerchief. "She is at least free of suffering."

"But she didn't suffer," Neela protested. "She died suddenly."

"I mean what she went through being a widow and having to deal with . . . him."

Mohan and Neela were silent, and Kavya pretended to be thumbing through her novel.

Kavya brought herself back into the present. *Stop thinking about all that.* She rested her foot on the bar stool next to her and focused on her sketch. She drew Ajji in her sari, the pallu turning into a paisley design that went off the edge of the napkin. She swallowed the last drop of her drink and looked back at the corner table. The laughing woman leaned her head on the man's shoulder, with her eyes closed and an easy smile on her face.

* * *

As Kavya walked home from the bar, she FaceTimed her sons. While the phone rang, she checked her balance one more time. Still walking steady.

"Mom."

"Mama."

Oh, they were so exquisite! She was secretly thankful that the only thing they seemed to have inherited from their biological father was their lanky builds. They were truly all hers, and only hers.

In the screen, the two were mashed together in a beanbag in Kabir's dorm room. It was so endearing that they had decided together that they would go to the same university. She watched them elbow each other and remembered them as a tangle of little arms and legs and hands, eating each other's food, stealing each other's toys. Even during those rough high school years, they would read or play video games next to each other on the couch, their long hairy legs all jumbled up.

Kabir leaned into the phone. His face filled the screen. "How's it going, Mom?"

"Mama," came Samir's voice from the background. "Could you get Janet Auntie away from Instagram already? She finds all this strange stuff that's obvs so cringe. Seriously, the two of you and what you think is funny."

"This again? Janet Auntie and I have a great sense of humor." She unlocked her door and entered her house.

The three of them talked over each other, as always. After half an hour of laughing, interrupting, teasing, they hung up. Calmed by the conversation, she settled in for the night. Ajji hung around a little but in a way that felt okay.

Usually on Saturday nights, she was hanging out with friends, or making plans for Sunday picnics or movies. But she had been avoiding all of that since the panic attacks started. Today made her realize how much she had been hiding away from the world and especially Ming-ming, whom she had not seen since that failed movie date. Kavya texted her an invitation to brunch, determined to show her friend that she was going to be perfectly fine.

* * *

The next day at noon, Kavya waited in front of an unassuming restaurant on Ditmas Avenue. Mothers hurried along on their errands, yelling at their children in Urdu, Bengali, and a few other languages Kavya couldn't quite place. It had rained during the night, and the entire road smelled like damp dirt and asphalt.

Mingming appeared out of nowhere, a gigantic yellow umbrella tucked under her arm. They embraced and hurried inside the restaurant, as gray clouds moved in ominously.

They sat down to laminated multi-page menus at a narrow, red vinyl booth. Kavya laughed after they ordered some of the new Chinese-Indian options. "This is really us being walking stereotypes. Fusion friends, fusion food!"

"Coming hard with the dad jokes I see." Mingming chortled, smoothing down her already silky hair. "I'm glad you contacted me. My ass would have stayed in bed all day. Well, until my team calls me. There's always work to be done." She rested her face on her palm.

Kavya saw that underneath her friend's eyes were deep, dark circles, like half-moons sitting on top of her high, shiny cheekbones.

A man stopped by with drinks. Looking around the restaurant, Mingming played with the straw in her can of ginger ale. "Hey, where are we taking our trip?"

Kavya pulled out her phone and read aloud what she had researched about Nova Scotia. They usually planned their annual summer vacations several months early. Something to look forward to.

The waitress brought out the food, and Mingming peeled the wrapper off the chopsticks. "Nova Scotia will be so beautiful in the summer, and everyone tells me the seafood is phenomenal." She pointed her chopsticks at Kavya. "Now, all I have to say is to pack clothes for cold weather this time. I'm not roaming around the northern Atlantic coast with you whining about being frozen. The nights will be even colder than they were in Vermont."

Kavya shrugged. "Aww, you didn't like lending me your clothes last time? I liked wearing Nirvana and Pearl Jam sweatshirts all night. I felt so grunge."

"Don't say grunge." Mingming narrowed her eyes and shook her head. "That's so denigrating to the complexity of that music."

As they discussed their trip, they were interrupted by a small boy pressing his face into the window and sticking his tongue out at Mingming. The mother yanked him away. Mingming laughed and turned back to Kavya. "Anyways, where were we? Oh, by the way, how are you?"

"Well, I'm very excited. I'm going to start researching the link between Partition and the generational pain that families carry because of it. I just have all these ideas!"

"Right, right." Mingming nodded, looking unimpressed. "I meant how's your anxiety. I haven't seen you since that whole incident." She gave her a knowing look.

Kavya spooned tamarind sauce onto her plate. She knew Mingming thought she should just get on some super-strength cocktail of meds and call it a day. "Maybe it's connected? My therapist sort of got me thinking about my dysfunctional family and my anxiety. We've been talking about intergenerational and historic trauma, and I think I can research that, and it will help me somehow."

Mingming moved the broccoli around with her chopsticks. Kavya could see her irritation.

"Meh. I don't know," Mingming finally said. "So trendy to have trauma these days. It's a cop-out."

"Why?" asked Kavya.

"My grandma's descending into dementia, and she is just living in another time when she was in China. Her whole life she has just hated on the Japanese, right? Like she would disown me or something if she knew that I hung out with Janet *and* her mother when they came up here. Two Japanese women at once? Blasphemy! But now it's just consuming her. My grandma yells at my mom when she takes care of her, and my mom yells at me. And then when I tell her to stop, she's all, 'Your grandmother has so much trauma. Your father gives me trauma. What am I supposed to do?' Like, Mom, get some support for my grandmother's condition and stop talking to Dad."

Kavya replied sadly, "I didn't know about this. That sounds stressful for everyone."

"Whatever," Mingming said coolly. "I'm too busy to think about it much." She shook her head. "My mom says the word trauma, but it's not like she ever answers my questions about the details of what happened to anyone. She once let it slip when I was in high school that my father's father died from starvation. Then she acted like it was so forbidden to talk about that I had to go find books to learn anything about the famine."

"The famine ... before the Cultural Revolution, I assume?" asked Kavya.

Mingming nodded.

As Kavya dolloped her veggies with an array of sauces and chutneys, she suppressed an inappropriate excitement about what her friend just said. Maybe everyone had to play detective with their own families.

"Umm, Mingming. You don't have to answer this if it's too personal. But do you think your dad being so rough on you and your family has anything to do with his own shit with his father dying like that? I'm not excusing it at all, I swear." She stopped herself. She had not too long ago thrown a fit because Helen had mentioned her father, and here she was getting into her friend's business.

"Whatever. I'm sure it affected him in all kinds of ways." Mingming rubbed her eyes. "But there are plenty of people whose parents died of starvation. They didn't all become angry jerks, did they? If my dad dared to talk to me about trauma, after treating us like shit all these years, I'd fucking punch him. There's your trauma."

"I get it. More than you know," Kavya said softly.

Mingming gave her a resigned smile.

They changed the subject, but Kavya couldn't focus, aware of an impulse to poke Mingming to hear more about her family.

Kavya dipped a steamed momo into chutney and stuffed it into her mouth. As she slowly chewed, the tender pork melted into the sweet tomato. She swallowed and dabbed her mouth with her napkin. "God, I forgot how delicious this place is."

After she finished off the momos, she said, "Listen, I'm sorry I brought up your dad. My therapist talked about these books, like one is called *The Body Keeps the Score*, you know?" She drifted off, hoping her friend might ask questions.

"My former therapist mentioned that book." Mingming wrinkled her nose. "Remember when I got those hives when I went to go visit my brother, after he told me at the last minute that my dad would be there? My therapist said, 'Oh, Mingming, your body is letting you know that it remembers his anger. Let's listen to your body, she is sharing her wisdom.' And I was like, listen to me say I'm never coming back here."

Kavya laughed. "Okay, so all the therapists talk about it then."

"Must be in their manual."

Kavya gestured with her fork. "So, why don't you think trauma is something worth looking at?"

"You don't have to convince me it's important. Are *you* convinced? You're the one talking about it."

"I am not convinced at all. But the thing is that I felt so hopeful when I thought about researching events that my own family lived through. I'd have some kind of answer to everything that's always bothered me. That must mean something, right?"

The happy din around them grew louder as the brunch crowd swelled to fill the restaurant.

"Not sure it means anything except that you're an academic." Mingming was skeptical.

"But you just said you had to go seek information about the famine. Would you ever want to research other people's stories about that time and fill in some of the gaps that your own family never told you? And then you would . . ." Kavya wasn't sure anymore about what she wanted to say. But she could hear how desperation laced her words. She needed Mingming to tell her to keep going, to approve of her ridiculous plan to research her way into sanity.

Mingming smiled sadly. "I just want to tell you about my screwed-up family and know you'll get it and then go back to living in denial."

"I always want to live in denial," Kavya responded emphatically. "My body has given me a hard no on that though." She tried to ignore the tears brimming in her eyes.

Mingming looked out the window. The rain had started. "Kavya, honestly, at the end of the day, despite everything, I love my family. Maybe from afar, but I still love them. I sometimes think about what it's like for them, to have experienced what they did and to now be in the U.S. It must be so unreal."

Kavya was silent. She blinked several times and used her fingers to quickly flick away any hint of tears. Did she love her dad? What about Neela? She did love them, but it was a hungry, ugly love. She felt some air leave her body, like someone had punctured her lungs and they were slowly deflating.

Mingming turned back to Kavya. "I mean, I was born here and still don't feel like this is my real life. It's like when I'm calling you about every stupid thing these white people say to me—the partners, the associates, the clients. Is it still just a microaggression when people look right at you if they mention COVID? Or say mocking shit like, 'Oh Mingming, cancan youyou helphelp?' That's just straight up hostility at that point, isn't it?"

Kavya nodded, forcefully pushing the weight of Neela off her chest. She took a deep breath. The steady drumming of the rain on the roof and windows was soothing. "Yeah, it's hostility. But if you dare say anything, they say they were just kidding, or they were misunderstood, or they don't remember doing it. Or they act like you're unhinged. Only their feelings matter."

"Bingo. And then you try to explain to the white people who do love you for real. And you can tell they're just continuously upset and surprised that you're experiencing it. Take Charles. The closest he got was when some idiot friend asked him if he has an Asian fetish. But he doesn't get what it's like at a cellular level. You do." Mingming's face fell.

"You okay?"

"Yeah, just, it's a thing I wish didn't come in between me and him. He doesn't get what it's like to try to be your own person and be nothing like your family but realize that you're completely intertwined with your family because you're always standing up for them, or at least people like them, against the racists."

They were quiet. Yeah, Kavya remembered the racist comments at school events, at the store, and so on when she was growing up. Sometimes she argued back and defended her aunt and uncle. But she also remembered Neela and Pramod's reprehensible running commentary about "the illegals." Plus, she spent most of her time hoping someone would stand up for *her*. Every summer, she used to silently pray that Ajji would admonish Neela. But her grandmother always treated Neela gingerly, speaking in a sorrowful, almost guilty way.

A baby's high-pitched squeal abruptly brought Kavya back to the table. She watched her friend for a moment before asking, "Can I say something kind of weird to you?"

"When do you *not* say something weird to me?"

Kavya leaned forward, peeling her back off the sticky booth seat, which released a ripping sound. "Oh, jeez," she said. "When's the last time this thing was cleaned?"

"Anyways, this 'cellular level' feeling?" Kavya stared intently at her friend. "And all this immigrant family shit? Do you ever feel like we're swept up in something that started before we were even born but that no one will explain to us?"

"Are you saying there's like an ancestral presence or something?"

"No, I don't think so."

Mingming smiled. "Well, I believe in ancestral spirits. Don't you?"

"Wow, I don't know if I do," Kavya said, surprised. "Okay, yeah, I very much believe in some of the Hindu goddesses, so I guess that's something." Her voice started shaking. "But I wish I felt my mom's presence, like desperately. Or my grandmother's. But don't you wish someone could just tell us what the hell happened before we were even born? What really happened?"

"Well, let's just be grateful you and I can talk about this kind of stuff, ancestral ghosts or not." Mingming responded with a smile that was warm but also tired, like she was ready to talk about something else.

Kavya changed the topic. And she decided to focus on her relief that despite the heaviness in her body, she was finally having a meal at a restaurant without that agonizing feeling that she was tilting, that the room was falling out from under her feet.

BREAKTHROUGH

Kavya could not help but start rereading Partition literature as soon as she got home from seeing Mingming. Over the following weeks, the nightmares and panic miraculously started to recede somehow, mucking things up somewhere in the depths of her brain but not enough to disrupt her days. Were these Partition stories distracting her from her anxiety? Were they *solving* her anxiety? Was she doing better because she was meeting with Helen twice a week now? Who cared what the answer was. She attended all her classes in person and even some committee meetings, singing her gratitude every minute of it all.

On campus one afternoon, Kavya saw Yandelis by the bike racks, twirling her spiral curls around her finger and wearing a glum expression on her face.

"Hey," Kavya called out, guilt washing over her as she walked through clouds of cigarette smoke and loud snippets of conversation. She arrived in front of Yandelis, who immediately smiled.

"Yandelis, I am really sorry, but I never followed up with you about changing your major and your mom being upset at you."

"You're good. It's just stupid parent stuff." Yandelis scratched her arm with her long blue nails and looked preoccupied again, chewing her gum with her mouth open.

"No, it's not stupid at all," Kavya replied. "And I'm here to talk to you about it. Do you want to?"

"No, it's okay. My mom's always riding me for something or the other, like every day." Yandelis looked forlorn.

Kavya wanted to make the poor kid feel better. "Yandelis, you know I have been reading those letters I had you all do. Remember that letter project assignment? Yours was so brilliant."

"Oh, thank you!" Yandelis beamed. "Yeah, I had fun with that one."

"Well, I've been doing a ton of research for a little project for myself on intergenerational experiences with global politics. You know, like 'the personal is political,' but focusing on families."

"Whoa." Yandelis blinked several times.

Kavya blurted out, "I'm confronting some things in my own family, and you know, they went through colonialism and Partition and all that. It's stuff like abuse, mental health issues, and colorism." *Where the fuck did that come from?*

Yandelis took it in stride, as if her professors regularly confessed their problems to her. "Oh yeah. My family's got all of that. Plus, other stuff." She blew a bubble, popped it with her nail, and kept chewing loudly.

Something pushing the words out of her mouth, Kavya continued, "Do you want to be my research assistant, maybe?"

"What?" Yandelis gasped. "Me? Really? What would I do?"

Kavya laughed, mostly at herself because she hadn't planned to ask this of her student. "I don't know!" She leaned against the bike rack. "Okay, I'm thinking out loud. So, trauma gets perpetuated if we don't resolve it, right? And the world keeps trauma going through ongoing political conflict or oppression, which then reopens both political and family wounds. What if we did a semester-long series of letters about who is responsible for or a witness to the global events that result in intergenerational trauma? You could research any firsthand stories about that pain within families, like partner violence, silence, child abuse, estrangement, trying to protect each other, all that stuff. Also, you can be my teaching assistant for the fall International Relations class!"

Yandelis blinked and adjusted her glasses. "I would love that. Like, all my best friends deal with family drama, and, you're right, a lot of times it's connected to historic, political things going on, like their parents were refugees or whatever. Doing something like this would be so validating!" Her blinking increased along with her excitement. "Can we also do campus-wide student workshops for anyone to do letters? We should come up with a workbook or toolkit for anyone to use, like to raise awareness about what you're describing. Please? This is so important!"

"Yeah, I'll figure out a way to do the workshops," Kavya said, running through ideas in her mind. She moved to the side as a student next to her struggled to lock his bike. "I'll find a way to compensate you for all this work, by the way."

She hesitated before spitting out everything floating around in her head, "I could write a few letters so the students have some examples. I also need to throw myself into the process for this idea to really work. I'll send you the letter I end up writing on colonialism, Partition, and family trauma." Kavya ended the sentence with a confident nod, even though she didn't know what the hell had come over her. *What am I doing?*

"Great! I can't wait to read it."

They chatted a bit more before Kavya had to teach. She entered the building, walked near the wall through the lobby, and then held firmly onto the staircase railing, fully expecting to tilt, or hyperventilate, or completely lose her mind. But she didn't.

When she got through class and back home in one piece, she stood in front of her computer. She was starving and wanted to shower, but she couldn't stop herself. She sat down and began a letter to the company that produced and marketed skin lightening cream throughout South Asia. And she wrote, read, rewrote, all evening, all Friday, and throughout the weekend.

Sunday night, she poured herself a glass of wine. She emailed Helen the letter she had written. Then she sent it to Yandelis. She was almost giddy. Thank goodness for being an academic. Thanks to a research deep-dive and one little letter, she was the closest she had ever been to facing her family shit. The beauty of the letters was that they could be cathartic even with just a hint or gesture at the more intense rumblings underneath. This brief experiment was even enough to make her feel like maybe she was finding her way back to herself. She sipped her wine, a wide grin on her face.

DEAR BOARD OF DIRECTORS

Dear Board of Directors of Hindustan Unilever,
One day, I came across Indian writer Hema Gopinathan Sah's poem, "Kali," which captures the colorist treatment she experienced due to her darker skin tone. You should read about

everything she was supposed to give up, like swimming, wearing bright colors, mental health, and physical health, for the sake of light skin, for the punishment of having dark skin.

Since you market and sell skin-lightening products throughout South Asia and its diasporas, you might balk at this accusatory letter about the harm your products do to people's bodies, minds, and souls. You might tell me that you're inclusive now. You now proudly call your cream "Glow & Lovely" even though it took you until 2020 to stop using "Fair & Lovely." And it still aims to "brighten" the skin.

I'm here to tell you about the intergenerational trauma you perpetuate with your product, no matter how you market it. It's time we talk about where colorism comes from and name it as a form of abuse.

Allow me a little detour first. Partition made us fear and detest the Other, made us obsess over borders and unmapped land. Look at the governments' machinations to appropriate even the tiniest, most uninhabitable pieces of contested land. Loss of territory can feel like the loss of one's own sense of self, and it can even feel like an assault on one's body. All that fear is still alive today, as you can see with the border tensions between Pakistan, India, and Bangladesh and with ethnonationalism throughout these countries.

You probably know about the rampant sexual assault of women (and many men and children) during Partition, and how assaulted people were rejected by their families for being "impure." Those legacies continue. You probably know our societies continue to attack and kill people for having sex, for being queer, for deciding what to do with their own flesh. To socially ostracize, diminish, and humiliate "bad" loved ones is a way to sanctify defiled families and countries. Bodies, as we feminists like to say, are where we all work out our agendas. Feeling emasculated because you can't get a job or you're totally distraught by your fucked up country or because you couldn't stop your daughter from being raped or you don't know where your worth comes from? Get a sense of control back by beating the shit out of your family!

But here's the thing. Bodies are covered in skin. Skin is meaningful. It's the intimate protective layer upon our flesh that is read by the world. It's the first field of contact with others. It's not just "sexual purity" but also skin tone that marks our inherent value, our social capital, our way of asserting our dominance when we can't control the never-ending political aftermath of Partition. And I think back to Sah's poem. Sah knows, just as you do, how too many people interpret dark skin as catastrophic. To have dark skin can condemn one to being the target of endless violence. You know that dark skin is why women are taunted and harassed by in-laws for more dowry money, are murdered so that men can remarry someone lighter, are called kaaliya or black when being beaten by their families. Who wants to be dark when we're supposed to be light to signify our greatness and our proximity to the very white supremacists who decided we were too small and stupid to determine our own lives?

I know about too many mothers who cry about why their daughters are too dark. People shocked that someone's darker-skinned partner is kind or smart. The darker-skinned children singled out by their own loved ones to be taunted and psychologically tortured. Their skin color matches the dreaded "before" pictures in your old advertisements (and who are we kidding, your new "inclusive" ones as well)? These victims of colorism all throughout the diaspora may never recover, maybe internalizing that they don't deserve to be seen, maybe continuing the cycle of abuse. Don't you know that what you're selling keeps alive our Partition nightmares?

From Kavya, a non-fair, medium brown, never-customer

HUMILIATE

Kavya sat next to her colleagues in the boardroom, watching as the provost, Linda, impeccably dressed as always, and the associate provost, Mark, arms folded, already aggravated, sat next to each other at the end of the long table. As the white president of the university mentioned every chance he could, they were both "diverse Latino administrators," whatever that meant.

Of course, he also made Linda and Mark take the heat for any controversy remotely related to race, which is why they were addressing the faculty today.

Linda cleared her throat and placed pearl-adorned reading glasses on the tip of her nose. The buzz in the room gradually receded.

"I would like to read a statement from our university president." She proceeded to speak quickly and quietly, in a monotone voice, as if no one would notice or care about what she said.

"Two years ago, the entire country faced a racial reckoning after the murder of George Floyd. Our African-American students rightfully demanded change. We listened. We hired a reputable organization to build a comprehensive series of workshops and training. These interventions were not designed to be attended by senior leadership so that we could focus our resources on those who primarily interact with students. Unfortunately, faculty members over the past few weeks have falsely claimed that senior leadership did not attend due to our alleged lack of commitment to anti-racism. We regret that we did not better communicate our intentions, and we reiterate our commitment to becoming an anti-racist institution."

Murmurs and whispers. And then several hands, including Kavya's, shot up in the air. Mark looked at Linda and nodded. He uncrossed his arms and roughly shoved up his sleeves. Tufts of dark brown hair unfurled, released from the confines of his too-tight pinstriped shirt.

Mark spoke in his usual brash style. "It seems some staff members are the ones who recently and erroneously told you that we were supposed to attend this training. Then, you all immediately decided to attack our characters and complain so incessantly that we had to call this meeting." He looked around. He picked up a pen. Twirled it as he let the words slide off his tongue without any thought as to where and how they would land.

He added scornfully, "You never thought that the staff were mistaken or speaking out of turn? Now we have to put some changes in place to make sure there are no further leaks or misinformation from our offices. I hope your hysteria was worth it."

Kavya quickly looked around. Almost everyone lowered their hands. Linda fidgeted with her glasses and stayed quiet. Kavya kept her hand raised.

Mark rolled his eyes, like an insolent child. "Okay, yes, Kev . . . Kaviya?"

"It's pronounced Kavya," she corrected him. He twiddled the pen between two fingers. "Mark, your office first sent out a memo two years ago proudly claiming that even senior leadership was doing the training. It's signed by you and Linda. So, I don't see this 'miscommunication' as our fault and especially not the staff's fault."

She looked around to see some of her colleagues nodding. One made a motion with her hand, as if asking Kavya to keep going. Buoyed, she continued, "I feel like when you say that you're going to stop leaks, and also the way you're communicating with us right now, it just creates fear and damages our morale." She looked around again, but no one met her eyes this time.

The room was quiet. Mark's neck turned red, the crimson creeping into his face, releasing blotches of anger all over his skin. He leaned forward, looking straight at Kavya. "You don't know what you're talking about. You and your buddies here need to grow up."

Kavya spoke through gritted teeth, trying to sound calm, even though her voice shook. "I do not think it is appropriate for you to speak to me this way."

"It is appropriate for me to correct you when you are trying to create a hostile work environment," Mark said icily.

Kavya's throat and chest burned. A voice deep inside of her begged, *Shut up.* "You . . ."

Linda quickly jumped in. "Okay! I think now is a good time to table this discussion. We will circle back to everyone." She droned on for several more minutes, by which point Kavya could barely sit still in her seat.

The meeting ended, and Kavya practically ran out of the building so that she could fume outside. She paced back and forth, with her messenger bag flapping angrily against her hips. She checked her phone. A voicemail about fraudulent activity on her credit card.

An ancient, well-worn sensation came upon her. She knew what it meant and rushed to the bus stop.

As she waited, her phone lit up with texts from her colleagues, all tenured and senior to her, who had just watched her get scolded.

Good job with Mark! Proud to call you my friend. Sorry I couldn't really chime in. Here if you want to talk.

I can't believe how he acted. You held your own. It's hard for me to know what to do in the moment.

Brave to do that when you don't have tenure yet.

She ignored the messages and checked her app to see that an express bus was on its way. Perfect! Because that familiar feeling was getting stronger. Something from long ago that she should never ignore.

The bus rolled to a stop. As she started up the steps and held her bag by the handle, her foot got caught in the bag strap. While she managed not to fall on her face, she twisted her ankle badly. So much so that even the bus driver said, "Oh shit! That's gonna hurt tomorrow."

"Thanks," Kavya muttered as she limped to a seat. She pulled out her phone and opened her emails. She typed in Mark's name with the subject heading, *Today*. And then she proceeded to write out a self-loathing, obsequious email in which she apologized for not being more collaborative and committed to a "great working relationship" moving forward. She pressed send.

She got home, wrapped and iced her ankle, called the credit card company, and nervously refreshed her emails. It was not until 11 p.m. that she saw a response from Mark. She opened it only to read: *Great. Always willing to work with cooperative partners. See you on campus.*

The relief hit her quickly, that old sensation dissipating but leaving behind its usual residue of regret and disgust. What had she done?

* * *

The next day, Kavya recounted the incident with Mark in Helen's office.

Helen's mouth dropped open. "I'm so sorry he spoke to you like that. And I wish you didn't feel like you had to apologize."

This week's scent seemed to be vanilla, but the artificial kind—was there even such a thing as vanilla essential oil?

"Yes!" Kavya coughed to clear her sinuses of the sickly-sweet smell that seemed to be settling into her nose and throat. "I had to send the email so that, you know, nothing bad would happen. I had such a horrible sense of dread I had to get rid of."

"Magical thinking! We've talked about that a bit. How can you offer a corrective to yourself?"

"I can tell myself that the credit card thing and the ankle were coincidences. They weren't punishments for 'speaking back' to Mark. He didn't cast a magic spell on me. I can tell myself that I can tolerate it if someone is upset at me." Kavya didn't quite believe the words she was saying. *What if, what if.* She wanted to close her eyes and stop all the noise inside her head.

"Did you experience magical thinking like this when you were with Ranjeet?"

Kavya stopped for a second. "Well, I mean, I guess I did actually get punished when I disagreed with him. But at the same time, he seemed really attuned to my abandonment crap. He always told me where he was going and called when he got there, even if it took him forever to find a phone. And he eventually bought us both those flip phones, back in the early days before smartphones. He was surprisingly understanding about my childhood fears." She swallowed. Ugh, she had been so grateful when Ranjeet had shown her the phones.

"Can we talk about what scared you as a kid?"

"Nice one, Helen. I didn't even realize I set myself up with that one."

Helen laughed. "Well, I walked right on in with the opening you gave me."

Kavya considered Helen's question. *Should I answer?* She thought about the sessions she and Helen had spent talking about her present-day safety with her chosen loved ones. And she allowed her mind to deliberately go to Neela.

Neela had always been in a fighting stance, always ready to bite off someone's head, chomping down hard, in response to any perceived insult.

How many times had Neela said, "It's so hard to take care of you. What did I do in my life to deserve you?"

How many times had Neela left the house in a huff, yelling, "I never want to come back here! I'm going to kill myself!" Each time her aunt left, Kavya stayed by the window. She counted to ten, then backward. She snapped her fingers with each number. Over and over again. *Please come back. I'll be good.*

One time, Neela screamed at Pramod about how she hated being in the house with him and Kavya. She put on her shoes and seethed, "You will only appreciate me when I'm gone. I'm going to die *now*."

Kavya threw herself at Neela's feet, sobbing. "No, don't kill yourself!" Her terror at last overrode her usual impulse to quietly begin her routine at the window.

Neela snarled back, "I'm just going to the store, stupid."

After Kavya shared these fragmented memories, Helen asked, "What was your magic ritual of counting and snapping fingers supposed to do?"

"I don't know," Kavya said, sulking. "Undo whatever bad thing I had done to cause her to be upset at me. Summon God or the universe to make sure she was happy and alive."

"And what did you think would happen if you didn't do your magic ritual?"

"That maybe she would die. Or maybe I would get punished for daring to . . . for trying to . . ." Kavya gazed past Helen at the wall, focusing on a framed oil painting of a mountain and lake.

"Daring to exist?" Helen suggested.

"Daring to be myself, instead of using all my energy to make her happy."

"She said such horrible things to you about taking care of you."

"I guess," Kavya said as she shrugged. "Maybe she never wanted to be stuck with her brother's kid." She hated saying the sentence aloud. She hated that this was her story.

"Whatever she felt or didn't, she had no right to make you feel like you were a burden," Helen said passionately.

"She couldn't have biological kids and maybe I was just a reminder of that. But who knows. I don't really know about how she felt about anything except contempt for me." Kavya sighed. "When I was a teenager, I did ask her why she threatened to kill herself when I was younger. She ignored my questions and said, 'Why are you always focusing on the past? You're not right in the head.'"

She cradled her head in her hands, put her elbows on her knees, and leaned forward until her hair fell over her face. She didn't want to cry and especially not in front of Helen. But she almost *wanted* to cry, to get a release from the stinging grief spreading through her throat, cheeks, eye sockets, ear drums. Her entire face ached.

Helen said quietly, "That makes me so angry and heartbroken to hear. How does it make you feel?" She moved to the edge of her seat, so close that Kavya could smell mint on Helen's breath.

Kavya leaned back into her chair and grunted. "Huh. It is what it is. What did you think about that letter I sent to you?"

"So passionate!" Helen seamlessly followed Kavya's lead. "Fantastic bibliography I want to dig into. Your students are so lucky."

"Ok, yeah, yeah, I'm *awesome*," Kavya said sarcastically. "What did you think?"

Helen hesitated. "I think I would like to know more about what it has to do with your family."

"But . . . I did . . . what?" Kavya sputtered with indignation. She took a breath and tried to speak more evenly. "If you want me to spell it out, my great-grandfather lived through colonialism and Partition, and he targeted Neela with colorism and his anger. So that explains her being messed up and fucking with me. And that's why I'm messed up. There you go."

Before Helen could speak, Kavya abruptly said, "I did look inward for this. There was an entire line about dark-skinned children being picked on. Hello? That's fucking Neela." Her head pounded. She could hear children screaming happily just outside the window.

"Yes, I understood what you wrote," Helen remarked patiently. "I get it. But you wrote this letter to the board of directors of a company that sells skin-lightening products."

"So? They need to be held accountable, don't they?" Kavya raised an accusing finger and said incredulously, "Oh wait, did you expect me to write a letter to Neela? Well, hey, why don't I just send a *real* letter to her? Why don't I invite her over for tea and a sleepover?"

"No, I'm not asking you to do anything with Neela," Helen said gently. "The letter was a great first step, but it isn't a substitute for talking about your experiences as a child and how you feel about it. I think we're ready."

No, we are not fucking ready. "I get that you didn't see my specific emotions in what you read. It's not the most amazing piece of writing ever. But I did what I do best. I researched and analyzed. I wrote. My student Yandelis told me she loved it, by the way, and it's making her reflect on colorism in her family. And guess what? Somehow, I am now feeling better." Kavya pointed her hands upward and looked up. "Thank God!"

Helen was quiet. The children's laughter and the steady dripping of the fountain punctuated the silence.

Kavya eventually said, "I've been teaching in person and doing better, as you know, so maybe my instinct to do this letter about intergenerational trauma, or whatever you want to label it, was right. Isn't this all good?"

"Yes, it's good. Your nightmares and panic attacks seem to be less frequent. But there's still this intellectualizing or distancing that's happening that is a part of your suffering."

"You just said my letter was passionate. Now you're saying I'm intellectualizing. You're contradicting yourself. And obviously I'm suffering," Kavya said forcefully, her voice rising. "Do you know what it's like to grow up with someone who is constantly talking about their death?"

"Oh, Kavya, yes," Helen answered kindly. "It's far more common than you might know. It's absolutely unnerving for a child."

"I think I did a great fucking job with that letter because at the back of my mind, I even felt a little bit of compassion for Neela. I don't understand what you want from me." Kavya choked on the words.

Helen replied calmly, "You did do a great job. But I still want us to process your experiences. I don't want you to see yourself or anyone else as messed up. I want to get you to something more, where these childhood fears don't rule you."

Kavya realized that she didn't want anything more. She didn't want to rock the boat any more than she already had by dredging up the past. "Helen, you have to stop."

As she watched the puzzled look on her therapist's face, she sensed the images and sounds of something that had happened long ago. Every detail was etched into her body. And to this day, she was surprised she didn't have recurring nightmares about *this*.

* * *

Kavya remembered that she had been putting together her poster for the ninth-grade science fair.

Neela had yelled out from the kitchen, "Kavya, get in here. The spaghetti is almost ready. I have to cook your American food for you, and you can't clean up after yourself? How many times have I told you to clear the table of all your school crap?"

"I'll do it! I'm in the middle of something!" Kavya shouted as she rolled her eyes.

"Get in here when I tell you to. You can't do one simple thing. Everything I do for you. Lazy girl."

Kavya threw her markers down and stomped toward the kitchen, griping along the way, "I'm doing it now, okay? I'm coming right now."

She stepped into the kitchen. She saw Neela, holding a pot with her green potholders, the ones that were slightly frayed, one with a big brown stain. Clouds of steam billowed out. She saw Neela mouth *no* as she slowly tipped the pot onto her body. Kavya turned her head away. She heard sizzling and the clatter of the pot as it hit the floor.

She turned back when she heard the thump of Neela's body on the ground. She was writhing and beating at her chest and stomach, with her potholders still on her hands.

Neela screamed, "Kavya! What did you do?!"

Kavya ran out the back, pushed open the fence door, sprinted across the grass, and pounded on the neighbor's door. Just as Jenny, the neighbor, stepped out, Kavya found she could not speak. Jenny took one look at her face, and they both raced to Neela's house. They stared at Neela's curled-up body, clumps of noodles all around her.

Kavya ran into the living room, wailing. She could hear the neighbor say, "Oh God, Neela. I'm calling the ambulance. You will be okay."

* * *

Kavya found herself talking aloud, saying frantically to Helen, "But it's what happened!"

"Wait, what? What was?"

Kavya stared at her, realizing she hadn't meant to speak. *Shit, shit, shit.* Her breathing quickened and became shallow.

"Kavya," Helen questioned, "are you okay?"

Kavya was shaking. The room began to move. *Is this really my life? Is this happening?*

Helen put a foot forward, as if she was about to get off the chair. "What's going on?"

"No. No." Kavya tried to steady herself. She looked around for her water bottle. It was nowhere to be seen. She caught Helen's eyes, which were wide with worry. Had Neela ever looked at her like that? Helen reached her hand out.

And then a sickening flood of words spilled out before Kavya could stop it. "Do you know what my aunt did? She said it was an accident, but I saw her do it deliberately. I heard her describe the incident to others, and she completely made up this story that she was trying to get dinner ready quickly because she was so excited and proud to work with me on my science fair project, and that's why she ended up spilling everything on herself. But I saw her. She did it, and in a way that made me feel like she wanted me to see her do it and wanted me to blame myself. And

65

then she pretended she didn't do it. She told me that I had an overactive imagination. I don't know which part of this story is the most fucked up. Do you hear me?"

"Whoa, slow down. Do what deliberately? Do what?"

"She poured boiling hot water on her own body." Kavya punctuated each word, her face contorted in pain.

Helen recoiled. "Oh, God. Kavya."

Tears immediately rolled down Kavya's face. She said, as her voice wobbled, "This is why I hate talking about my past. Don't you get it?"

The room was hot and sticky, and she listened for the sounds of the fountain. She looked at the oil painting and tried to find the brush strokes. Her throat seemed like it was closing.

Kavya placed a hand on her chest to try to push down the humiliation she had spent her whole life trying to live with. Helen's look of alarm reminded her of the same mortified reaction of a friend from childhood.

That friend had come over to play. But out of nowhere, Neela showed up, screamed at them for making a mess in the kitchen, and threw their plates against the wall.

"Oh no, I want my mom. I need to go," the friend said, hurrying out of the front door as Kavya watched helplessly.

Neela then moaned, "Now everyone knows what a horrible person I am," and collapsed into agonizing sobs.

Helen leaned forward, her fast movement bringing Kavya out of that shame-soaked memory. "I'm sorry, Kavya. I just felt your pain and emoted."

"No, you're disgusted. You should be." Kavya's body shrank as she cried.

Helen put her hands up. "No, no, not at all."

Kavya contracted even more into herself, her hand still at her chest, until she became concave. She cried even harder. She cried for herself, for when she was a child. She cried with rage at Pramod and Mohan for not helping Neela, or for at least not keeping her away from Kavya.

She finally spoke, tears filling her mouth. "Sometimes when I think back to that night with the spaghetti, I can replay every single detail. But there are times when I'm not sure. Maybe I remembered it all wrong, my entire childhood, and convinced myself of something. Maybe *I'm* the one who doesn't know what reality is."

She licked her lips, as tears and mucus slid down her face. Panting from the exhaustion of weeping, Kavya grabbed a handful of tissues on the table next to her and wiped, smearing snot from one side to the other.

Helen quickly but firmly said, "I trust you. I believe you. And you know what's real."

"Well, I don't believe myself," Kavya said. She blew her nose and used another tissue to dry her face. "My friend Mingming said something about how life in the U.S. is unreal if you're a person of color. It is, because you just have to detach so many parts of yourself to try to make a life here. So, then what is real? Whose history? Which stories? Maybe that's why I got so into this letter project idea. I know what it's like to doubt reality. I just needed some stupid project to talk about what's real and say this shit fucking happened and still does! Stop denying it!"

Helen asked slowly, a hint of sorrow in her voice, "Can I say something?"

"Yes." Kavya clutched the soaked tissues in her hand.

Helen responded, this time with sadness filling the room, "I never knew that your aunt made you question reality. And I am so sorry that happened to you."

"It was terrifying. Down was up, up was down. Nothing ever, ever felt okay." Chills shook Kavya's body.

"I want you to know that you are safe now. We will keep working together, step by step," Helen said encouragingly. "We will help you tolerate the feelings you have when you speak up for yourself. And I love that this letter project became almost like a *container* for your pain, as if it's a safe way to talk about very difficult stories, some of which resonate with your own story. Am I getting it right?"

Kavya nodded. They sat silently for a few minutes, as she took more tissues out of the box.

Helen stood up, signaling the end of their session. "This was really heavy. Just call me if you need to talk. I'm here. You're not by yourself in this."

Kavya started to walk out the door but then turned and asked, "Have you heard stories from other patients like . . . the spaghetti one?"

"Sadly, I have." Helen looked pensive. "You know, your letter really was powerful. It hints just enough at a kind of pain that no one wants to talk about but plenty of people have experienced. I think you should keep going with this project. People like to know that they're not alone."

2

Winter

TELL ME IT'S OKAY

Kavya walked into the classroom on the last day before winter break. As she headed to the table where she usually dumped her coat and bag, she stopped for a moment. She blinked and stared at the floor. Was it tilting? Oh no, were the attacks coming back? She excused herself and scurried out of the classroom and around the corner, out of view of the students.

She leaned against the wall and looked around to test herself. No moving walls or floors. No lightheadedness. She thrust her hand into her bag to grab her mixed nuts, raisins, and M&Ms. Chewing methodically, she willed the protein and sugar to stabilize whatever disruptive energy was possibly waking up.

She walked slowly back into her classroom, trying to keep her feet glued to the ground. She placed her belongings carefully on the table and turned to face the class.

* * *

A few hours later, Kavya practically skipped through her front door, giddy at how smoothly the day had gone.

She surveyed her house, wondering where to start cleaning. Her boys would be coming home in a couple of days for their winter break. She zeroed in on the piles of books on the floor from her earlier aborted mission to organize the bookshelf. She worked for an hour and just as she was about to stop, she came across bell hooks's *Teaching to Transgress* peeking precariously off one of the shelves. She flipped through the book, studying the Post-it notes scattered throughout. She stopped to read one of her favorite passages.

> ... the academy is not paradise. But learning is a place where paradise can be created. The classroom, with all its limitations, remains a location of possibility. In that field of possibility we have the opportunity to labor for freedom, to demand of our-selves and our comrades, an openness of mind and heart that allows us to face reality even as we collectively imagine ways to move beyond boundaries, to transgress.

The sun was coming in from the window, shining right on the book. How lucky she was. She already had her paradise with her students. Yan-delis was even emailing her all the time to express excitement about the letter project.

As she touched the open pages, she thought about how ridiculous she had been the whole semester. She could pay her bills. Her sons were healthy. She couldn't even hear any traffic on her quiet block. The big-gest problems she had were sleep deprivation and being too neurotic, which just meant she was officially a New Yorker. Maybe it was even perimenopause.

She put the book back on the shelf. After choosing a playlist on her phone, she headed to the kitchen to start cleaning. As she danced around the table, she felt only her body move, not the rest of the room. Maybe now that she had spilled her guts to Helen, the worst was truly over. She did a spin. The room stayed still. She turned the music up.

* * *

One week later, Kavya soaked in the bliss of feeding more than just her-self. Janet and her little family were here for a small vacation with Kavya and the boys. The people she adored the most in the world were filling up her house with their warmth and silliness, and she couldn't be happier.

She set the pots of food on the table and placed the serving spoons next to them. As she folded napkins, she peeked out the back window at the garden. She could see the backs of Janet's and Fiona's heads, leaning into each other. Fiona's seven-year-old daughter Lexi danced in front of them, bubble wand in hand, her little blue plastic eyeglasses sliding down her nose. Kavya moved to the window for a closer look. Lexi handed Janet the bubble wand.

Kavya pushed her palm against the window, feeling the cool glass against her skin. With Janet and her boys here, the days of walking around frazzled and frightened seemed like a lifetime ago.

"What are you thinking about?" Samir's voice came from behind her.

"Oh," Kavya said, spinning around. "Umm, just thinking that I'm glad Janet married a woman with such a sweet little kid."

"I love Lexi. She's so smart. We even bonded about how we both basically had sperm donor dads."

Kavya stared at her son's sweetly eager smile. "Oh, yes, that's great. Hey, can you help me get the drinks?"

* * *

The boys were eight years old when it had become a "thing" that they didn't have a father. Having a cool aunt Janet was no longer an adequate response to the kids who asked, "Where's your dad?"

"Why are we being raised by you and Janet Auntie?" Samir asked one day, just as the boys came home from school. "You're not even a lesbian."

"What?" Kavya responded, baffled. She hurried over from her stack of student papers to help them with their backpacks. She peeked out the door to wave her thanks to the neighbor who always picked them up from the bus stop.

Samir handed her his lunch box. "Okay, Janet Auntie is gay, but you're not two mommies. If you don't have a dad, then you have two mommies. Or a grandma. You can't have an aunt who's not even related to you."

"Who says?" Kavya asked. She smoothed Samir's hair down and let her hand rest on his cheek.

"Well, everyone says we don't have a dad." Kabir shrugged. He continued in his matter-of-fact way, "I guess they don't realize every family is different."

Kavya had been preparing for this conversation for a while. She led them to the couch and asked them to sit. "Well, yes." She took a breath and plunged in. "I've always told you that you don't have a dad. Do you remember earlier when we talked about where babies come from?"

Both boys immediately made faces. "Eww!" Samir said.

"Okay, okay," Kavya continued. "There was once a man, and his sperm helped my egg make the two of you. And I will always be grateful for that, forever. And sometimes someone shares their sperm or an egg or even a uterus, but they're not the parent. You become a parent by promising to always take care of the child."

Samir nodded slowly. Kabir looked skeptical.

"Who was the man who gave you the sperm?" Kabir asked.

"A man I knew a very long time ago, but only for a day. I was living with Janet Auntie and then gave birth to you."

"So that man is our dad?" Samir asked.

"He gave the sperm, biologically speaking, but he is not your father because he isn't part of the promise to take care of you. It was just something that happened." Kavya smiled at them. "But the most important thing is I love you enough for a million parents."

Then both boys seemed to lose interest, asking to watch TV and have snacks. But after that, things were not quite the same. Samir wanted Kavya to sleep in his bed more often. And Kabir seemed a bit moodier, losing his temper more than usual. But maybe those changes were coincidences? Over the years, only a few times did the topic come up, with a reference to "the man who gave the sperm" or "the guy who's not really our dad."

Kabir asked for the man's name a couple of times.

"It's Vinay. I don't know his last name," Kavya answered sheepishly each time. The boys never sought more answers than that. And she never offered them.

* * *

Kavya watched Samir place the bottles of wine and seltzer on the table, as she thought back to him as a little boy asking about his father. She tried to get up the courage to ask him what exactly he had said to Lexi.

But then the little girl came bounding inside, singing loudly.

Kavya asked everyone to take their seats. As they all dug into the food and talked loudly, she scrutinized Lexi and Samir. What did they tell each other? She also wondered what she never dared to ask. Did her sons ever wish they had a father? Would they ever want to track down "the man who gave the sperm"? Was she enough for them?

Samir threw his head back in laughter, relaxed as ever, and she felt silly for fretting about what was probably an innocent conversation.

After dinner, Fiona took Lexi upstairs for a bath and then to sleep in the boys' old room, where Janet's family was bunking for the next few days. Everyone else moved into the living room.

Kabir poured another glass of wine for himself and sank into the couch with a groan.

Janet laughed. "One semester at college and you've got an old man sigh already."

"Nah." Kabir chuckled. "The end of the semester about did us in. Final papers. Our campus jobs. All of it."

"Okay, so tell me the scoop. You're not very good at calling your old Janet Auntie."

"Sorry, sorry. The latest is that I'm sticking with political science for my major." Kabir quickly added, "And it has nothing to do with Mom."

"Who said it does?" Janet patted his hand affectionately.

"There are some cool people to hang with," he continued. "Oh, and I'll try to score a job or something with my suitemate over the summer. Maybe volunteering on a campaign."

"I'm still thinking English for my major," Samir chimed in. "I can't decide. Did Mama tell you I almost failed Bio?"

"Yeah, but you didn't!" Janet responded encouragingly.

Samir shook his head sadly. "Lab science sucks. I'm going to take a couple of the harder requirements over the summer so I can take my time. I'm not getting into that position again."

"Very mature of you, sweetheart," Janet said.

Kavya nervously played with her earrings. She could see that her sons were already other people, their own people. They even looked different. Kabir had just decided to grow a full beard for the first time. Samir had been hitting the gym for stress relief, his wide shoulders, inherited from Kavya, even broader than usual. Their voices seemed more assured. Even when they came home for their November break, a quick trip with them bent over their laptops the whole time, even in the weekly video calls, they weren't like this.

"Are you guys keeping up with old Houston friends?" Kavya asked. "Now that most are in college too?"

Kabir shrugged and topped off his glass.

"I don't know," Samir said. "It's not the same with some of our old friends. At least, the ones who stayed there for college. You can tell that some of them want to escape, you know?"

"Escape is the way to put it," Janet said. "I want to escape Texas."

"But why?" Kabir cut in. "Fiona's whole family is there. *Your* parents and brothers are there! Your brothers were literally texting me the other day about coming up to New York again. *Their* families are there too!"

"You know who else is there? My queer family!" Janet said sharply. "Oh, and did I ever tell you all about how my wife got cyberbullied by the *parents* of Lexi's classmates? For the horrible crime of liking a Facebook post? It was back when that disability rights group filed a lawsuit against our evil governor's stupid ban on school mask mandates. All those idiots knew Lexi is immunocompromised but hey, personal liberties and all that, except for who you sleep with and your right to abortion."

"Is Lexi still masking in school?" Samir asked.

"No, not anymore. She didn't want to be different, you know? But at least now she's vaccinated." Janet let out a sigh. "Oh, and thanks for testing, you guys. And for getting that." She gestured toward the wall, where an unsightly whirring gray box flashed a blue light to indicate purified air.

"Well, I still don't get this concept of escape," Kabir said. "Lots of people are staying and fighting back."

"I think you're naïve, sweetheart." Janet shook her head. "I don't get your idealism."

"Idealism? You're the one who wants to escape. And leave behind everyone else to protest and resist. Look at the fascist shit happening every day, everywhere. You think people in Brazil or the Philippines or . . ."

"Okay, Kabir, just because you took some political science classes, you know everything now?" Janet crossed her arms indignantly.

"Why are you coming for me? Do I make fun of your velour sweatpants?"

Samir let out a "Ha!" and then quickly covered his mouth.

Kavya clapped a couple of times like she was a grade-school teacher getting everyone's attention. "Alright, y'all. We're on the same side here. There's no right way to respond to this kind of repression. Everyone does the best they can, right?"

"Yeah," Samir said. "Like, some people left Texas because they felt it was too unsafe, and other people are sticking around and doing things like getting people to Mexico for abortion care. I respect both choices."

Kabir rolled his eyes. Janet gave Samir a warm smile.

A little later, after the boys left to head to a restaurant to meet up with old high school friends, Janet scooted over to Kavya. "Alright. Now you. Tell me what the hell is going on with you."

"Sure thing."

Janet pulled her in for a hug. "Let me check on Lexi and Fiona first. Let's stay up and talk!"

A few minutes later, Janet strolled back into the living room. She poured a large glass of red wine. As she quickly sipped, a purplish hue stained her teeth and bled onto her lips. She talked about Fiona's parents while Kavya listened.

"But Kavya, wait," Janet said, interrupting herself. "You need to tell me what's up with you. I'm worried about you."

Kavya had not meant to, and maybe the wine was getting to her, but she spoke nonstop. She told Janet about her conversations with Helen. The letter project. The spaghetti incident.

As she spoke, she kept her eyes focused on Janet's glass. She watched the level go down, and then back up with the refill, down, and back up once more. She talked to the chip on the rim, from the time she had accidentally hit the glass on the drying rack. She talked to the stem. She talked to stubborn bubbles that were not popping.

She didn't look at Janet once. "Okay, umm, I'm done."

She kept her focus on her coffee table, thinking that Janet would say, *Why didn't you tell me any of this? Why are you always so closed off? If you can't even tell your best friend, what's wrong with you?*

Instead, Janet hiccupped and then belched. "Oops. I'm a bit buzzed. Do you have those salt and vinegar chips?"

Kavya laughed. She hurried to the pantry and pulled out the chips from her stash of snacks she had purchased just for Janet.

Walking back, she tossed the chips to Janet, who didn't even attempt to catch them.

"Girl, I'm with you, you know?" Janet slurred her words. "Kavya, I love you, and you should stay in therapy and just keep doing your thing. Just keep doing this shit."

Kavya burst out laughing. "I will, I will!"

Janet picked the bag up from the floor where it had landed, ripped it open, and inhaled deeply. "Ahh. Salt. And. Vinegar."

As Janet crammed chips into her mouth, she spoke again, little bits of food flying out. "So, you did a letter about colorism and colonialism. What's the next one going to be about?"

Kavya thought for a moment. She suddenly remembered the package that had arrived that week and wandered over to the bookshelf to find the book. Thenmozhi Soundararajan's *The Trauma of Caste* had been released the previous month.

She showed the book to Janet. "This just came out. Super lucky timing for me. I guess it's a sign that I look at casteism now."

"So cool." Janet smiled then abruptly grimaced. "Okay, I feel kind of gross. I think I need to go to bed."

Kavya giggled as Janet gathered herself and her blanket, gave her a kiss on top of her head, and shuffled away. Kavya mentally took note, as she used to, of how much Janet had eaten that day. Breakfast, lunch, dinner, snacking. Indulging sometimes, always at ease. Her face full and healthy, her torso squishy and warm against her when they hugged, her hands steady.

* * *

Sometimes, Kavya would play back the worst fight of her friendship with Janet. Their junior year of college, Kavya had grown suspicious of Janet's frequent "stomach bugs." And how she had stopped joining her for meals in the student cafeteria.

And how she kept brushing her teeth and chewing gum. And how she always ran water while in the bathroom, two flushes in a row. And disappeared on the weekends for "church" events.

Kavya finally confronted Janet one evening. "Something's been up with you for a while. I know that you're struggling with food. Please tell me what's wrong."

Janet was fuming, the angriest Kavya had ever seen her. "You're spying on me?"

"No, I was trying to figure out what's wrong. I don't understand how you have been doing this to yourself all this time! You have everything going for you. Please tell me what's wrong!"

"I don't like how you're talking. Like nothing could be wrong with my life?" Janet paced back and forth in their room.

"Janet! I don't mean it like that. I just mean that your family loves you so much."

"People with fucked up families can have fucking eating disorders. People with loving families can have fucking eating disorders." Janet clapped her hands to emphasize her words. "Don't you get that? You don't even see me as a person. You think I have a perfect life just because you're jealous of my family. And they are not perfect and maybe even a little fucked up. You don't even see me!"

"I do see you!" Kavya insisted. "Yeah, I'm envious of what you have. So what? But I see you! I'm the one who saw all of this first!"

"What the hell are you talking about?"

"Wait. Back up. You *know* you have an eating disorder?"

Janet slammed her hand against the wall. "Yes! I've had bulimia since I was thirteen. Sometimes I relapse. I'm in an outpatient program right now. I might go on a small medical leave, too."

"But why . . . Janet, why didn't you tell me?"

"Why nothing. You're not the one who saw all this first. You're the one who snuck around, hoping to catch some kind of crack in me. You just want to feel better about yourself!"

They screamed at each other until they were both hoarse and bawling. Until the dorm director knocked and asked, "What's going on in there?"

Janet left their room that night and stayed on the floor of a friend in another dorm. Then she moved home. Some weeks later, after Janet finished her program and medical leave, Yumiko and Bob arranged for Kavya to come over so that the friends could make up, which happened within the first five minutes.

Ever since then, Kavya promised herself to remember what Janet had said. So, she tried to *see* her friend. She tried not to entertain any of those small, selfish thoughts. *At least her parents want her. At least her mother holds her. They all loved her even more when she came out. What could be missing?*

And after that fight, they settled into a more "even" friendship. Kavya idolized Janet less. She supported Janet through an almost-relapse in their early thirties. But sometimes she did wonder, could she see *anyone* as complex and contradictory, or could they only be "healthy" or "fucked up," "good" or "evil"?

* * *

Kavya pushed herself off the couch to grab the new caste book sitting on the coffee table. Caste was undoubtedly evil. She wanted a simple story about evil people who did evil things. Those kinds of stories were as familiar to her as a nursery rhyme.

As Kavya curled up, waiting up for the boys out of habit, she read through the first chapter of the book.

ECHO

Kavya had first learned about caste from her grandmother.

One summer evening in Mumbai, she had been relaxing with a book on the balcony of Ajji's apartment. When her grandmother emerged with a bottle of coconut hair oil, Kavya smiled and slid to the floor. There was nothing in the world as comforting as Ajji kneading her scalp.

Kavya asked her grandmother, "I heard you say the other day that we're savarnas, and then you said we're Brahmins. Which is it? What does that mean?"

"Lord Brahma created us all, and so we all come from him. Brahmins come from the head because we are the priests and teachers. Kshatriyas are the warriors and rulers, because they work in the government and the army, and they come from Brahma's strong arms! Vaishyas come from Brahma's sturdy thighs. They hold up the body by doing the work of being merchants and traders. Shudras come from Brahma's feet, and they do farming and service jobs."

"We are each a body part?"

"Yes, child! Do you see how we have a special, God-given role for everyone in society?"

Kavya was silent for some time, almost intoxicated by the coconut scent enveloping her. "The people in the street are Shudras?"

"The sweepers? The beggars? No, no. If they are cleaning streets and latrines, doing manual scavenging, or living there like that, they are, they were called Untouchables. These days they call them Dalits."

"They don't come from Brahma at all, then? Are they savarnas?"

"O-yo! No, only Brahmins, Kshatriyas, and Vaishyas are savarnas. Savarna means twice-born. Born to our parents and born to God. We have a special relationship with God."

"Why don't the Shudras and Dalits have a special relationship with God?" Kavya persisted.

"It was their karma. It's the sins of their past lives. Their souls were polluted."

"But Ajji, that's not their fault. Why . . ."

"Stop asking so many questions." Ajji sighed, irritated. "Also, no one really cares about caste anymore. Lots of Dalits even have good jobs and go to university these days."

"So now people who are Brahmins might be on the street sweeping and picking through the trash?"

"No, no, it doesn't work like that."

Kavya tried to turn toward her grandmother, but Ajji firmly moved her head back to face the railing and dug deep into her hair. She backed down like she always did when her grandmother shut down her questions. Ajji was the one person in her life who seemed interested in her. Why be a nuisance?

She often sat outside of Ajji's apartment to read, hoping her grandmother would come out with hair oil. She could see the Arabian Sea in the distance and hear the shouts in the street as vendors marketed their wares. Plus, the adults inside never realized that their voices carried right to that balcony, the air pouring both humidity and secrets right onto Kavya.

She could hear her Ajji's concerned voice one time. "She asked if her mother's family is still in Pune. I said no."

"Fine. Leave it at that," Neela answered in her angry staccato.

"Neela. Child. She deserves to have some connection to her mother's side. This is very strange. I am feeling we are being very rotten to her."

"Why don't you think about how I feel? You never care about that."

Kavya's mouth turned dry. She leaned toward the doorway to hear Ajji's muffled response. "You're my daughter. Why are you always saying that?"

* * *

Kavya tried to brush away these echoes as she sat on her living room couch. She did not want to think about Ajji's small and calloused fingers caressing her hair. She did not want to wonder how Ajji felt about Neela. She needed to focus. She didn't have time for these stirrings. So, Kavya kept reading about caste, pen in hand, hovering over passages, ready to make notes in the margins.

When the boys were growing up, while Kabir was always out playing basketball or riding his bike, she and Samir had pens in their hands, writing stories together. Kavya always told Samir that holding a pen meant being able to create and communicate anything.

But the pen meant something else now. As the book was reminding Kavya, Brahmins were scholars, with special access to knowledge that they denied to everyone else, especially Dalits. They were still the top caste, the superior caste. And they intended to keep it that way.

She wondered how to get this book to speak to her. Because her pen was going wayward, unable to write, unwilling to scribble thoughts on the pages.

Finally, at last, she came upon a short paragraph that she easily circled:

And yet when you talk to dominant-caste people, despite them having materially better conditions, you find that there's all sorts of trouble and misery going on behind the curtains. This is because, again, the truth about violence is that it destabilizes everything. The truth about othering people is it slices your spirit in half. Half people can't have whole families or whole relationships, least of all with themselves.

She put the book aside, allowing the words to settle in.

She checked her watch and resisted the urge to text the boys in a way that would only annoy them. *Oh, just a breezy check-in, all okay?*

Her eyes moved to the front door, and she went around and around on a carousel of memories, of waiting by the window as a child, counting forward and backward.

Neela had threatened suicide so many times that Kavya had been convinced that one day she would disappear. And then Kavya would disappear.

Neela's spirit was clearly split in half.

Maybe caste was why Neela hated herself and hated me. The couch was too cozy to bear the weight of such a thought.

She wandered into the kitchen in search of snacks or beer as a nagging ache spread across her forehead. She found a box of cookies, ripped the top off, and crammed a few into her mouth. As she circled her table, walking aimlessly, she wiped crumbs from her shirt.

Several memories started zooming through her brain. She tried to catch one and examine it. But they were like the round balls of air on bubble wrap. A little bit of pressure, and they popped.

She set the cookie box on the counter and hurried to her computer to create a new document called "Caste." She hastily typed the disparate thoughts racing through her head.

Caste is about purity. Dominant caste (Brahmins, Kshatriyas, Vaishyas) = savarna = oppressor. Out of caste = Dalits, Adivasis/ Indigenous, and others excluded from caste(ist) society because their very presence was considered to be polluting, like Ajji talking about the alleged sins of their past lives. Even Dalit converts to other religions are mistreated in those communities simply for being born Dalit. You have to marry only within your caste. Comply with hygiene and food rituals according to your caste. Purity means being clean and light-skinned. Colorism is also about caste. Neela hated herself. She hated me for not complying with her warped ideas about what it meant to be good (i.e., give myself entirely to take care of her emotionally). Did she want me to magically make her feel worthy of being Brahmin? What are the different ways dominant caste people absorb the violence of what we are?

Neela and everyone else in our community called the kids bhangi if we didn't clean our rooms. Bh*ngi = casteist slur. Caste is also in the U.S., not just India.

Pramod's friend Raj Uncle was over once. Laura came over and we played cards with Uncle. Laura went home, and he washed his hands raw. He said Mridula Auntie was trying to get pregnant and they couldn't take any chances. Laura had cerebral palsy. Not just appalling, ableist bullshit but also casteist fear of being "polluted"?

All the stupid boys and their thread ceremonies that were supposed to be about a second birth to God. Rite of passage only for dominant caste boys.

Ajji had to bring her abusive father-in-law into her home. Why is being a widow considered bad? Only dominant caste people get troubled by the existence of widows. You're a burden. You should not get remarried and waste some dominant caste man's chance to be with a virginal savarna.

Kavya leaned against her chair as she thought about how trapped Ajji must have felt, even while clinging onto the idea of Brahmin caste pride. She kept typing.

> Neela was over the moon when Ranjeet and I met. Why did everyone in the community say we were a match? Because Ranjeet and I had lots of academic credentials. Grandmothers knew each other. His family knew about Ajji's reputation with the printing press. My father and Ranjeet's dad had both gone to the same prestigious school in Mumbai. Amma allegedly from "good" family. Neela made sure that horoscopes/birth charts matched. Same subcaste. Everyone split in half. All of us.

Kavya paused. She spoke openly and critically about caste with her boys but as if it had nothing to do with her. Like the time she told her boys about Ranjeet without once considering that caste was a part of that dreadful story.

* * *

It was probably 2017, about a year before the New York move. Samir and Kabir were starting to go out on group dates with their friends.

One day, Kavya sat them down in the living room. A musty smell hung over them from the still damp bedsheets hanging here and there because of the broken apartment complex dryer.

She started to speak, trying to sound stern. "Now that you're getting into the dating world, I want you to promise me, both of you, that you will always treat any partner you have with respect. They never have to do anything to be worthy of that respect, and neither do you."

Kabir looked bored. Samir chewed on his nails while eyeing the TV behind Kavya, as if willing a show to come on.

"Don't worry, Mom, we know what you're saying," Kabir finally said.

"No, listen. If someone had warned me about how dating can go wrong, I'm sure I would have ignored it. Who thinks that will happen to them? But then I met someone who seemed wonderful. And once, he humiliated me in the grocery store because I got the wrong sauce. When I told him to stop, he became so angry and just let me have it. He wouldn't apologize and said it was my fault for making him react that way. I made lots of excuses and tried to see only the good in him. But he still treated me very badly."

"That guy sounds like a dick!" Samir exclaimed. He immediately looked a little thrilled, as if he couldn't believe he said "dick" in front of his mother. Kabir was quiet, but he set his jaw and his eyes darkened.

Kavya observed how small they both still seemed, even while or maybe because they were having this "grown up" conversation.

"Yes, he was awful," she eventually said. "You may think you're strong enough to never end up in a situation like that, but it can happen to anyone. He hurt me a lot."

Kabir glowered, pointing a finger. "What do you mean? What did he do? Did he hit you?"

"I broke up with him. And well, everything's fine now. See?" She pointed at herself, hoping she was convincing them. "I'm fine. But do you understand what I'm trying to teach you?"

Kabir was scowling. Samir seemed confused. He looked down at his chewed-up nails.

"Do you understand what I'm trying to say?" Kavya asked her sons, one more time. "In our family, we value others, and we value ourselves."

* * *

Kavya watched the blinking cursor on her computer screen. She put her hands on the keyboard and let the words pulse through her fingers.

> Ranjeet seemed proud to be Indian but what if, actually, he liked being Brahmin? He didn't like when I disagreed with him. Didn't like when I disagreed with his mom, or when he perceived I made him look bad. I had to always be grateful and fawning. He tried to mold me into his mother so that I could eventually be a good mother and pass on my intellect, Ajji's reputation, my "good" caste position. He got to own it all, every good thing about me. He seemingly supported my ambitions and my feminist work. He didn't bat an eye when I said I didn't care about marriage. He said maybe we'd do a quick religious ceremony to placate everyone after I got my doctorate. What went wrong? I was a misfit. He was always picking on me, as if I was too disruptive,

like I was upsetting the natural order of things. Oh my God, yes, the "natural" order of caste hierarchy. We were supposed to be a good "match." When savarnas say good "match," they really mean making sure their caste is protected from outsiders, or from anyone lesser than. He and his mom thought they were better than everyone. Is that caste? I know caste is about hurting and oppressing those in a "lower" position. But you have to hurt people within your own caste, too, because how else would you uphold the rigid boundaries of it? Look at Great-Grandfather tormenting Neela for not being light-skinned enough. And she raised me in a way that normalized violence, and I accepted violence in Ranjeet, and she in turn reinforced that I should accept it. It was caste all along. Caste helps to explain what he did to me. I never saw it until now.

Her joints ached from the fury with which she hammered out the words. She stopped to do a breathing exercise. Then she closed her laptop and organized her desk.

An hour later, the boys finally got home and rolled out sleeping bags in the living room. She gave herself permission to go to sleep. She lay in her bed thinking about what she had just read and written. *Ajji, why did Great-Grandfather hurt you so much? Was it his personality? Was it colonialism? Was it from being dominant caste?* She thought about Mingming's grandmother in the throes of dementia and yet remembering the violence of war and occupation, and her grandfather's death by starvation. How much of those horrors shaped Mingming? Like her strained relationships with her parents, or her fierce ambition, acerbic comebacks, and unabashed love of speaking Mandarin? How were you supposed to know for sure?

She turned off the lamp, at last understanding that the previous semester wasn't an aberration. She was in the middle of some kind of reckoning.

BURN

"I'm supposed to light this on fire now?" asked Samir. He held papers in his hands, a match ready, standing over the grill on Kavya's back deck.

"Yes," Kavya said tentatively. "I think so."

Samir hesitated.

"It's fine, hon. I own this place. There's no landlord to yell at us." She regretted the words as soon as she said them.

Her father had helped her buy the house. She fought the offer so vehemently until Janet convinced her to accept the kind of love he was extending. Kavya told him at the time that she would pay him back. But who was she kidding? It was a sizeable down payment.

Maybe she took the money in the first place because she believed herself to be entitled to his wealth, the kind of wealth that dominant caste families accumulated over generations.

She thought about how to correct what she just said to everyone. But they were waiting for her, rubbing their arms to stay warm, wondering why they were gathered there.

She cleared her throat and told them that on December 25, 1927, the Dalit civil rights leader Bhimrao Ambedkar set fire to a copy of the Manusmriti, the "Laws of Manu," the "first man." These Hindu scriptures explained the divine ordaining of caste and patriarchy. And since 1927, every December 25, on the day known as Manusmriti Dahan Din, protests by Dalits around India have focused on burning the Manusmriti and committing to the annihilation of caste.

"Mom, I don't know what this will do," Kabir noted with concern. Lexi looked up at him, pushed her glasses up her nose, and shrugged.

"Okay, I don't either, but let's try." Kavya cleared her throat. "Let's play our role in destroying caste. We just can't be silent." She pointed to Samir.

Samir held the match to the forty-two-page double-sided English copy of the Manusmriti they had downloaded from a random website with endless pop-up ads. As he did, Kavya scrolled through her phone until she found the vows that she had copied from *The Trauma of Caste* book.

"Repeat after me, everyone," Kavya said, instantly aware of the eyes on her.

I do not believe in the Chaturvarna (four-varna caste division of society upheld by texts).

I do not believe that caste biologically makes people distinct from one another.

I believe that untouchability is an anathema, and I will place all my efforts in the direction of destroying it.

I reject any Brahminical text-based restrictions on food and drink and culture.

I believe that untouchables must have equal rights to water, schools, and all other public amenities.

When they were done, everyone looked at each other. As the acrid odor quickly spread, Kabir slowly poured a pitcher of water waiting nearby onto the burning paper. Plumes of ashy smoke billowed until he put the lid on the grill.

Lexi started jumping around the backyard. While bouncing, she yelled out, "Auntie Kavya, how do you feel?"

"Good question, sweetheart. It's not about how I feel. It's about realizing I'm part of something that is not fair."

Lexi stopped and nodded her head as if she understood perfectly. "When can I play with the Legos that Santa brought me?"

Everyone laughed, and Fiona scooped up Lexi. "In the morning, love. Time for bath and bed, munchkin!"

As mother and daughter went inside, Kavya stared at the grill, the smell of burned paper still so heavy that she could taste it. The others seemed unbothered or were just being polite.

Janet leaned over. "Now what?"

"I don't know. I feel like I just pulled some meaningless stunt, to be honest. I still feel so uninformed, even after reading that book, even after always trying to learn about caste whenever there have been workshops or webinars by Dalit activists. Caste is obviously everywhere and still oppressing millions of people, but we never talked about casteism when I was growing up. I feel like I'm catching up still. But that's like a white person saying they weren't brought up to talk about race and then acting completely helpless."

"Damn!" Janet chortled. "Are you going to stop making fun of white people now that you have all this caste guilt?"

"I'm always here for the jokes. At my expense as well." Kavya let out a half-hearted chuckle. She didn't know what else to say.

She watched as Kabir lifted the lid of the grill and then used a stick to poke at a few embers.

A gnawing feeling that had arisen the other night started nibbling at her conscience again. She realized what she needed to do.

She turned to her sons. "Do you remember a couple of years ago how that neighbor was venting to us about wanting to cancel a plane ticket to see her allegedly 'racist' family?"

They looked back at her blankly.

"You remember," Kavya said impatiently. "And I said something about how even though she didn't want to deal with her family, she had to. Because it was a luxury as a white person to step away from dealing with racism. People of color don't have that choice."

"Yeah, and?" Kabir asked.

"I have to take my own advice." She tugged at her sweater nervously. "Y'all, I think I'm going to reach out to my dad for an honest conversation here, face-to-face. About caste. I have to do it."

The boys looked surprised and then worried. First, their mother was burning Hindu scriptures in the backyard, and now, she was purposely reaching out to a man she seemingly only tolerated for their sakes.

"I just want to ask him some questions about our caste history," Kavya explained.

The boys were doing that thing where they snuck quick glances at each other whenever they thought their mother was being a bit off.

"Mama, are you okay?" Samir asked. He looked to his brother for backup.

"You can tell us anything," Kabir added. "We know that things haven't been great."

Samir noted, "We're not little kids anymore."

Kavya exhaled loudly. She knew that she had probably seemed like a woman on the edge over the past few months. She wanted to be honest about everything that had happened but didn't want them to be distracted when they went back to school.

Janet sensed Kavya's frustration and pulled her in protectively. "Don't worry, guys. Your mama is on a journey. She's allowed to do that. And we should trust and support her." She looked pointedly at the twins. "And if your mom decides to talk to your grandfather, then we're here for her. Right, guys?"

The boys nodded in unison, breaking out into smiles and murmuring words of encouragement.

"Thank you," Kavya said, blushing, as she watched a struggling wisp of smoke while it slowly dissipated into the sky.

Janet rubbed Kavya's arm. "Well, we show up for each other when one of us needs it. That's what family does."

LEAVE

Just one month before Kavya's defense of her PhD dissertation, she was a nervous wreck. It didn't help that the damn project had already consumed her every waking minute during the first half of 2003. But now she was imagining every possible worst-case scenario. Staying up through all hours of the night, she obsessively went over index cards with her notes.

Ranjeet was supportive. He did all the cooking and cleaning. He sometimes kept late hours to help her review or to distract her with a TV show.

Two weeks before the defense. The pressure was building. She had headaches every day and was in a perpetually foul mood.

One day, Ranjeet came home from work later than usual.

"What's for dinner?" he asked casually.

Kavya was indignant. "I thought you were going to cook. This is also late notice. I don't need any more stress, like deciding what to make for dinner."

"Relax! I had a hard day. Let's just do takeout."

Kavya tried to agree but was crawling out of her skin. "I feel like shit. What's wrong with the air conditioner? Can you check it? It's been way too hot all day. I bet that's what is making me feel so awful." She grabbed the front of her shirt and fanned her body, as if to make the point.

Ranjeet sighed. "Anything else, Your Highness?"

Kavya usually would have apologized. She would have checked herself. But she was sleep deprived and moody. Without thinking, she said, "I hate how you talk to me sometimes." She stormed off to their room and slammed the door.

She had barely stepped into the room when Ranjeet swung the door open. "How do I talk to you? I've been taking care of you this entire time. How do I talk to you?" he asked quietly.

Kavya answered him with unmistakable disdain. "It's about time you realized that you talk to me like I'm shit. You treat me horribly. Not just now but always. This is the biggest moment of my entire life. And you're doing what any supportive partner should do. You want a trophy?"

Before she knew it, she was in the air. She landed on her back, hard. She lay there, stunned. Her entire jaw had seemingly realigned, only an eerie space when she tried to get her rows of teeth to touch. An excruciating, stabbing pain radiated through her tailbone. What had just happened? Her feet had actually left the ground.

He had pushed her. No, he had thrown her. Oh God.

This had never happened before. She heard a boom and then a crack. Ranjeet had kicked the door so hard against the wall that the knob had broken through the plaster.

He glared at her, his round eyes large. "You're psychotic."

"No, I'm not!" Kavya wept as she slowly sat up, still reeling.

Ranjeet shook his head. "Psycho." He took off his belt and threw it on the ground. And then he turned and left the room.

Kavya stood up, quivering and in nauseating pain, but resolute in an anger she could barely recognize. "You're the psycho!" she screamed. "You're deranged. Look at you! Do it again, motherfucker!"

He kept walking and locked himself in the bathroom. Kavya heard the shower running. She leaned against the wall and waited. She had no idea what had taken over her.

As soon as he emerged, she hollered, "Why did you do that? You *threw* me as hard as you could."

"Stop it. Always overreacting. Nothing happened."

She stood in his way before he could enter their room. "Something happened! Something happened!" And she shrieked those words over and over as loudly as she could, for the last shred of dignity she had left, but also for that time when she was ten and Neela had shoved her when they were standing in the driveway. She couldn't remember what they were arguing about. And Kavya fell hard, deep bloodied scrapes on her palms and face. And when she later asked Neela why she had pushed her, her aunt had said, "What are you talking about? You tripped."

Ranjeet muttered, "Excuse me," and went inside the room. He threw the towel on the bed and changed into a shirt and shorts. Then he ordered a pizza.

They sat at the dining room table, eating in silence. Kavya leaned at an angle on her left butt cheek because her tailbone hurt so much.

She stayed at the table when he finished. He drank a beer in front of the TV and then went to bed. She moved to the couch.

She stayed up all night, staring at the wall, trying to breathe through the waves of pain surging throughout her body. The sickness that had descended upon her during the past month came up violently into her mouth. She repeatedly went to the kitchen sink to spit out the bitter saliva pooling behind her teeth.

The next morning, Ranjeet got ready for work and left without a word. He called when he arrived to let her know he got there safely.

Kavya waited for an hour before calling Janet. As soon as she heard that hoarse, "Hello," she started to cry.

"Janet. I don't know how to say this."

"What did he do? What happened?"

Kavya tried to explain, even though she herself could not understand what had happened.

"I'm going to fucking kill him," Janet bellowed. "What if your head had hit something?"

"No, no. It's not like that," Kavya quickly said. "It's just that this has turned into a toxic relationship. I really had a go at him, too. I don't even know why I'm so angry."

"You're not about to blame yourself."

"I just need to figure out how to make it better. I think he must be stressed, and I'm so preoccupied with my dissertation."

"Like I said, Kavya, I will not let you blame yourself."

"He has never been to therapy," Kavya said desperately. "I think that would help. He hasn't processed his father's death. He was only seventeen. He was just starting his life."

"So were you when your mom died!" Janet sounded like she was crying.

"I can't just give up on him. He has been so tolerant of all my issues. He makes sure I never have to worry. Even now, he called to tell me that he got to work okay. I'm not easy to live with."

"Bullshit! Don't forget that I lived with you." Janet let out a long exhale. "Okay, so he doesn't make you worry or threaten to leave you. That doesn't make him a prince. I would like *you* to threaten to leave. Better yet, I want you to leave. You can leave him, Kavya. You can leave."

Kavya gasped. "No, I'm not going to be like my dad. Doesn't loyalty count for anything?"

"Be loyal to yourself, Kavya," Janet said quietly. "Not to him, not even to me. To yourself."

They hung up, after going back and forth. Janet's words, *you can leave,* wormed their way into Kavya's body, and she could feel their imprint even though she didn't want to.

* * *

It was the day of her PhD defense. Kavya woke up feeling queasy.

Janet called her, as she had been doing every day since the incident.

Kavya was at the breakfast table with Ranjeet and answered the phone cautiously. She stepped away from the table just in case he said something nasty. In case Janet yelled at him.

As she walked away, Ranjeet said, "Wait, stop, sweetheart."

Kavya froze.

He came over and gently touched her cheek. "I'm off to work. I'll check in with you from there. But call me as soon as it's over. Don't forget your phone." He kissed her and then as he walked away, he turned and said, "I'll see you tonight for our celebration, okay? You're my champion."

She wanted to say to Janet, *See? That's the real him.* But she didn't. Janet would just say, *He's putting on an act.*

Instead, Kavya said, "Sorry about that. Umm, Ranjeet was just saying bye."

"Mmm-hmm." Janet made her voice cheery. "Listen, my parents said good luck. They said they will be praying for you. They said to take something with you to remind you that you are loved."

Kavya almost cried then. "Oh, tell them I love them. That's so sweet."

After hanging up, she went to her room to get ready. She thought about Janet's words and rummaged through her overflowing jewelry box while sitting on the bed. As she rifled through each section, she came across a small, laminated print of Goddess Lakshmi. She picked it out and put it next to her. Looking through each of her pendants, she tried to find one Ajji had given her.

And then she found a tiny three by five photo of her Amma taken when she had just arrived in the U.S. She wore a royal purple sari in front of the airport, a tentative smile on her tired face. Kavya took the pictures of Lakshmi and her mother and tucked them gently into her wallet.

She had never carried a picture of her mother with her. But it turned out to be her good luck charm because the defense went incredibly well. The committee enthusiastically praised her, and Kavya excitedly called Janet and then Ranjeet, both of whom were ecstatic.

As she left campus to go home, she let herself speak out loud to her mother. "Amma, I did it." How strange. Maybe she should try talking to her more often.

* * *

That evening, for her celebration date with Ranjeet, Kavya wore the deep chocolate silk dress that he loved. She carefully placed a rose gold brooch in her hair. She sprayed on her wrists Ranjeet's favorite perfume, slightly woody with a hint of bergamot. Before she walked outside to wait for him, she put her wallet into a small gold purse. She stuck her hand inside, pressing the wallet, knowing that Amma was inside.

When Ranjeet opened the car door for her, they embraced tightly. She barely reached his chest and looked up at his face. He smiled and said, "I love you."

They got into the car. They grinned at each other at the stoplights. Kavya took a deep cleansing breath, feeling like the night would be something to treasure.

Ranjeet drove up to his favorite restaurant. She always told him she found the dishes there too rich, not delicate enough. She shook off the disappointment.

As they walked through the parking lot, her stomach gurgled unhappily. She hesitated and checked to see if anyone was around.

"Ranjeet, thank you for tonight. But sweetheart, do you mind not getting that oyster dish you always get here? Usually I wouldn't mind, but I'm not feeling well for some reason."

She instinctively flinched.

He looked at her for a moment. Then he put his hand on the back of her neck, pressing his fingers deep into her flesh, steering her so that she walked right next to him. He leaned his head in and spoke steadily. "You really need to get it together. Here I am taking you out, and you're complaining. Here I am . . ."

She listened, as she always did. And then he stopped, as abruptly as he had started. He dropped his hand down from her neck to her hand. They entered the restaurant, holding hands, smiling. She swallowed the humiliation, which slid down her throat and splashed down into the stomach acids already sloshing about.

He flirted with the hostess, who ate it up, smiling and blushing, turning around several times as she led them to the table. *Why does he save the best for everyone else?* Ranjeet's friends and co-workers all seemed to adore him, basking in his charming glow. Her own friends, except for Janet, found him fascinating. None of them would have believed what he had done to her just weeks before.

A server arrived at the table with notepad in hand. Ranjeet looked at the woman and then asked for the charbroiled oysters, winking. "Oysters are an aphrodisiac after all."

The button eyes gleamed. He bit down ever so softly on his bottom lip. He ran his fingers through his hair. Despite the embarrassing display, the woman bent over in laughter. She was still tittering when Kavya asked for the linguine.

Kavya took a gulp of water, forcing another mouthful of indignity down her throat.

The food arrived, with the waitress smiling only at Ranjeet.

Kavya picked at her food. As she sat, pain traveled down her legs, the residue of being thrown to the ground by a man twice her size.

"I know you, Kavya," Ranjeet said. "You're upset because I ordered the oysters. Or maybe you're jealous of the waitress." He shook his head. "The world has to revolve around you. You feel sick, don't you? You lost your appetite, didn't you? You're the one who ruined this special night."

He was grinning. He slurped the oyster. The buttery garlic sauce dripped down the side of his face.

He licked his lips, his black-black eyes still on her, and slowly lowered his head to take a sip of his wine. The thin sheen of the buttery sauce seemed to be spreading.

Kavya spoke quietly while trying to point discretely. "Honey, you have a little something on your . . ."

"Shut up. Eat your food."

And that's when Kavya decided.

I get to leave. I can leave.

She looked out the window next to their table and smiled.

Ranjeet leaned forward. "What? Why are you smiling? Damn, you're weird."

She was mostly quiet for the rest of the meal, asking Ranjeet about his day, sharing only small details about the defense, as if it weren't *her* day.

After dinner, they climbed into the car to see their mutual friends for drinks.

"You know what?" she said. "I'm just feeling sick. You go ahead and have a great time."

He made a face. "That's stupid. The drinks are for you. What am I going to do there?"

She smiled at him. "Everyone there loves you. You were as much a part of this accomplishment. Go have the time of your life."

She didn't have to do much to convince him.

"Fine. Dave is gonna be there, and I'm dying to talk to him about some work stuff." He kissed her and looked down at her. "I'm so proud of you. You're a good girl."

She laughed despite herself. "Yes, yes, I am." Something awakened inside of her, something she had never felt before.

He dropped her home.

She looked around the apartment. She changed her clothes. Then, as if in a play, as if this were someone else's life, she pretended she was a strong woman. With unsteady hands, she dragged out her suitcases and placed her shoes inside. She pulled clothes out of the closet and threw them on the bed.

Ranjeet called to say he had reached the bar safely.

After packing everything she could, she made several trips to put the suitcases and clothes-stuffed trash bags into her Honda Civic.

Then she went to the building manager's office and asked to use her phone. She called Janet.

"I didn't recognize the number. Kavya, I thought you'd be out getting wasted."

Kavya spoke as calmly as she could. "I didn't want to use my cell phone or the landline. Can I come over tonight? I mean, can I stay with you?"

"What do you . . . Oh, shit. Oh, Kavya. Please come. Come."

Kavya went back into the apartment and left her keys on the counter. She used her cell phone to call Ranjeet. "Hi, I just wanted to let you know I'm going to bed. Have fun and give my love to everyone. Okay?"

"Great!" He was relaxed.

"Great," she repeated. She left the phone next to the keys.

She went into their room for one last look. As she walked out, she impulsively grabbed the bottle of the perfume she had worn that evening and threw it out their bedroom window, hard.

When she got back outside, she saw the shattered glass all over the sidewalk, releasing citrus notes into the air.

* * *

A few hours later, after driving straight from Austin to Houston, Kavya arrived at Janet's apartment complex. She parked and stuck her head out of the car window.

Seeing some teenagers hanging out in front, speaking loudly even though it was the middle of the night, Kavya hesitated and then yelled, "Janet!"

One boy noticed her and said, "I'll get her for you, mami." He hollered, "Janet!"

A light turned on. Janet's face appeared at the window. Minutes later, she appeared outside, in her usual tracksuit outfit.

Janet looked at Kavya and said, "Pop the trunk." She lifted out the suitcases and bags. They quietly moved Kavya's belongings into the guest bedroom.

Kavya sat on the bed when they were done. "I left. For the first time in my life, I left someone."

Janet stroked Kavya's hair gently, smiled, and said, "I'll be right back."

She could hear Janet speaking quietly into the hallway phone. Who was she calling at this hour? She wanted to listen in but was too exhausted and lay down for a fitful sleep.

The next morning, Janet greeted her with coffee and then flopped into the rocking chair next to the bed. Peering through her bangs, she announced, "Kavya, I talked to my mom and dad last night."

Kavya almost dropped her mug. "What? Why would you do that?"

"They have experience supporting people who have left abusive relationships."

Kavya stayed silent. All those times Janet had pointed out why she despised Ranjeet—she regularly called him an asshole to his face when she visited, and he'd just pleasantly smile and say, "C'mon Janet, you love me."—she had never said the word "abuse."

Janet continued, "You just escaped domestic violence, right? We need to end this right here and now."

Kavya sat for several moments. She let the words linger in her head. Domestic violence? No, he had some kind of anger problem. That was all. Kavya feared how quickly things were moving toward a point of no return. "What are your parents going to do?"

"They are going to call Ranjeet and, if need be, his mother. They'll respectfully tell him to let this all go and to move on. The end."

Kavya set the coffee mug on the nightstand. "Janet, this is like poking the bear. It's too aggressive. Plus, that's too much to expect from your parents. Why are they getting so involved? Just stop this." She secretly wondered if she would give him a chance if he apologized. He had never apologized to her for anything, but she had never walked out on him before.

Janet stood up. "No, I'm sorry. We can't." She started to walk out and then turned around. Kavya saw that her face was wet with tears.

"My parents and I waited so long for you to be able to do this." Janet's voice shook.

"You've all been talking about me behind my back? This isn't the real him. He's just . . ." Kavya trailed off. She had just defended a dissertation based on feminist theory. About gender violence! What was she doing?

"My dad and mom handle shit like this every day. He's a priest for crying out loud. She's always there with him for these situations. He'll know how to do it in a calming and deescalating way. Let them do this."

Kavya hugged herself. *These situations*. Janet the sitcom sweetheart was now in an afterschool special, the hero with the plan. And that not-so-old feeling, that she was not worthy of Janet and her family, resurfaced.

She wanted to prove that she could solve her own problems. She wasn't some pathetic woman the perfect Christian family had to rescue. Why were they even meddling in her life?

"No, it's a bad idea, Janet."

Janet sat down on the bed. "Kavya, why are you here?"

"I don't know what I'm doing. It seemed like what I needed to do at the time. I was being crazy. I've been really moody."

"You can be all those things. We both know how he talks to you. We both know that he hit you so hard that your body went airborne."

"He was supposed to be there for me. We were supposed to create a life together. This isn't how this was supposed to go."

"If you want to call him right now, let's do it. If you want to go back, I'll drive you myself. What do you think you will have with him? What will you have to be in order to be with him?"

Kavya fell quiet again. Her Amma surely would have raised her to live up to the feminism she professed, right? To stop making excuses for Ranjeet and to stand up for herself.

"Okay. Tell your parents they can talk to him." Kavya was petrified about what would happen next.

* * *

The next day, Yumiko called.

"Hi, sweetheart," Yumiko started. She always had a cheery voice regardless of the news. "Okay, we haven't had a chance to deal with Ranjeet. But he must have contacted Neela because she called me wanting to know where you had gone. Now, I asked God to forgive me for lying, but I covered for you and said you had left the state. I wanted you to know that they have no idea where you are."

But after they hung up, Kavya drove to a gas station. On the way, she was both grateful for and frustrated with Janet's parents. Why would they even pick up a call from Neela? Now she had to go deal with that. *She's going to be so mad at me.* She called from the pay phone, dialing *67 to make sure the number didn't show up on Neela's Caller ID.

Neela answered on the first ring.

"It's me," Kavya managed to say.

"Stupid girl. What is this temper tantrum you're having? You don't even have the decency to go see his mother and explain yourself? Or me and your uncle?"

"I . . . well," Kavya stammered. "I'm not . . ."

Neela continued, "Everyone has problems. You have to grow up and learn to deal with them instead of running away. You need to go to him and explain yourself if you want to save this relationship."

"He was really mean to me. I can't." Kavya struggled to get the words out.

"You are throwing your life away, idiot! You won't ever get someone like him again. How do your uncle and I explain this to our friends? What did I do to deserve all of this?"

Kavya heard the dial tone.

And as if still held by the impetuous force that brought her to this gas station, she called her father, also blocking his Caller ID. She unleashed on him the anger she was afraid to show Neela.

"Listen to me, Dad. I broke up with Ranjeet and have left Austin. But do not try to find out where I am. And if you try to help Ranjeet, or his mom, or Neela find me, I swear that I will completely cut you off." She didn't wait for a response. She slammed the phone into the cradle.

"Fuck!" she screamed into the parking lot.

A couple of days later, while Kavya drove Janet up the wall with going back and forth about what should happen next, Yumiko called again.

"Hi, darling," Janet's mother said in a happy voice that belied the entire shitty situation. "I want to let you know that Ranjeet's mom seems ready to move on and find a new 'match,' as she called it. Her son will do what she wants him to. That was clear."

Kavya couldn't focus on anything after that. What did Yumiko and Bob say to Ranjeet? Why did she let them swoop in like that? She tried not to feel the ache of Ranjeet replacing her so quickly. Why didn't Yumiko and Bob just try to counsel him? Didn't Ranjeet love her at all? He wasn't even going to fight for her?

Janet was standing at the end of the hallway when Kavya hung up.

"So, it's done, right?" Janet asked.

Kavya nodded, numb.

"I know you," Janet said. "You think this is too much fuss."

Kavya looked away.

They were both quiet until Janet asked, "That time you had a busted lip, it was because of something he did, right?"

Kavya whipped her head around, startled. She had told people that she had fallen while being a clumsy idiot rolling around on a swivel chair. But really, Ranjeet had kicked the top of the chair while she was sitting on it, after she had been short with him. She remembered how forcefully her face had slammed into the desk.

She quietly answered, "Yes." She couldn't stand the silence that followed, so she said, "But it's over, so we don't have to think about this again. His mom will probably arrange a marriage immediately." She spoke as if in a trance.

"You still rejected him," Janet said slowly. "He may want to do something about that. I won't let him. So, I'm going to figure something out, just to throw him off if he starts asking around, until he moves on."

Kavya looked at her friend as her mind raced. She wished she could just think on her own.

Some weeks later when Janet traveled to a conference in Seattle, she dropped in the mail the stamped postcards she had asked Kavya to write out to her close friends in Austin. Every card had the same message. *I'm sorry I left without saying goodbye. I had a bad breakup and am starting my life over in France. I am sending this while on a trip to the U.S. I will always remember you.*

Janet thought it was a great plan, and Kavya complied to make her feel helpful. But what did Janet or her family know? If Ranjeet wanted to find her, make her life hell, kill her with his bare hands, he could. He could do anything.

CONFESS

Winter vacation was over. Kavya watched Janet, Fiona, and Lexi wave from the back of the taxi taking them to the airport, while the boys headed to the subway station to then get the train back to college. She wanted to run after them all to tell them, *Come back. Stay with me forever.*

That evening she forced herself to go out to dinner with friends. On her way back from Williamsburg, on a whim, she got off at the Bedford-Nostrand Avenue stop and walked north along the wide sidewalks. A few people still in scrubs or suits were dragging their trash containers to the curb. Brown slush from a winter storm a week before lined the streets.

She rang the buzzer of Mingming's building. Her friend poked her head out of the window and yelled, "I'll let you in!"

Kavya made her way up the three-story walk-up, deftly stepping around strollers and piles of boots. Children were laughing, crying, and fighting behind the doors, with an occasional adult yelling.

Mingming was waiting with the door open, wearing a Pearl Jam concert T-shirt. They hugged, and Kavya handed her the plastic bag from the restaurant.

Mingming peeked inside and tossed the bag on a table by the front door.

"Kavya, seriously, why do I want your half-eaten tiramisu?"

Kavya laughed and wandered over to the fridge to look at new pictures of Mingming's niece. "Where's Charles?"

"Off on some snowboarding trip. He'll be back in a few days. How was the visit with everyone?"

Kavya sat on the plush rug on the floor as Mingming's aging dog Lulu lazily sauntered over, sniffed her, and lay down next to her with a big sigh. She mindlessly scratched the golden retriever behind the ears and was rewarded with a groan of deep satisfaction. Kavya relaxed into the warmth of Lulu as she recounted Lexi's antics.

Mingming settled on the floor on the other side of Lulu. She picked sleep out of the dog's eyes. "This pup is requiring more and more attention every day."

"How old is she now?" Kavya asked.

Mingming put her face into Lulu's fur. "Twelve." She raised her head. "She's my baby."

Kavya smiled. "By the way, where's that T-shirt from?"

"Wrigley Field, Chicago, 2018."

"No, I saw that, but you went to that concert?"

Mingming nodded, her face lighting up. "Of course. It was before I met you."

"I knew you were kinda obsessed with them, but you still go to Pearl Jam concerts? It seems like a disgruntled bro crowd."

Mingming's eyes widened. "What? That's not true! Looks can be deceiving." She then went into a twenty-minute monologue about song lyrics, political protests, the fan club, and on and on. Kavya wasn't really following but loved seeing this side of her friend. Mingming finally finished and declared, "And case closed."

"You should leave your job and become a Pearl Jam groupie."

"I wish."

Kavya got up, feeling the exhaustion in her body and the sadness of missing her sons. "Well, it's getting late. I think I'll head out. I just felt like swinging by to see you."

"No! You just got here," Mingming protested. "We can talk about music you like. Missy Elliott? Tori Amos?"

Kavya sat back down and leaned against Lulu. "I'm so tired though. But yeah, I do have good taste in music." She saw Mingming getting worked up and quickly added, "And so do you! Truly."

"Okay, in all seriousness," Mingming said. "What's been up with you? How's the panic attack and therapy stuff going?"

"Panic attacks are way better. But remember back when I told you a bit about my ex Ranjeet? I'm trying to figure out why he was abusive."

Mingming raised an eyebrow. They could hear a dog yapping from across the hallway. "Does it matter?"

"Yes! That caste book that I was texting you about made me think about how being dominant caste makes you . . . violent. And I think that explains him and maybe why I shouldn't ever again date anyone who's dominant caste."

"Whoa. That sounds very simplistic."

"Not really. You're the same person who's sitting there nodding when Kendra and Sarah say that 'whiteness is violence.' They've both told us over and over again why they will never date white men. You never have a problem with that." Kavya heard the edge in her voice.

Mingming frowned. "What's with you? Two Black women saying they don't want to date white guys because of racism is very different from what you're saying."

"Shit, I'm sorry." Kavya waited for Mingming to meet her eyes. "For real, I'm sorry. I was trying to draw a connection between white supremacy and Brahminical supremacy, like with Brahmins upholding casteism and caste oppression. Like, whiteness is violence and Brahminism is violence. And I fucked up the comparison."

"Okay, fine. But what did Ranjeet do that makes you think it has to do with caste, versus being a misogynist, an asshole, whatever else? Why does it matter? He's been out of your life forever!"

"It matters!" Kavya wished she could find the words to express that particular anguish of being trapped in the past. She wanted to bang her head into a wall until she destroyed every sordid memory. "You asked about my therapy and anxiety, okay? I'm a bit better, but I'm still so uneasy. I have to understand so I can truly move on. I can see more clearly the violence all throughout dominant caste communities. I will never date a Brahmin man and participate in this caste shit again!" Kavya's tone was defiant, but she was flustered and confused.

"Kavya, I get it. It must have been horrific to be with Ranjeet. And you met some losers when you moved up here. It happens. But Freddy was good to you, right? Listen, first you said that if you studied intergenerational trauma, you'd feel better. Now you're saying you'll be better if you understand caste. This search for an explanation happens to a lot of survivors of domestic violence, and also when you've had a shit family life, believe me, and it's not your fault."

Kavya bristled. Why was everything coming out so lopsided? But she also ached at the mention of Freddy.

"I'm not talking about Freddy. He's Puerto Rican, obviously, and has nothing to do with this. Listen to what I'm saying. I think I fooled myself into thinking there was some kind of cultural familiarity with Ranjeet and all along maybe it was a case of 'caste recognizes caste' type of thing. And it caused this dynamic with expectations to uphold caste, and I didn't do it well enough, so he became violent, and that's part of how caste operates."

Mingming looked at her, unconvinced.

Kavya sunk her fingers into Lulu's fur, rubbing deep. She steadied herself. "I don't get it. You and I *talk* about this all the time. We are always talking about what it's like to date a white person versus a person of color, or the kind of stuff that comes up when we date someone in our community. Why won't you let me talk openly? Why can't I draw the limit on who I will and won't date?"

"I've never said, 'I won't date Chinese guys.' Do you think I don't care about Chinese men just because I had bad experiences with a few of them? Those men are in your community, Kavya!" Mingming's voice broke. "What about my brother? Even after becoming a parent, he isn't careful and gets into these stupid situations. Every time there's another anti-Asian hate crime, I can just picture it happening to anyone in my family. But also him. Especially him."

Mingming looked away. She brought her knees into her body, hugged herself, and picked at the nail polish on her toes.

Kavya teared up. "I don't want to fight with you. Of *course* I get what you're saying. My kids are brown men! All I'm saying is that it can be two things at once. You can experience racism but also uphold the caste system here in the U.S."

Mingming sniffled as she continued to look at her feet, amassing specks of purple paint on the rug.

"I'm not saying what you think I am, Mingming. Please. And I want to hear about all this with your brother. What's going on?"

"No," Mingming said petulantly. "I don't want to talk about it, and I'm not done with you. What about Kabir and Samir? You want to warn all the Brahmin Indians out there not to date these two Brahmin guys? As if all they are is their caste?"

Kavya stammered, "I mean, no, because I'm just talking about me, and I hope that, umm . . ."

"Oh, okay, so those two Brahmin guys are fine. Everyone else is bad?"

"No, but I do think I should have this conversation with them. I'm saying that dating within your caste or other people who are dominant caste inevitably reinforces caste in ways that you can't see if you have that caste privilege. It's not just Brahmin men. It's also Brahmin women. We're all raised with supremacy and ideas of who's worthy and who's not.

Even if you have the sweetest family or relationship possible, or even if you proudly say you're anti-caste, you're still dominant caste, you're still part of this . . . thing."

They were quiet, until Kavya protested, "No offense, but you don't know enough about caste. Why are you pushing back so hard?"

"Because you're oversimplifying things, which is not like you. Oh, and I'm a lawyer. What do you want me to do?" Mingming bobbed her head around and made a silly face. "Should I just nod my head and listen along?"

Kavya exhaled. The air between them was thick. The yapping dog in the other apartment was now whining nonstop.

"Okay, and why do you think you ended up with dominant caste guys?" Mingming asked. "What does that say about your awareness of caste? What does that say about who you're attracted to?"

Ouch.

Kavya conceded, "Yes, you're right. I've moved in dominant caste circles." She hesitated. "I think part of me wanted a guy like Ranjeet to prove something."

"Like what?"

"That I'm . . . that I belong?" Kavya shook her head. "Honestly? It was about trying to prove that I'm not some kind of pitiful weirdo without a proper family. That someone from my community thought I was important. Because when I was growing up, I knew that everyone in my ridiculous Brahmin community felt sorry for me." As she said the words, she abruptly remembered what things were like right before she met Ranjeet. She grimaced and turned away. She never should have brought any of this up.

* * *

During Kavya's first few months of graduate school, back in the late 1990s, a relentless and suffocating anxiety started to wrap itself around her, python-like. She had called the gas company to her apartment multiple times, convinced there was a leak that explained her endless headaches. She had rearranged her life so she could avoid elevators because the small space and closing doors would send her into dizzying waves of terror.

She went to Neela and Pramod's house one weekend, encouraged by her aunt's invitation upon hearing about Kavya's symptoms. "Home cooking will fix all that," Neela had said. Kavya was dubious but always said yes to any kindness extended by her aunt.

By that Saturday evening, Kavya was surprised to feel slightly more settled. She was resting on the leather couch watching TV when Neela sat next to her.

"I know what's causing these issues," her aunt said.

Kavya lifted her head, leaned on her elbow, and lowered the volume with the remote. She braced herself for the verdict Neela would deliver.

"Kavya, you need to get married."

Kavya laughed. "That's the kind of thing that would stress me out even more."

"No. Even that Shalini with the big nose is engaged. You're better than her. A nice boy from a good family will make you feel steadier and calmer inside yourself."

Kavya tried to hide her annoyance because she knew Neela was trying to look out for her, and the mere thought that her aunt wanted her to be happy warmed her more than she wanted to admit. "You're right. I shouldn't just be studying all the time. I should try to have a life." She added, "And the food has been delicious this weekend. Thank you for doing all of that." She smiled up at her aunt.

Neela smiled back, and for a moment, Kavya wanted to slide over and rest her head on her lap.

"Yes, you need to cook more of our food for yourself, Kavya. None of this American junk food. It's very important to nourish your body properly to get rid of all this stress. I'll give you some special recipes."

Kavya's body rippled with giddiness. Oh, it was so lovely when Neela was like this.

But then, Neela kept going. "You've never been right in the head. I thought all the time of taking you to a psychiatrist when you were a child because there was something very wrong with you. But it's really important to fix yourself now. No man is going to want you like this."

And just like that, the python was back. Kavya's insides curdled as they pressed up against each other. She was enraged and devastated all at once. She wanted to strangle Neela. She wanted to shake her into being nice for fucking once.

But instead, Kavya nodded and lay back down, turning the volume up.

Her anxiety remained a constant, but she visited her aunt and uncle less and less, which also meant she saw Mohan less. She settled into a quiet existence for a couple of years.

And then an old high school friend from the community invited her to a party for Indian graduate students. In a moment of fuzzy-headed thinking, Kavya accepted.

At the party, she noticed a man looking at her. He approached her confidently, while she watched him carefully. He stood in front of her, and she could not look away. Maybe it was his easy command of the conversation, even though she was awkward and clearly nervous. Or his quiet chuckle. His casual inclusion of Marathi words after he asked about her background. He eventually introduced himself. "My name is Ranjeet by the way. And I can tell you right now that you and I are going to end up together. I've found the person I've been looking for all this time." And she was smitten. *See Neela? I did find someone who wants me just as I am.*

* * *

The shame was overwhelming Kavya now as she sat with Mingming. How pathetic. She had found someone from the community to validate her, so that Neela could finally be nice to her, so that maybe Mohan could finally love her, so that she could stop feeling like a project for Janet's family, so that, so that, so that . . . She was always chasing after some kind of approval, just like Neela. *Am I like her after all?*

Mingming interrupted the cascade of self-admonishment. "I am hearing you, okay? C'mon. Don't look like that. I'm sorry. Maybe we're both just a bit off tonight and not hearing each other." She paused. "This 'I'm important' thinking is sounding like a way to cope with being in a racist society. Shit. All that model minority crap that makes us go crazy, you know?"

Kavya leaned back against the wall. She was too tired to try to explain anything else. That memory of Ranjeet walking over to her at the party, that excitement and anticipation, now seemed more like the cliched beginning of a horror movie.

The annoying dog across the way had finally shut up. Lulu was snoring heavily now, probably bored by Kavya's hand-wringing.

"Listen to me," Mingming said earnestly. "I have to say this because I love you, Kavya, and you would do the same for me. You haven't forgiven yourself for what happened with Ranjeet. And you're scrambling to do this academic analysis instead to understand it."

It was exactly what Helen and Janet always said to her. *Forgive yourself.* As if it were so easy. As if forgiveness didn't require sitting with the very worst you thought of yourself, and then, inevitably, the very worst you thought of the others who had hurt you. As if forgiveness wasn't just a path right into the darkness that always threatened to end you.

"It's all good. I'm really going to think about everything you've said." Kavya was ready to just move on. "And the offer still stands for us to talk about your brother."

She was met with silence.

She reached out and let her hand rest on Mingming's arm. "Hey, forget all my whining. Maybe I'm just a bit embarrassed. I have to confess that I've always been kind of a bad feminist."

Mingming gave her a half-smile. "Is there any other kind?"

Kavya laughed so loudly that Lulu startled awake. They cooed over the confused dog to settle her back down.

After tucking into some chocolate ice cream and the leftover tiramisu, and chatting a bit about their Nova Scotia trip, they hugged goodnight. Both held on for just a bit longer than usual.

As Kavya headed for the subway, she paused and looked around. She had been to this neighborhood so many times over the past years to visit Mingming. Bought beer from the bodega a few steps away that always smelled like fresh coffee grounds. Got her eyebrows threaded in the dilapidated store down the street that had somehow survived the COVID shutdown. But some of her favorite haunts were now shuttered.

Everyone always said they had been changed by the pandemic. Some were significantly more desperate for connection, or focused on their careers, or understanding of their children, or enchanted with New York, while others were less so. Some were utterly unnerved by the physical and emotional tectonic shifts that the pandemic had caused. Kavya was used to feeling rudderless and unsettled, so she wasn't as thrown off as everyone else.

But now everything was definitely different for her. Old Kavya would have bounded down the steps of the subway, reminding herself to come back on another day to take care of her eyebrows as they grew dangerously close to her hairline. This Kavya descended into the subway, steadying herself in case she lost her balance, even though the nightmares and panic attacks had both largely subsided. This Kavya thought about inviting her father to her home and locking the door behind him so that he finally had to talk to her. So that she could root out the ancestral darkness inside of her, so that she never again relied on Brahminical thinking to fill her up. Or to heal her.

DERAIL

Kavya kept turning over in her head her conversation with Mingming. She clearly needed to talk this caste stuff out with someone who had the patience to sit deeply with the topic. She did her best to ignore Mingming's claim that she had to forgive herself. No, her friend just didn't get it.

After a few days of stewing, she emailed Yandelis that she was going to soon send her a letter about caste for their project.

One week later, Kavya happened to see her colleagues Lynn, in Art History, and Teri, in Economics, deep in conversation in the university courtyard. That's when she realized that she could ask them to help with the intergenerational trauma student workshops that Yandelis wanted. They ran a popular and well-funded "race talks" series at the university. Perfect.

The problem was that Kavya found them insufferable. She usually avoided the "White Women Brigade," as she called them when venting about work to her friends.

Lynn, deceptively casual in overalls and a worn-out tote bag slung over her arm, was always ready with a word salad of diagnoses and insults. Like the time she ambushed an unsuspecting colleague to say, "After you aggressively critiqued my idea at that meeting in front of the dean, I thought about filing a grievance about your psychosocial difficulties, but I decided it was best if I gave you another chance."

Lynn also saved her best compliments for herself. Once, in a faculty meeting to discuss student well-being, she detailed how she selflessly nurtured her students. Then she paused dramatically before breathlessly asking, "Let's guide ourselves by asking, are we really being our activist ancestors' wildest dreams?" What a brazen act of plagiarizing Black folks' words about being *their* ancestors' wildest dreams! Who the hell were Lynn's "activist ancestors"? Because her actual *white* ancestors probably did dream about their descendants consuming all the oxygen in a room, suffocating the voices of everyone else.

Teri, constantly tugging at her clothes and fussing with her hair, followed Lynn around and specialized in passive-aggressive asides, like, "It's not for me to say who counts as an ally, *but* I just would have made better choices." She batted her eyes and sucked her teeth in a way that made Kavya's skin crawl.

Lynn and Teri were both pros at inflicting verbal wounds and then flitting away to serve on panels as self-appointed experts on the topic *du jour.*

Kavya jolted back to the present. *Do it for Yandelis. Just go up to them.* She quickly approached their table.

"Hi!" she said, trying to sound casual.

Lynn and Teri both looked up, surprised.

Kavya cleared her throat and pulled up a chair. She tucked her coat under to protect her from the cold metal as she sat down. "Okay, I'll get straight to it. I'd like to do a mini-series on intergenerational trauma for the race talks. I'd like to serve as co-facilitator with a student of mine to have some critical conversations about how to name the historic trauma passed through families."

Lynn smiled a little too widely. "Oh, Kavya, I'm glad you've started to care about the emotional well-being of the people in our community."

"You know that I'm really involved with our students. I don't think that's accurate to say I've *started* to care." Kavya tried to speak calmly.

Lynn still had that shit-eating grin on her face. "Oh, don't take it personally. We all bring different strengths. But you're not really, you know . . ."

Kavya took the bait. "Not really what?"

Lynn tilted her head, her brown-black eyes piercing right through Kavya. "You're not really the nurturing type. Your interpersonal style is more avoidant. But, hey, that's okay! You have a lot of other skills I admire."

Kavya opened her mouth, about to shoot off. *Stop. Not now. I'll regret it. She's just trying to throw me off balance. Again.*

* * *

Kavya's spinning mind was propelled back to those days at the beginning of the 2020 shutdown.

Amid a flurry of activity to support students through that frightening time, she and five other feminist colleagues had created a group to strategize on a "feminist ethics of care" to assist students who were struggling.

To Kavya's chagrin, Lynn and Teri showed up to the first video call meeting. Monica from English raised the issue of students, especially queer and trans ones, now trapped in abusive homes.

As they all brainstormed resources in a shared spreadsheet, Lynn unmuted herself and proclaimed, "We are the ones who must be there for these students. Some of these students are in the tri-state area. We can easily go to them and do the kind of care work perhaps the whole family units need."

The others nodded.

"That's very thoughtful, Lynn," Kavya said. "However, I'm not sure going to students in crisis is appropriate. We can absolutely talk to these students and check in on them. But I think visiting them, especially if there's any indication they're in an abusive environment, is a step too far. We don't have the skills or resources to support an entire family system."

Lynn's eyes flashed, as she shot back, "These are not normal times. We have to do things we wouldn't normally do."

"But even if the students let us, we can't just roll up to someone's house like some vigilante group."

Lynn ignored Kavya. "Okay, so who is with me? We'll contact the students, and we can make care packages to take with us."

"Let's first please discuss this," Kavya interrupted. "I'm uncomfortable with this idea, even if a student invites us. We could end up doing more harm. Living in an abusive household is very complex."

"Oh, I see that you're very triggered, Kavya." Lynn half-heartedly attempted to suppress her snickering. "What I usually try to remember is that I must suspend my hang-ups and focus on what really matters. Whatever is stressing you out doesn't mean you forget basic human decency, right? I just thought you were more empathetic than this."

And Kavya was immediately teleported to Neela's living room, as her aunt lectured her, "Why did I end up with you, Kavya? Selfish bitch." So yep, she was triggered.

"Lynn, it's not . . ." Kavya stammered. She meekly objected, "You can't speak to me like that."

Everyone else on the call remained silent. The feminist crew, always talking about care and solidarity, had nothing to say. Some looked away.

One changed the subject. Others remained expressionless. Teri focused on fluffing her bangs and looking at herself from different angles. Lynn smiled, almost triumphant.

Kavya excused herself and exited the meeting. She sent a quick group text to some of the others, sans Lynn and Teri, trying to extract some kind of camaraderie from them. *Hey, what was that? I'm pretty taken aback by how Lynn treated me. It felt like she was mocking me. You know me. I think my point was valid.*

Rookie mistake.

After all, it was the academics who wrapped themselves up in "feminist," "anti-racist," and other such labels, who most quickly shed that skin, slithering around and away from the difficult shit. That's why the others either ignored her message or wrote patronizing responses.

I'm sorry you're so upset about this. I value you as a colleague. Maybe you should take care of yourself?

Oh, she is just passionate. It's not a big deal, is it?

* * *

Even now, Kavya could feel the sting of that entire incident as she watched students, clad in down jackets and winter boots, walk through the courtyard. Lynn and Teri were still staring at her. She steeled herself. *No, I'm not going to let Lynn derail me this time.*

Kavya took a deep breath and said, "What's different about my idea is that I'll walk the students through a letter project to explore intergenerational trauma. Can I tell you more details?"

"Thanks for the suggestion. Lynn and I will think about facilitating something about that topic," Teri said. She then lined her mouth with a glossy stick. She smacked and rubbed her lips together.

"But I know that you've had guest facilitators before. I would like to do it."

Lynn and Teri exchanged glances.

Kavya quickly added, "I really appreciate this program you've set up, and you have such a huge listserv and the funding from the dean. Why can't we collaborate?"

She paused but they didn't say anything, so she continued, "I think a mini-series would be good. One should deal with caste, since it's a way to 'other' people within a group as 'less than.' And we've had that large influx of international students from India, and I'm sure casteism is playing out in ways we may not see. I'm dominant caste myself and, well, there's quite a few companies and universities in the U.S. that are finally seeing caste as a part of equity work. There's this new book on caste and trauma that also talks about race, and there's so much to discuss." She waited. *Look at them. Show confidence.*

"Trauma is an intense topic, Kavya," Teri sniped. "It's not something you can just show up and talk about without any experience or training. It sounds like you want to take advantage of the resources we have cultivated for some personal project." She looked down as she fiddled with her waistband.

Be calm. Kavya looked back and forth between the two. "My student and I are already working on this project for my fall class, and this would be a way to involve more students. It was my student's suggestion, and I want to support her. This isn't group therapy or something invasive. It's like what we do when we talk about race, right? We talk about the impact of oppression. And I am no more or less qualified to talk about this than any other faculty member involved with any of the race talks so far." The last sentence sounded sharper than she had intended.

Lynn clasped her mittened hands. "I am feeling really attacked right now. Kavya, I think you should ask yourself why you are not able to trust us to do this topic. It doesn't seem to me like you're seeking collaboration with us at all. We always amplify faculty of color, and no one has ever complained."

"We will take your suggestion under advisement," Teri added. "If we do a week on trauma, we'll be the facilitators. We'll get someone from Psychology to help."

They both looked at her.

Kavya stood up, mumbled a goodbye, and quickly walked back inside. She lingered behind a column and looked through the window at Lynn and Teri as they chattered, no doubt, about how they had just demolished stupid, uncaring Kavya.

As she leaned against the window and nervously tapped her fingertips on the glass, she wanted to go back out there and scream at them. *Stop saying I don't care about others! It's not true!* But she had listened enough to Helen to know that right now, she couldn't distinguish whether the intensity of her pain was about them, or about Neela.

And yet, she couldn't stop her mind from crafting what she really wanted to say to them. *Who the hell do you think you are? You just want everyone to make you feel important. You collect people of color to validate you, so no one sees that you don't really know anything! You don't know how to talk about despair or about what people do to each other to live in the worlds we were born into. You only said no to me because you can't stand me. That's because I see through you. I know what you are.*

Kavya slowly walked to the entrance of the building, trying her best to calm down. What the hell kind of hold did this letter project have on her? Why did it feel so vital to plan, talk about, share these letters? Why did it matter so much to Yandelis to get other students involved? Kavya had blown the chance to do the workshops, but she still had to do right by her student.

When she got outside, she called the university operator and connected with the Office of Internal Grants. She left a message asking to set up a meeting.

* * *

A few days later, she was in the administrative wing of the main building, after climbing eight flights of stairs so she didn't have to use the elevator.

Trying to catch her breath, she sat down at the large desk across from Jacey.

"Why don't you tell me why you're here?" Jacey was a humorless woman who got way too close to the webcam during Zoom calls so that you could count every nose hair. She was clearly miserable, in a position that didn't at all match her enviable skills in data analytics. Now that Kavya could see her in person, she noticed that Jacey was as apathetic as she seemed on screen.

Kavya answered, "I want to try something a bit experimental, and I was wondering if my project would be eligible for the classroom and pedagogy grant."

Jacey's face didn't change. "Okay."

"I would like to use the money to hire a student research and teaching assistant. We want to pilot a project on intergenerational trauma in my fall International Relations class and create a community toolkit for anyone to use."

Jacey sighed and pumped hand lotion into her palm. She rubbed the cream on each finger, slowly and deliberately. "Okay, so what's the experimental part?"

"We are not going to focus on student learning outcomes. We're not going to be assessing some kind of cumulative growth."

"But how will you know if the students got anything out of the class?" Jacey sighed again.

"I'm going to challenge that idea of getting something measurable out of learning. Some students will experience a release by getting in touch with anger and frustration. Others will find validation in stories that acknowledge what their own families have endured. Maybe someone else will learn how much global politics matter and find their voice. So, bell hooks wrote . . ."

"Yeah, sounds good. Fine, go ahead and apply."

Kavya was startled, expecting far more pushback. "Oh, so it's eligible? I wouldn't fill out the usual rubric if I were to get it."

"Does it matter? Write up some kind of reflection. No one looks at the rubrics anyways. It's just paperwork. You should know that by now."

This unexpected honesty threw Kavya off-balance. She kept probing. "Do you need me to spell out my qualifications and approach? Because trauma studies is not my field. But I would draw upon the literature I teach, like human rights, postcolonial and decolonial studies, and feminist theory."

Jacey stood up. "I've got to take a smoke break. Listen, just apply."

Kavya scrambled to gather her things and follow her out. As they walked silently to the elevator, Jacey fumbled around in her purse.

"Take it from me. No one is paying attention, Kavya. The selection committee goes through it, and they're not exactly picky. Then, there's a couple of us who sign off if they say yes. Mark does the final signature. Usual workflow."

Shit. Mark.

"Jacey, there was this faculty meeting about anti-racism training, and Mark and I sort of got into it at one point."

Jacey smiled, as her lips disappeared, and her yellowed teeth showed themselves for the first time in the conversation. Her always sleepy eyelids even slid up. "Oh, yes, I do remember that. I was there that day, you know. He was very angry with you."

The elevator doors opened. Kavya's breathing quickened, but she forced herself to step inside.

"But he deserved it," Jacey continued. "He is such a child, threatening to stop leaks like that. Did you know his assistant has to organize everything for him because he's so incompetent? She's the one who finally told him to tailor his pants and not drag the bottoms of his suits all over New York."

"Will he take our argument out on me and turn down my application?" Kavya nervously held onto the bar inside the elevator, keeping close to the emergency button.

The doors opened again, and a crowd of people streamed inside as Kavya and Jacey elbowed their way out.

"Mark's signature is just a formality, Kavya. He signs so much paperwork every day. Just submit it." Jacey stuck a cigarette between her lips as she walked to the exit.

Kavya stayed behind and stood against the wall, watching people walk past the elevator bank. Okay, submit the application, maybe get the grant, and move forward with the letter project.

And then a million questions assaulted her. *Should I send Mark a nice email, just in case? What if Yandelis and I do all these letters and I just end up having panic attacks again? What if no one likes the project because it just brings up too much stuff? Who the hell looks to research and teaching to feel better? Writing a letter about caste won't and shouldn't make me feel okay. Who am I to teach an entire semester about fucking trauma? I'm as bad as the White Women Brigade.*

That floating feeling was starting up. Shit.

Kavya walked quickly to the same exit Jacey took. She was really losing it. As she walked on the sidewalk, unsure of where she was headed, she pinched her skin, hard. She smelled roasted peanuts. She heard the high-pitched beep of a truck backing up.

When the light turned green, she sprinted across the street, holding her breath and hoping she didn't lose her balance.

Now she was in City Hall Park. She stood helplessly and watched as an older woman threw pieces of bread to a squirrel. She and Freddy used to meet here and scarf down food cart biryani. She wanted to be doing that again instead of whatever was happening now. It was sort of that slingshot feeling. But she was so tired she couldn't even figure out what she was remembering. But it was also sort of that tilting feeling. But more like when you first step onto a rocking boat, and less like the world was going to end.

Was the panic attack over? Was it even a panic attack? She couldn't tell.

She sat on the bench, near the woman with the bread. She exhaled and watched her breath turn into vapor in the cold air.

She pulled her phone from her pocket and called Janet.

"What the hell, Kavya. I was just thinking about you!"

"What's going on?" Kavya tried to sound casual.

"Just tell me. Why is this seven-year-old child outwitting me?"

"What happened?"

"Ugh," Janet groaned. "Before Fiona goes on these work trips, she says, 'Lexi, listen to Janet.' But since we're in the middle of my adoption process, I'm still just Janet, but I'm also soon to be legally and officially responsible as the co-parent, too, right? It's confusing, and I think I send mixed signals or something. And so now, Lexi's refusing to shower. She lies about doing her chores and then says that I was the one who messed up her room. She always has some argument ready!"

Kavya consoled her. Janet *was* always the "cool" one in any household, definitely with Samir and Kabir, which sometimes made her all the more anxious about how to be the serious grown-up. Kavya listed all the ways that Janet had been a calm, guiding force and deftly handled all kinds of shenanigans with her brothers and Kavya's boys.

"Janet, be confident and assured in yourself. It's a power struggle, and she wants to see how you'll react."

"I guess. Thanks for the advice. Even though I was right there in the trenches with you all those years, you still teach me about kids. You're the best mom."

Kavya winced. She *was* pretty proud of herself for the kind of mom she was. But Janet would take back that compliment if she actually knew everything about her.

The confession that was always alive, always ready to spill out, crept along, ready, ready. *Not yet. Not yet.*

Kavya quickly changed the subject. "I've been thinking about the trauma stuff all week, and I'm applying for a school grant to work on it some more."

"Girl, get that coin!" Janet cheered.

"It's to pay a student named Yandelis. But maybe I shouldn't pursue this."

"Oh stop, what happened now?"

"The letter project has been so pivotal for me. But I'm questioning the idea of going all out with a whole semester on intergenerational trauma.

Maybe I'm opening a can of worms I can't handle. Maybe I'm making a big mistake."

"Kavya, why are you always beating yourself up? You literally just told me to be confident in myself." Janet's frustration with her was evident.

Ugh. Could Kavya not ever express one fucking doubt to anyone without getting lectured about how she "treated" herself? This was about academia. About how to teach and talk about violence and oppression in people's lives without causing harm. Why wouldn't anyone tread carefully when talking about trauma?

But Kavya gave in. It was easier that way. "Yes, you're right. I'll work on that. So, while you're wrangling Lexi, how's Fiona's work been?"

Janet excitedly told her about Fiona's promotion.

"Fiona is so awesome, you know?" Kavya said. "Tell her and Lexi I send my love. And I'm going to find more bobbleheads in the souvenir stores to send to Lexi."

After they eventually hung up, Kavya got up from the bench and walked down Broadway to her bus stop, feeling the rattling of anxiety a little bit less. *Try to believe in this project. Fuck all the noise.*

When she got home, she created a new document for a letter on caste. She read and took notes until her eyes were dry and itchy. She glanced at her window, opaque from condensation. Time for some fresh air. She put on her winter layers, pulled on her boots, and left the house.

As soon as she opened the door, the chilly air rushed into her nose and settled in her lungs. She wrapped her scarf tighter and hurried along the sidewalk until she reached Owl's Head Park. She trudged through the slush along the pathway, passing bundled-up people walking their dogs, until she reached the highest point. She squinted as her eyes, already watering from the bitter cold, focused on the Manhattan skyline in the distance. On her regular walks through this park, she sometimes conjured up different scenes when she really wanted to clear her mind. Yes, let's pretend that sewage plant isn't there. And let's imagine that the moonlight is shining into pristine water and there's a mountain range on the other side of the Hudson River.

She lingered under a lamppost. Her mind drifted away to her father.

Her entire life, she had referred to her relationship with her father as "strained," "estranged," or "complicated," depending on the day. Her first memories were of calling out to her adoptive parents, Neela and Pramod, as her aunt and uncle. After she left Austin, she used only their first names, to make it known they no longer had her respect. Yet, the person who signed away his rights to her was still Dad, even Daddy when she was little. Sometimes she thought she called him that as a way to wake him up, to make him remember her. It was never too late to become her father.

The wind picked up, and she turned back to go home. As she shuffled down the hill, she thought back to that summer visit with Mohan that started the horrid panic attacks. How could the nothingness and boredom of interacting with her father have sparked all of that?

As soon as she got home, she tore off her gloves and took out her phone before she could overthink it. She quickly texted her father, *Dad, please call me when you get this. I would like to invite you to New York to visit me.*

Underneath the hope that he could tell her about her family, lay a secret wish that he could figure out why he had woken up her demons. And that he could make them go away.

REUNITE

Kavya's father set the dates for the trip to New York very soon after receiving her invite.

And just one week later, Kavya received a text from Freddy. It was like every other message he had sent after their breakup. *Hey K, I'll be back in the city for a bit and crashing at Joe's sublet. Want to meet up? Hope you're good, Freddy.*

Every other time she had made up an excuse as to why she couldn't see him. She didn't want to open the door to getting back together, or worse, see that he had moved on happily without her. But her rules for herself were all over the place now. Her father was going to stay in her home, for crying out loud. So, this time she accepted Freddy's invitation. Why the hell not?

* * *

Kavya and Freddy had last seen each other three years before, in 2020, a couple of months into the pandemic.

They had met up at the park. Kavya settled on the bench, knowing that home was just around the corner if she needed to make a quick exit. Freddy removed a mask from a new package and tried it on, pressing down onto the bridge of his nose. He slid the top of the mask up so that it rested right underneath his glasses. He looked at Kavya as his lenses immediately fogged up, obscuring his dark eyes. She could only see part of his golden-brown skin. He removed his baseball cap, revealing his curls. He used a finger to clean his glasses, but then they fogged up again. He finally took them off and squinted at Kavya.

"That's not the right kind of mask," she said.

"I have to be ready for any time a work thing comes up, and I got these in bulk." He shrugged. "Anyways, that's not why I asked to meet. I don't understand why we can't be together. I don't understand anything that happened. I asked to move in, you said no. Okay, fine, we won't live together, but then why the hell did you dump me?"

"You're going to be on the road all the time, Freddy. You're going to be gone for weeks or months at a time."

"So? There are these things called phones and computers. The whole world is Zooming."

"I don't know."

"I don't want to be with anyone but you. And that won't change. I'm in love with you." His voice softened. "I'm in love with your kids. We're all so good together. Don't you feel the same way?"

Kavya scanned the park, watching families, groups of friends, and couples in their own imaginary bubbles as they walked down the paths or settled underneath the oak trees dotting the hilly stretch of grass.

What was she supposed to say? *Well, Freddy, I do want to be with you. But you screwed it all up by saying you want to know everything about me. That means that one day, you will figure out that my aunt fucked me up. And you'll finally notice how I track my sons with GPS. You'll find out how scared I am. And maybe one day, you'll get fed up. And a switch will turn on, and you will morph into someone nasty and unrecognizable. I won't let that happen again. I won't let it happen to my children. Still love me now?*

Finally, she replied, "I keep saying no. And you keep pressuring me."

"I'm not saying we get married tomorrow. I'm saying let's give it a shot."

"Why are you talking about marriage? You never brought that up before."

"I said I was *not* talking about marriage!" Freddy spoke loudly.

"See? We're already fighting."

"Who's fighting?"

"Listen, I'm just connecting all the dots." She avoided looking at him as she spoke. "And you know, I didn't move my entire life and uproot the boys so that I could sit around and wait for some guy."

"Some guy?"

"Not like that. But you want me to sit at home, and, you know."

"Who said you're sitting at home?"

"I just see where this is going," Kavya answered forcefully.

They bickered back and forth until finally, Freddy, his eyes wet, said in a strained voice, "I can't convince you. I have to go."

He left Kavya on the bench, where she tightened her own mask and slipped on her sunglasses so that she could finish crying by herself before she went home to her sons.

* * *

A few days after Kavya responded that, this time, she could meet up with Freddy, she found herself standing outside of a restaurant next to the outdoor dining section. She uneasily played with her hair as she studied the couples shivering under the barely functioning heat lamps. She checked her lipstick in the window reflection. Watching the street, she wondered if she should just go back home. Then she saw him.

Three years after last seeing him, Freddy still had that same thick corduroy jacket, the one he had placed around her shoulders at Kung Fu movie night in Prospect Park. He had grown out his beard. He had cut his hair in that weird flopping-over-the-eyes style that her own boys now wore. In the most recent FaceTime call with her sons, she had used all her might not to say, *Cut your damn hair!*

As Freddy walked up to her now, her stomach churned a bit from the excitement. Or maybe anxiety. Or hunger. He leaned down to hug her, and she moved her arms up the familiar ripples of the jacket. They walked inside to the table Kavya had reserved.

And even though so much time had passed, they fell back into their jokes. Taking food from each other's plates without asking. Finishing each other's sentences.

Kavya had prepared a speech for when Freddy questioned, *What have you done with yourself since we broke up? Do you miss me?* But he didn't ask.

Instead, they reminisced, wiping away tears and gasping for air as they laughed.

"Freddy, Freddy! Do you remember when we busted our asses to help with that event, the one where you taught a free photography lesson?"

"Ha! It was to raise money for an immigrant rights group or something?"

"Yes, yes! We did all that outreach. We hit the pavement. We were the ones who secured the space and the equipment."

"Yes, and then it's the day of the event. We're looking around like, where the fuck are the people in charge?"

Kavya giggled. "You were so mad. The two organizers came well after the event started, when everyone was leaving. They just rolled up like there was no hurry at all."

Freddy slammed his hand on his table. "Oh shit, yes. They were so late." He shook his head in disbelief. "Yeah, you're right. It was two hours at least. I think you called one of them who kept saying they were on their way."

"You remember how pissed you were when they finally came?"

"Yeah, I gave it to them."

"Yeah, but remember what you said?" Kavya asked excitedly. "You said, 'Next time, I'm not teaching photography. Instead, we're doing woodworking. A clock-making event.'"

Freddy leaned back in his chair and snapped his fingers. "Shit. Yes. They got so angry, and the one kid came at me. First of all, I'm a big dude, so don't try it. Second of all, it was a justice event!"

"He tried to slap you and missed!" Kavya squealed, and they both burst out laughing again.

When they finally calmed down, they reached for their drinks, coughing and giggling.

"Those assholes," Freddy said. "But I shouldn't have gotten so angry. We knew they'd be late—okay, not that late—but late for sure. That's how brown folks do. That's how my people do. That's definitely how your people do."

"True." She mindlessly pulled an ice cube out of her glass. She popped it in her mouth and crunched. Still sucking on the ice cube, she said, "But I'll take it over the alternative."

"What's the alternative?"

Kavya smiled. "The White Women Brigade."

"Whoo!" Freddy yelped. "What happened now?"

She detailed the encounter in the courtyard, being careful not to share too much about the trauma part. She ended with, "But whatever, I won't do the student workshops. Too much drama."

"No, do it. It's not like there can only be one race discussion program in a university. Yours will be better."

"No, Lynn and Teri will lose their minds over it. They might sabotage me. Or do who knows what." She had never told him about her magical thinking and wasn't about to now.

"So? Who cares what they say?"

"Freddy, I'm going up for tenure. They both have tenure and could throw their weight around. I don't want them starting anything."

"But . . ."

Kavya shook her head firmly. "No, Freddy."

Freddy was quiet for a bit, swirling the wine around in his glass. "Do you remember why we split up?"

"What do you mean? Umm, we wanted different things." Her heart started to pound.

"You assumed I wanted to get married and keep you trapped at home. No matter what I said, you didn't want to hear it. You made up your mind, and you were out."

"That's why we're having dinner? So that we can argue about why we broke up three years ago?" She tried to sound annoyed, but she was rattled. Sweat dripped down the back of her neck.

"Nope. But it's like you hear one thing, and you make it mean something different, and then you're off to the races. I'm offering a suggestion for your work because I know you can do it, and you're backing down from something important that your own student wants, just because I suggested it. And of course, just giving in to Lynn and Teri goes against everything I know about you."

Kavya flushed. "You haven't seen me in ages. What do you know about me?"

Freddy stared at her incredulously. "I know that you're a badass at work. But also that you don't want to accept others' perspectives. You think it takes something away from you or makes you weak or something."

"Oh, well, I'm so thrilled you have me all figured out," she seethed. "So, if I don't say, 'Yes, Freddy, whatever you say, Freddy,' there's something wrong with me?"

"Not at all. I'm *supporting* you. I'm confident in what you could do. At least try to set up your own workshops, even if things get a bit uncomfortable with Teri and Lynn. Okay, maybe they get mad or something. Maybe not. See how things unfold. Live in the gray." He looked like he wanted to say something else but stopped himself.

He reached his hand out to rest on hers. "I'm on your side, Kavya."

He looked right at her. A small, thrilling surge. She wanted to pull her hand away but didn't. "So just live in the gray," she said, both asking him and commanding herself.

"I do hear what you're saying and why you don't want to mess with them. But you know, you're a force. They shouldn't want to mess with *you*."

She sat quietly. She was lightheaded. Staring at his hand, she counted the hairs on his knuckles and compared the lengths of his fingernails, focusing on anything she could because she didn't want to cry. First Ming-ming, then Janet, now him. Why couldn't anyone just allow her to be?

Or was she just so incapable of receiving unconditional support that it was suffocating when others actually fought for her? She considered all the times she woke up from the past months' nightmares thinking, *Thank God Freddy isn't here to see this.* But now she wondered, why didn't she ever wish he was there?

She started to say something. But she wasn't sure what.

And then he motioned to the waiter for the check.

"Do you want to . . ."

"Yeah, I guess it's late?"

"I mean, if you . . ."

"Yeah, no, you must be needing to head back."

"Yeah, yeah, I should go."

"No, that's cool. Yeah, that's fine."

Freddy removed his hand, and Kavya carefully folded hers in her lap. They immediately transformed into the awkwardly polite exes she had imagined they would be. She nervously chattered about how much the neighborhood had changed, and he feigned great interest in the bill as he mumbled about gentrification.

Kavya threw money on top of the bill. "I got you. No worries!" She practically fell off her seat in her rush to get out.

When they were outside, she stood on her toes and reached out to hug him. "I'm glad we did this."

"Thanks for coming out, Kav." He hugged her tighter. "Take care, okay? Tell the boys I said hi."

She pressed her face into his neck. She wanted to tell him all about her father and how she had invited him to come up. She wanted to tell him about her panic attacks. She wanted to ask if he was seeing anyone. She wanted to tell him to come home with her. She wanted to say a thousand things.

But instead, she said, "I will. You take care of yourself, too."

They pushed each other away, or maybe pulled themselves away, she couldn't tell. And she turned, forcing herself to just focus on the sidewalk, to focus on her steps, to keep her feet on the ground. She didn't know if an attack was coming on, or if she was mourning, but she couldn't give in to it now. As she walked, she kept staring at the sidewalk, stained with dog shit, cigarette butts, and scratched-off lotto cards, willing herself to stay upright.

DEAR COLLEAGUE X

Kavya sat across from Molly, the chair of her department, who was scrolling through Kavya's tenure portfolio. As she waited, she looked at the framed photos all around the office. In each one, Molly, her husband, and their four pale, strawberry blond children smiled preciously at the camera, arms wrapped around each other and their dog. In each photograph, everyone was always color coordinated, even the dog with its bandanna.

"I want to see the executive statement by the end of the semester, okay?" Molly noted.

"Of course."

"But other than that, you're in great shape. It was a good move to hit the ground running when you first started here. It set you up well for a smooth path to tenure and promotion."

"Thank you!" Kavya brightened. "Anything else?"

"Not related to this, but I do need your help on something else."

Kavya tried to smile, but Molly's requests never led to anything good. She was a nice white woman, the kind where you could disagree with her without her getting all fragile and defensive about it. But Kavya could never tell if Molly was testing her with endless requests for assistance on "special projects." So, she always said yes, just in case. The last time, Kavya ended up participating in a painfully horrible recorded skit that one of her department colleagues had written to entice students to major in political science. Kabir and Samir still made fun of her for it.

Molly continued, "Sneha mentioned something at a meeting about wanting to partner with somebody to put together career preparation workshops. It's not until the fall. I thought you would be perfect?"

Oh damn. Sneha was an Indian-American woman in Sociology who worked on urban planning. They even used to hang out during Kavya's first year. Then Sneha straight up told her one day that she was sure Kavya "meant well," but she was too "radical," whatever that meant. And it turned into yet another awkward relationship with a colleague.

Molly quickly said, "It's not because you're both Indian! I apologize! You both have had success in getting students into internships that led to job offers."

"No, no, I wasn't thinking that at all. Happy to do it." She tried to sound light so Molly couldn't sense her irritation.

After trading anecdotes about having children in college, Kavya left, wondering why she always struggled to understand her colleagues. But that's when it hit her. She got home, marched right into her office, and typed out the caste letter, with Sneha as her inspiration.

Dear Colleague X,

I am writing to you because you, like me, like too many dominant caste people, are afraid to call out casteism every chance we get. Caste always finds a way to weasel its way into any South Asian context and thrive. We make excuses to avoid this topic because we don't want to face what we are. We don't want to face that our families are responsible for a heinous system and the intergenerational trauma that results.

Do you remember when I invited you to attend a workshop held by a Dalit rights group? You said it made you feel uncomfortable because they were "anti-Hindu," and that they blamed us savarnas "without proof." You asked me to not be so radical. You said I should consider getting involved instead with a "progressive" Hindu organization that was fighting against Indian Prime Minister Narendra Modi's Islamophobia and Hindu nationalist extremism. I didn't challenge you that day because you know way more about Hinduism and Indian politics than

I do. I chickened out because I was afraid of looking stupid, because heaven forbid we look like we don't know everything in front of each other.

But let's pick up where we left off. Because you can't have Hindu nationalism, with all its hypermasculinity and brutal violence, without the Brahminical patriarchy that is the engine of caste. I know a lot more about Modi now, like how terrifyingly good he is at amassing political power through the manipulation of caste identities. Modi himself is not dominant caste, as he is from the Ghanchi caste, designated as Other Backward Caste. As a young boy, he joined Rashtriya Swayamsevak Sangh, the right-wing paramilitary Hindu nationalist organization, maybe as a way to feel important. That experience shaped his "Hindu unity" approach to bringing the out-of-caste, lower caste, and even Dalit converts to other religions into the Hindu nationalist fold as voting blocs. Modi is so skilled at naming historic trauma (let go of your colonial mindset, he recently said) by blaming Muslims as a whole for all that ails India and giving everyone else the promise of an impressive future via the Hindu Nation. And he does this all while enacting draconian anti-Muslim measures and happily allowing the Hindu right wing to foment and exacerbate the repressive social mores of caste.

In addition, did you know that he was the first prime minister since Indira Gandhi to travel to Fiji because it is part of the indentured labor diaspora? All those countries to which Indians were shipped by the British are now part of Modi's grand plan for connecting the diaspora through Hindu nationalism. Why is he doing this? To find out, I've been reading about South Asia and its indentureship diasporas. Some caste-oppressed people saw indenture as a way out of caste! And dominant caste indentured workers found that their very departures from India alongside the caste-oppressed allegedly "polluted" their caste status. These different caste experiences led to divergent trajectories among the descendants of indentureship, as caste intersected in all kinds of ways with race, class, sexuality, and so on. But regardless of the differences and nuances, some of the descendants have something in common: they suffer from the historic and family traumas of the cruelty of indentured labor and are finding solace in Modi's pledge of "greatness." It's fascinating how countries try to capture the loyalties of people scattered all over the world by promising to convert pain into a sense of belonging.

And yet, those promises notwithstanding, all I see is how caste morphs and mutates and somehow still stays the same. Over and over again, Dalits are assaulted and murdered for stepping out of their place and socializing with or being educated alongside the caste-privileged. Dalits are bullied into suicide in our name. No inclusion in the great Hindu Nation will change that. So, you see, to confront Modi means to confront caste.

Anti-casteist savarnas have been there all along, putting their bodies on the line. We have to learn from them because the more I learn about caste, the more I see in myself some of the clue-lessness, entitlement, and performativity that I critique in white feminists.

Caste is a catastrophic, murderous beast whose violence seeps through the generations, who is nourished by ethnonationalism, authoritarianism, misogyny, and hatred. We can't be silent. There's another anti-casteism workshop coming up, and we could go together. Can we?

Yours in solidarity,
Kavya

Kavya's insides pulsated. It was like after she wrote the first letter about colorism, when she felt like *herself*. As she sat in front of the computer, she at long last realized something. There was nothing special or earth-shattering about the letter she just wrote. And sure, maybe like Helen suggested, these letters were a container for her anxiety.

But each letter was also a portal she could enter whenever she wanted to. She could join a chorus of messy, imperfect people who were also trying to deal with their sorrow. Instead of waiting to be tossed around by her wonky brain and fretting that she was stuck in the past, she could find comfort in how time was maybe not supposed to be linear.

Maybe she could be back in 1972, before she was born, alongside beloved feminist poet Adrienne Rich just as she was writing that the "sleepwalkers are coming awake, and for the first time this awakening has a collective reality; it is no longer such a lonely thing to open's one's eyes."

She could go back and forth in time with Rich, or anyone, to find kinship with others in pain, to corroborate others' stories, to seek reassurance that it was worth it to confront violence and oppression. And it wouldn't have to be such a lonely thing.

She remembered that when she was a girl, she would read nonstop and then write notes to the characters and even form friendships and share her secrets with them. A kid from her school once found the notes and made fun of her for being weird. Yeah, so she was a weird kid. Good! Writing those letters probably saved her back then, just like right now.

Before the beautiful sensations could pass, she sent the caste letter to Yandelis.

SAVE

Once upon a time in Texas, a woman in Kavya's community downed a bottle of pills. The husband discovered her just in time. When everyone found out, people rushed to her bedside. Neela also visited her, taking twelve-year-old Kavya to the woman's house with several containers of food.

After they came back home and got dinner ready, Kavya asked, "Why did she take all those pills?"

"Who knows. She looked like a pathetic zombie, medicated like that." Neela could not hide her contempt.

Kavya tentatively offered, "Maybe it's good we went then. Maybe she hurt herself because she was lonely."

"I know how she feels," Neela said quietly. "But you never care about what might happen to me. Who cares if I die, right? I might as well try to kill myself too."

Kavya was still flustered by the visit to that withered woman and the husband who could not wipe the fear from his face. And she could not stop the words that she hurled at Neela. "I'm sick of hearing you say you're going to do something to yourself."

"What?" Neela, not used to Kavya challenging her, was shell-shocked.

"You just said you might as well kill yourself. Why would you say that? You just literally said it. This time, you can't deny it." Kavya was resolute, speaking loudly and clearly.

She stared at Neela's face then, full of gray splotches, an unnatural color, maybe from those goddamn lightening products. One of Neela's eyes twitched. Her mouth was in its usual frown, dry lips, garlic breath.

Kavya looked at her with disgust. "Whatever. You'll never admit to it."

Neela quietly said, "It's because I hate myself."

"What did you say?" Kavya held her breath.

"I hate myself. I hate myself. I should never have been born." Neela's mouth slowly opened as soundless sobs struggled to leave her body.

Kavya was fascinated and alarmed at the same time. She felt an urge to hold her aunt, to say, *No, don't say that*. But she couldn't move or speak. And Neela turned and left the room.

Had Neela ever made good on her threats, Kavya would have wondered for the rest of her life what she could have done to prevent it.

* * *

Kavya didn't have to wait long to hear Yandelis's reaction to the caste letter.

March 7, 2023

Dear Prof. Joshi,

OMG! Thank you for sharing your caste "letter" with me. I am already reading some of the stuff in the reading list you attached. I am ashamed that I never really knew what caste was. I started to read the Yashica Dutt book about "coming out" as a Dalit, and how she was moved to tell her truth in part because of the "suicide by bullying" case of Dalit student Rohith Vemula. I just can't believe this kind of thing goes on.

Yandelis

March 8, 2023

Dear Yandelis,

So first, I'm hoping to hear about the grant soon. Fingers crossed! And, yeah, Rohith's story is haunting and yet emblematic of what happens too frequently because of what Dalits face from dominant caste people. Thenmozhi Soundararajan's *The Trauma of Caste* says that caste-privileged and caste-oppressed people both have to deal with how caste has negatively impacted their bodies and their relationships at all levels. It does impact me in an embodied way to know, as Soundararajan says, that everything caste-privileged people have is because of violence against Dalits. I can also absolutely see the legacy of caste violence through the generations. For example, I know of a caste-privileged person who always threatened suicide. It left behind a brutal legacy for the child she raised. That child couldn't ever figure out why the person did that, and now, as an adult, she wonders if the brokenness that led to the suicide threats had something to do with caste. It's a system that, like white supremacy, fundamentally damages the perpetrators and victims alike. My father's coming up to visit soon, and I'm going to talk to him about caste. It will be soon after the first day of Spring. A time for something new, I hope!

Prof. J

Kavya pressed send on her phone. She pulled her puffy jacket around her, shivering but too lazy to get up from her backyard. As she used her boot to break up pieces of ice under the table, she thought about how freely she was talking about truly dreadful things with Yandelis.

Something about writing that caste letter smashed her impulse to keep hiding and evading. She *could* shake things up. She could tell the truth. She could demand the truth.

She quickly scrolled through her phone and forwarded the caste letter to Sneha before she lost her nerve.

Picking up a shard of ice, she stared at the crystalline shapes inside. She threw the ice on the ground and watched it splinter into its cool, jagged edges. She adjusted herself slightly, as the chill plus getting older meant that her tailbone was aching, a memento from her time with Ranjeet.

The real reason Sneha bothered her so much was that she was like too many academics, or, shit, too many people. If you pointed out something uncomfortable or too "real," they asked you for proof. But no proof was ever good enough for them, especially if it was inconvenient for them to acknowledge. If you pointed out the bigger, historic forces at play, they might tell you, *Stop blaming the ghosts of the past.*

But Kavya knew that ghosts didn't stay in the past. They could only be ghosts and do a good job of haunting you if they were walking right alongside you.

She finally went inside when she couldn't stop shivering. Shrugging off the jacket and slipping off her boots, she went straight upstairs into the boys' old bedroom. Two full-size beds were up against the walls with a long nightstand in between. Kabir's posters of cars and Samir's half-painted mural of the New York skyline watched over the room.

She sat down on Samir's bed and surveyed the room. This was where her father was going to sleep. He was going to be here soon. She was going to find out everything about him, her mother, her aunt, and everybody in this split-in-half family.

3

Spring

SPEAK

Kavya opened the door. Her father stood there, looking somewhat surprised to see his daughter, as if maybe this invitation was a prank.

"It's me," Mohan said.

A smile tugged on the edges of Kavya's lips. "Yes, I know, come in. I'll make you some tea."

He pulled off his loafers and set down his bag. He rested his hands uneasily in his pockets.

"Do you have instant coffee?" he asked.

"I don't. If you want, I can run over to the bodega?"

"No, no. I'll have your tea. Black, no milk or sugar. I must go wash my hands and face."

She directed him up the stairs.

Kavya turned on the kettle. She stood in front of the pantry and looked at the shelf overflowing with teas, chat masala, chakuli, barfi, and everything else she could find at the tiny Indian grocery store one neighborhood over in Sunset Park. She picked through her tea selection.

The house's old pipes released quiet tick-tick sounds as she heard the water running upstairs. A strange sensation came over her. *My father is washing his hands in my house.* The kettle whistled, and she prepared his tea.

When her father emerged, she handed the mug to him. "The boys say hi," she said.

He gave her a small smile. "Good. What are they doing?" He remained standing, holding the drink carefully with both hands.

Kavya filled him in about the twins' latest. She was somewhat anxious to get to the point of the visit but also wanted to delay the conversation indefinitely.

They sat down at the table so that she could show him pictures from her visit to Stony Brook during the first weekend of Spring Break. She realized she had never offered information or pictures of the boys back when they met at the Times Square café last summer. Why was she being so chatty and open now?

She pointed out how Samir was somehow now the taller twin. Then she scrolled through the pictures Samir had sent to her of his Appalachian Trail spring break trip for an environmental studies class. Then, the photos of Kabir's Pennsylvania visit with his maybe-girlfriend. Then, maybe-girlfriend and Kabir posing in Kavya's house on the way back.

"What is the girl?" Mohan asked.

"Huh? Are you asking what her race or background is?"

He nodded.

"Rasha's parents are originally from Egypt."

"Oh. Muslim girl?"

As firmly as she could, she said, "Dad, I asked you up here because I want to talk to you about some things."

"How is your retirement portfolio looking?"

Oh God.

"Dad, no. I could have asked you that on the phone if I wanted to. I have several questions for you, and I need you to answer them. And if you have to stay here longer, then I'll pay to change your ticket, because I need answers. This is just what has to happen."

"Okay." He was nonplussed, mindlessly tapping the table.

She put out a plate of snacks. As he munched, he spilled more crumbs than her boys ever had even at their messiest.

She started with her first question. "Is everyone on both sides of the family Brahmin?"

"What? Oh, definitely. Maybe some exceptions. But Kavya, caste doesn't really exist anymore."

"Nonsense, Dad."

"No, it's true." Mohan stared at her.

"Where's your thread?"

"My what?"

"Your so-called sacred thread. From your moonji."

"Ah, who knows, Kavya. I didn't keep that thing."

"Why did so many of our family friends wear them? Why did even some of the young men wear them?"

"Probably habit."

"Habit of what? Wanting everyone to know they're dominant caste?" Kavya peered at him.

"Why are you saying dominant caste?"

"Savarna," Kavya said patiently.

"Oh, okay. No, it's spiritual. It's your connection to God. I didn't wear mine because it was always in the way." He roughly wiped his hand across his mouth.

"And were you guys taught not to interact with Dalits or anything like that? Like, not to share utensils or bring a Dalit friend over?"

"Umm. I don't think anyone said that. I didn't know any Dalit person anyways."

"Okay, new question, but I want to come back to that. Why did Ajji make me read and then watch the serials about the Ramayana and Mahabharata? What was she trying to get me to believe?"

"Our religion?" suggested Mohan, looking utterly confused.

"Dad, look at that archer, Ekalavya, in the Mahabharata. This Dalit feminist writer Thenmozhi Soundararajan wrote about it. His guru first refuses to teach him because he's tribal and low-caste. Then when Ekalavya proves how good he is, the guy decides to be his guru but in exchange for his right thumb. As a child, I'm learning about Hindu mythology, so basically about how caste works, and how caste-oppressed people literally have to chop up their bodies to be accepted by caste-privileged people?"

"But I don't think people really do archery these days."

"Dad. That was not my point."

They went in circles for a long while, with Kavya suppressing a scream the entire time.

She finally said, "Okay, Dad, it's clear that you're pretending we're all casteless, as if we have nothing to do with the oppression of Dalits."

"I am not oppressing anyone. These days no one is oppressing anybody. Not like the old days."

"I wasn't saying that you, oh, never mind. Then tell me what happened in the old days. Everything you know."

Mohan threw a handful of nuts into his mouth. "Oh, caste was there to do a division of labor, according to people's natural abilities. It was not supposed to be this bad thing. Everyone was happy. You had to make the society run. Then, some people took advantage. But you don't see caste anymore. Maybe just in the villages."

"Tell me about the village your side originally came from. How did they get their land? Do Dalits still live segregated on the outskirts like they do in other villages?"

"I don't really know about all that," Mohan answered.

Kavya took a deep breath. "Let's try this. Let's talk about arranged marriages in our family. Arranged marriage exists to ensure caste endogamy, like the perpetuation of the purity of the caste, right? So why did you and Amma choose each other, or did you even get a choice?"

Her father's eyes darted around, lingering for a few brief moments on the back door, as if contemplating escape. "We were a good match. Our families of course found the suitable girl and boy. Very nice. It was very nice."

"And?"

"Are there any more of these nuts? They are extremely tasty."

Kavya grabbed the package from the pantry and practically poured the rest onto Mohan's plate.

"Keep going." She hovered over him.

He carefully dusted off a few of the cashews before chewing on them.

"Dad."

He swallowed. He reached for the cup and took a sip of the tea.

"Can you reheat it? I waited too long with the pictures and your caste talk. Now it is lukewarm."

"Jesus Christ." Kavya grabbed the mug and stuck it in the microwave. As she stood there, she used the safety of the distance between them to gather her courage. "Dad, you and I have never had a real conversation about our family. You have to talk to me now. Please."

She saw that her father's expression didn't change, that he was not moved by her words. Without thinking, she burst out, "Ranjeet did terrible things to me. And I'm still dealing with it. Maybe casteism was behind his behavior. Maybe casteism was why Neela rooted for my relationship with that ogre and why she was the way she was. I need your help in understanding what caste does to us."

"I thought you broke things off because it wasn't a good match. What terrible things?"

Kavya turned on her heel to give him her back. She stared at the microwave. "I'm not telling you anything. You don't tell me anything."

"Kavya." He sighed. "What is there to say? Things happen. The past is the past."

Kavya sensed the tears coming. No, he would not see her cry.

"Forget it," she mumbled.

She removed the mug from the microwave and slowly walked it over to him. She sat down and stared at him, trying to figure out what was going on in his head. She watched him swipe his napkin across his face. Maybe she had to ease him into this. Even though her questions were lined up, ready to leap out of her mouth.

"Dad, do you want to do something, like any sightseeing, while you're here?"

"Sure." He sipped the tea. "But first I need a nap. I woke up very early to get to the airport."

"Fine. Go ahead. When you wake up, we can have a late lunch. I'll take you to the botanical gardens because the flowers are blooming."

She watched him finish his tea. She couldn't help but stare at him, to look at every pore, every gray hair, every mole. *Who are you?*

Then she led him up the stairs to his room. "This is the boys' room. You've been to the bathroom. There's only one. Just make yourself at home."

"I know there's only one bathroom, Kavya. I did see the house specs."

Kavya flushed. He said it innocently enough, but a savvier man might have said it with some bite. To remind the ungrateful daughter that he was the one who made it possible to give her sons this home. That he paid for an agent and lawyer who helped her decipher the inspection and fees and everything else that came along with buying a house in a place like New York.

Wracked with guilt, she said, "I'm sorry I've never had you over. I have this home because of you." She quickly added, "My mortgage payments are actually cheaper than the rent of some of my friends. And with the boys going to a state school, after my tenure and promotion and then their graduation, I think I can find a way to pay you back." She didn't know what else to say. She had no idea how to save such a large sum of money.

Mohan gave her his usual, constrained smile. "I told you. It was a gift."

"Yes, I know." She paused. "All that stuff about caste. Well, it's kind of hypocritical for me to go on about it when I've happily benefited from it."

Mohan yawned. "I don't understand anything you're saying. Caste is the past."

"Caste is the past?" Kavya repeated.

"Yes. It even rhymes."

Kavya stared at him for a moment. "Okay, Dad. We'll talk about it later. Have a good nap."

She walked out and closed the door behind her.

She was too anxious to just sit around while he slept, so she occupied herself with cleaning the kitchen and cooking a rice and cauliflower dish. An hour later, she was chopping the cilantro for the garnish when she heard the bedroom door open. Her father walked slowly down the creaky stairs and then shuffled toward the kitchen.

When he appeared, she asked, "Was the bed comfortable enough?"

Mohan stretched his arms and let out a drawn-out yawn. "It was perfect. Very comfortable. I am refreshed."

"Well, I'm glad to hear that. You're just in time for lunch." She stopped herself. She was going to say that she didn't know what he liked to eat. But she had already planned Indian meals and snacks for his visit. "Umm. I decided to make Indian food for you. Is that okay?"

"Yes, anything is fine."

She sighed. How could there be so much distance and intimacy at the same time? He just slept in her child's bed. Sensing a wave of anxiety roaring toward her from the distance, she could not help but slide back into her agenda.

She handed him a plate and led him to the table. "Last summer, after the boys left for college, did you contact me so that it would just be the two of us?"

He sat down and immediately started stuffing the food in his mouth. Kavya couldn't remember if he always ate like this, so intent on shoveling in as much as possible. "Delicious," he said. "The lady I hire for my meals could learn some lessons from you."

"Dad?"

He guzzled his water and devoured another bite. "I just wanted to see you. What's so wrong?" He spoke with the half-chewed food in his mouth. Kavya stared at the spittle and the yellow-orange mash.

"Nothing's wrong. I want you to know that I was really confused because I am not used to being alone with you." She tried to keep her tone somber but not accusatory. "Since then, I have had lots of anxiety, worse than usual. Really bad dreams about Ranjeet, and sometimes Neela, and panic attacks, sometimes feeling like my life was going to end. I started to think about things that have happened in our family in a way that I never have before. The caste stuff, but also lots of things. I don't know why my anxiety got so bad after your visit."

She paused, exhaling noisily. "If I knew more about all of us, maybe I could understand. Can you help me understand?"

Mohan swallowed. He was quiet for a few minutes. "I didn't want to make you so upset."

"I know," she replied sadly.

She walked back to the counter, made herself a plate, and sat down next to Mohan. She focused on her food, suddenly feeling tired.

Mohan broke the silence. "Oh, this is nice. Being in your home, in the big city."

"Great. How about we finish our meals and then we get ready to go explore Brooklyn?" Kavya offered, resigned.

She plodded through the next twenty-four hours. The botanical gardens. Every floor of the museum. Dinner at the nearby Caribbean restaurant with the low ceilings. Home. A quick reassuring text to her sons that the visit was going just fine. Sleep. Wake up. Shower. Walk to the bagel store. A round trip ride on the ferry. Home.

She went through the motions, exhausted from keeping silent, from pretending, from trying to make her father comfortable enough to open up.

When her father went to nap, she retired to her room. She took out her diary and wrote.

Amma, I am sitting here trying to get Dad to talk to me. He's not telling me anything about caste. He's not telling me anything about you. I realized the other day that I pray to try to connect with you. I feel like, growing up, there was always some Hindu priest telling us what to do and how to do it. I never felt like I was a part of some spiritual community trying to comfort each other or help others. But I have always prayed. I think the Goddesses are so comforting. During Navaratri, I like chanting Aigiri Nandini and thinking about all these avatars of Durga Ma. Maybe at some level I think that if I can't have my Amma, I can have these Divine Mothers watching out for me. Now I'm thrown off because I'm reading these things about Hinduism being inherently casteist, which I always knew, but now I'm actively trying to figure out what to do. I don't want to do yet another ridiculous performance like when we burned the Manusmriti. Do I pray for Durga Ma to annihilate caste? Or better yet, Kali? I don't have much investment in Hinduism, but the Goddesses are the only way to feel a connection to you and also to Ajji.

Who knows what I can get out of Dad. Was he this bad at communication when you were alive? When I was a kid, I secretly wished he had died instead of you. I wish you were here.

I hate this fucking diary. It's just me searching for you.

* * *

Kavya went downstairs a few minutes after she heard her father open his bedroom door. When she got to the kitchen, he was standing at the back door, looking outside.

Before he could turn around, she announced, "I'm going to get lunch ready. But feel free to go hang out in the backyard if you want to."

He mumbled something without looking back and stepped outside.

She heated up the leftovers of rice and cauliflower and quickly sauteed spinach and garlic. As she did, she peeked out the back and saw him pacing around, looking intently at the bushes.

She spooned the food onto two plates. "It's ready!"

They wordlessly ate. Kavya listened to them both chew. How much longer could they go on like this? If it were up to her father, probably for the rest of their days.

She picked at her food while her father ate hastily.

"Well, Dad." She didn't know what else to say. She picked up his empty plate and walked to the sink. As she rinsed the plate, she watched out of the corner of her eye as he played with a coaster.

She walked back to the table and stared at her still full plate.

And then the room started to sway.

No. Enough.

Before she could stop herself, she went off script. "Why didn't you want to be with me after Amma died?" she blurted out.

Her stomach churned then, cramping strongly. She moved her hands down to massage her stomach, which kept clenching. She gripped her toes to the floor.

Mohan made a strange sound, like something was curdling in his throat.

"I'm sorry," she cried out. She grabbed her plate and fork and ran upstairs to her room. She shut the door and sat down at the vanity table and chair by the window. She focused on the breathing exercises she always did with Helen. Her stomach cramped again. She held on to the folds of flesh surrounding her belly button. She dug deep as she massaged, trying to reach for the source of the pain. *Stop, stop!*

She looked around for her phone. It was somewhere in the living room. She got up and walked around her room, back and forth between the walls, until her breathing slowed down and her stomach relaxed. Nothing was tilting at least.

She finally sat down in front of her plate. Pushing the cauliflower and spinach to the side, she picked out the mustard seeds and ate them slowly, one at a time, alternating with a few grains of rice.

Go back out there. Make him answer. Make him help.

Kavya put her hand on her chest to test how quickly her heart was beating. She looked down at her other hand to see if it was trembling. As she scanned her body, she realized that she was much calmer now. She left the room with her plate, throwing a quick glance at the small Goddess Saraswati painting hanging above the light switch. *Help me.*

When she got back to the kitchen, her father was still seated at the table.

"Hello," she said.

"Hello." One good thing about their bizarre dynamic was that she didn't have to explain why she had fled the room. And he wasn't going to ask.

He had already brought out the snacks from earlier. Spiced peanuts were scattered on his plate, and he was playing with the wrapper, crinkling the plastic.

She sat down next to him. Many minutes later, she finally said quietly, "I want an answer to the question I asked you."

Her father kept rolling the plastic, pulling it together and apart like an accordion.

"I asked you why you decided not to raise me after Amma died."

Mohan coughed. He set the wrapper down and stared at the peanuts. "Answer me. Dad, please."

He paused and then said to the peanuts, "I didn't want anything to happen to you, Kavya."

"What do you mean?"

"I didn't want anything to happen to you."

Kavya let out a frustrated grunt. "You can't just repeat the same sentence. Also, something *did* happen to me. You just got rid of me and sent me to live with Neela." Her voice cracked even as it rose, even as she spewed out the words. "And she was fucking crazy and made my life hell. Something did happen to me. Why did you throw me away like that?"

Mohan made a sound that could have been a gasp or a sigh. A quick inhale. He continued to gaze intently at the peanuts, his head now close to the plate, his shoulders up almost past his ears.

"What's the answer, Dad?"

"It would have been worse with me, Kavya."

She slammed her hand on the table. "What would have been worse with you? What are you talking about?" Her stomach started to cramp again. It roiled around violently, as if it did not want to be a part of this conversation and was trying to exit her body altogether.

He was silent.

Her chest heaved as she looked around at the table. She wanted to throw something at the wall. To smash his plate on the floor so he would stop looking at those damn nuts. To keep pounding her fist onto the table until he answered.

As her eyes flitted back and forth, Mohan said quietly, "I did not want you to end up like your Amma."

She stared at him. "What? Dead? Get in a car crash? What does that even mean?"

He made the strange half-gurgling sound again. He picked up the wrapper, twisting it with both hands. More wet sounds behind his pursed lips.

"Are you about to puke? What's wrong?" Kavya asked, bewildered.

He looked up, and she was shocked to see that his eyes were wet. He pushed his lips together, as if to keep his mouth shut, as if to stop whatever was bubbling inside from coming out.

She quickly got up and grabbed a cup that was drying on the rack next to the sink. She filled it with water and set it in front of him.

"Drink," she instructed as she sat down next to him. He slowly sipped. He looked into the water each time before he took another sip. Several long minutes passed.

He pressed his lips together again.

"Dad."

Finally, he was able to force a few words out. "It was not an accident."

SHATTER

"Amma." Kavya called out for her mother. She stumbled out of her chair and backed away from the table. She gripped the edge of the counter as the room spun. Her body started its familiar journey sideways.

Mohan would not look at her. "I didn't want to tell you."

She now let the tears fall. "What do you mean? There was no car wreck?" For a moment, she wondered if her mother was still alive. Maybe she had been hiding all this time? Was she out there somewhere?

He shook his head. "There *was* a car crash. Your mother died in it. But the car did not crash by accident."

She let out a guttural cry. *She's dead. My Amma is dead.* It was as if she had heard it for the first time. *No, it's not true! It's not true!* Her eyes raced around the room. *No, he's making it up. Liar.*

She breathed through her nostrils, feeling them flare and deflate.

"If that's true, how did the car crash? Was she murdered?" she asked desperately. But she already knew the answer.

He pushed his cup aside, stood up, stepped over to the counter, and gripped her hand. The sensation of his hand on hers was so odd. He had never physically comforted her before. And maybe he was not trying to soothe her but was holding on so that he could speak.

"Kavya."

He was silent. The two of them breathing.

He said, "She did it on purpose."

Kavya heard herself whimper. As unsteady as she was on her feet, she lumbered to the living room. She picked up her phone from the coffee table. She could hear her father clearing his throat and coughing. She stared at her phone. She was so lightheaded she didn't even know what she wanted to do. Who could she even call?

She threw the phone on the couch and realized she was hyperventilating. Just then, Mohan appeared next to her. He stood there, his arms stiff by his side.

"Kavya." He couldn't say anything else. He kept repeating her name. But it was in his usual flat tone. Not to calm her. Not to soothe her.

And then Kavya, tired from over four decades of keeping her unrelenting pain inside, exhausted from inventing herself to be stronger than she had ever felt, could feel her body start to collapse into itself. Her limbs hung heavy from her torso. And she started to sob. Her body heaved.

As she opened her mouth and the wailing got louder, the room got darker.

* * *

Kavya opened her eyes to find herself on the couch with a blanket tossed over her. She looked over to see her father rifling through her bookcase.

She felt something under her shoulder and reached around to find her phone. She had been asleep for about two hours.

Looking back at her father, Kavya studied how he scratched his face as he peered at the book titles on her shelves. He flipped through a book, scrutinizing what must have been Kavya's handwritten notes in the margins.

He was lying. Kavya was sure of it. Maybe Neela got some ridiculous idea into his head. Her mother died in a simple car accident. Yes, he had fabricated some story. Who knew why.

But the more she watched him touch her books, his usual hunch, his pants pulled up too high, the belt missing a loop, thick white socks, she realized that he was not making it up. He just wasn't capable of it.

It would have been worse with me. I didn't want you to end up like Amma.

He blamed himself for Amma's death. And as she deliberately formed this thought, letting it congeal and become solid and real in her mind, the pieces of her life started to shift. She had always assumed that her father never wanted her. But now, that part of her that always felt utterly unlovable dislodged itself and moved.

She rested on the couch watching her father. *All this time, did he think that if I stayed with him, I too would want to die?*

And then, that part of her that had always imagined what her mother would have been like had she lived, that part also started to move. Why did Amma feel that she had to die? What did Amma's family do when it happened? Did they blame her father—is that why he blamed himself?

Her entire childhood was about waiting for Neela to make good on her threats to kill herself. Those threats took on a new weight now, knowing that her aunt had to have known the truth about Amma. Kavya's lifelong fury and agony turned hot and alive.

What kind of monster threatened suicide in front of a child whose mother died like that? The level of narcissism, of Neela taking Amma's story for herself, was beyond what Kavya could have ever imagined.

She desperately wanted to ask her father what happened that day. Was there a note left behind? Did he just immediately take her to Neela's house and dump her there?

But the idea of trying to find out why Amma did it was like being buried alive in an avalanche. She wanted to dig her way out of the hell, but she might never reach sunlight, and everything could just collapse in on her instead. Maybe Amma did that because she didn't want to be *her* mother. That *I'm unlovable* part of her moved again, pressing up against her ribs.

Her father had shuffled over to the back window, a few books tucked into the crook of his arm. He had not once looked back at her. How dare he be so at ease.

But then arose a small, secret urge to wrap her arms around his middle and rest her head against his stooped back. She wanted to ask, *Dad, did you want to keep me?* She tried to imagine him alone, crying out for the wife and daughter he lost. But she couldn't see that scene. She didn't know how she should feel about this man. She never had.

She quietly silenced her phone so that her father wouldn't hear whatever she planned to do next. She was going to text Janet or Yumiko to find out her aunt's cell phone number so she could call her. She was going to break decades of silence and confront Neela. She was going to ask, *Why did my mother kill herself? Did you make her do it?*

Wait a minute. Did her father blame himself because his *sister* did something to her mother? Kavya rolled the possibility around in her mind.

As her fingers hovered over the phone, she realized she could not risk contacting Neela. Not yet. Any interaction with her aunt threatened to unravel her life entirely, even more than it already was. She couldn't be impulsive. Not now.

She cleared her throat. Her father quickly spun around and almost dropped the books.

"Oh, you are awake." Her father, the master of observation.

"Yes, yes. What are you reading there?"

Her father looked down at the books and shrugged. "Just some things you have on Partition. I like history books."

"Okay, of course."

She wasn't about to explain the letter project to him. But she and her father had crossed some border, where secrets were being revealed. She did not know what to do in this new terrain. It was like they were on the moon, bouncing around in spacesuits, speaking in muffled voices through helmets.

"Dad . . ."

"Hey, listen, do you have any dinner?"

She wordlessly pushed the blanket aside and walked into the kitchen. She took out the khichdee she had cooked and frozen a few days before. As she put the container in the microwave and pressed Defrost, she silently watched the plate rotate. Her father entered the kitchen and stood next to the counter. When the timer chimed, she went to the pantry and showed her father an array of pickles.

Her father, after much dithering, selected the hot lime.

Kavya set the table, placing the khichdee container, pickle, and yogurt in the center.

They ate dinner in silence. Kavya's head was swirling but in slow motion. As she picked at a torn bay leaf on her plate, Mohan leaned back, burped loudly, and stretched his arms. As if this was the most typical dinner in the world. A completely natural belch. Compliments to the chef.

They quietly took their dishes to the sink. Kavya avoided eye contact as she said, "I'm going to shower and go to bed."

"I'll stay here and read."

"Fine." Kavya was utterly drained.

* * *

The next morning, after an endlessly restless night, Kavya sat on her bed thinking about how her father was going to fly out in the late afternoon. She wasn't sure whether to extend his stay or to ask him to go to the airport right now and catch an earlier flight. She rubbed her temples.

When she finally forced herself to go to the kitchen, she heated up the leftover khichdee for breakfast. She was standing at the microwave when her father entered the room.

Once again, the pressure inside of her started to build. For a brief second, he looked her in the eyes, and before she got cold feet, she asked, "Why did Amma ..." It was too hard to say, so she just finished with a timid, "do that?"

Mohan shook his head. He dropped his arms to his side. He almost imperceptibly shrugged his shoulders.

"Please?" A child-like voice came out of her mouth. One that she didn't have even as a little girl. "Dad, if you care at all about me, please tell me something."

"I don't know why she did it. The police came and said she crashed into a wall at a very high speed. There was no evidence she tried to stop or turn the car." He spoke robotically, but the color drained from his face.

Oh, dear God. "Maybe it just *seemed* like she did it on purpose."

"Her seatbelt wasn't on. I had to get dentist records because, umm, the car hit at such a high speed, you know." He kept his head down.

Kavya's chest squeezed tight. "What about her family? What did they say?"

He shook his head again.

"Tell me, please." As soon as she said it, her stomach roiled. She wasn't sure she wanted to know. Oh, God. Fuck him. Why did he tell her anything if he wasn't going to tell her the entire truth?

"Kavya, what can I tell you? She was happy to move from her family and come to the U.S. She really didn't want to contact her family."

Previously buried memories spun around in her mind. The brief, tense visits to Amma's family in Pune, a few hours from Mumbai. Her maternal grandfather and her uncle Suresh would pick up Kavya and Ajji from the train station. They would go to their bungalow apartment in a complex with an enticing playground. Suresh's wife and kids and Amma's step-mother would bring them food and tea nonstop. Kavya had her first Fanta there, the start of a childhood obsession. Ajji would ask Kavya to recite poems she had learned in school or to tell everyone about what it was like to grow up in the U.S. But then, by the time Kavya turned eight or nine, they stopped their visits. The one time Kavya asked to go again, Neela had yelled, "No, you will not step foot in the house of people who think terrible things of us." And Ajji had walked away with tears in her eyes.

"Why did Amma's family let us visit, and then it all stopped?" she asked.

"You got a little older, old enough to ask them about what Amma was like as a kid."

She waited for the rest of the answer. None came. She tried to fill in the blanks. "Dad, they knew what she did? And they thought it was better to just cut off all contact with us?" She remembered again Neela's accusation about Amma's family and the "crackpots" and "idiots" insults over the years. "Did they blame you for what happened?"

He ignored the question.

"Dad, what did they say when it first happened?"

"I don't remember," he said quietly. "You were very little. My only focus was how to take care of you."

Kavya was taken aback. "What?"

She then proceeded, slowly and deliberately. "You could have kept me."

"No, I wanted you to be safe," he replied, his hands shaking slightly.

She thought about those intense times with her twins and the dark thoughts that sometimes invaded, like wanting to run away or drink herself into oblivion. But she always brought herself back from the brink. And one day, when it got bad enough, she went to a doctor and got on Paxil. Maybe her mother hadn't been able to get help like she had.

Her body ached. Her mind was racing in a million directions. She tried to think of something to ground her.

She looked around her home. She picked at her nails to hear the soft clicking sound. A whiff of cumin.

But her thoughts went straight to Neela. She indulged in the rage this time. It was so warm and familiar. She breathed in the bitterness filling up her body.

"You could have kept me. I know that it was Neela's fault!" she said, livid.

Her father's eyebrows shot up.

Kavya raised her voice. "Amma was upset or depressed one day, and Neela told her to hurt herself. She's capable of it, you know. What the fuck is wrong with that fucking woman?"

Anger coursed through her body. She wanted to beat at her own head and tear out her hair. "Do you know how many times I had to listen to that woman say she was going to kill herself? What is her fucking problem? I hate her!" She screamed again, "I hate her! It's her fault. I hate her!"

"Stop." Mohan's voice cut through her shouting.

She was startled into silence.

"Don't talk like that." He spoke without emotion, but as forcefully as he had ever said anything. "Neela did nothing to your mother. Your aunt did lots of things to care for you."

She scoffed. "How do you know she did nothing to Amma? You were ready to blame yourself to the point that you stopped taking care of me. What if she was the guilty one all along?"

He closed his eyes and dropped his head. Kavya knew this was probably the most taxing conversation he had ever experienced. Some small part of her felt pity for him. He looked so fragile and beaten down.

But she pushed forward. She couldn't help it. "What was Neela's relationship with my mother like?"

Strolling slowly to the table, he poured some salt out and ran his finger through it. He only barely looked at her. "Try not to hate Neela. Maybe try to think good thoughts. She tried a lot to be good and nice."

Despite herself, Kavya conceded, yes, surprisingly, that sounded right. Neela sometimes tried to be nice.

She recalled some nuggets of goodness she had squirreled away.

Once, during her sophomore year in college, Kavya had temporarily cut off contact with Neela. It was after an ugly fight in which she had told her aunt, "You just have to face that we are not good together."

At the end of that call, Neela asked, "Don't you think we could get along?"

And Kavya, afraid of more arguing, replied, "I guess I have the slightest glimmer of hope."

"Then that glimmer will burn bright for me. We could get along. I know we can. You're the only child I have." It was the gentlest Neela's voice had ever been.

Kavya forgot how much those moments once held her, no matter how bad it got. She used to think that Neela really meant to be kind but was too sad to be. She once felt a softness for her aunt, but over time, it had turned into wet cement. It became hard and immoveable and shoved her organs aside, becoming a part of her body.

Mohan interrupted her thoughts, "Maybe you should just talk to Neela yourself?"

"No," Kavya said quietly.

"If you want to know something, you have to ask her."

"I'm going to ask *you*. What did your grandfather do to her? What exactly did he do that made her so miserable?"

He fell quiet again.

"Physical violence? Insults about being dark? Right?"

He nodded. He pushed the chair away from the table and walked to the bookcase.

Carefully, she prodded a bit more. "This is awful to ask, but did he touch her?"

He grimaced. "I don't think so."

"What specifically did he do to her? What do you know?" She steadied herself in anticipation of a ghastly story.

But her father just pulled a book out and sat down on the couch with it. Kavya looked at his profile, noticing for the first time how short his nose was.

"How did Ajji let that happen? Couldn't she see that Neela was falling apart? Couldn't she foresee what would happen?" It was the first time Kavya allowed herself to name her grandmother's role in her family's tragedies.

"Kavya, what was she supposed to do?" he asked the book.

"Couldn't other family members take you guys in? Why did it have to be *him*?"

He shook his head. He wasn't the type to chide her for her naivete. He instead offered a simple explanation, "Kavya, you did what you were told. You did what society said. You had to think about what society would think."

"But what made him like that? I know about him pushing Ajji and also doing something to make her have a miscarriage."

He turned his head sharply to look at her. She nodded. "She told me. If I had to guess, deep down, was he resentful that he worked for the British? Was it a caste thing, like he thought he was too good for something like that?"

He turned back to the book and started flipping its pages. "No, no. He was proud to work for the railways."

He put the book down on the coffee table and clasped his hands, his face drawn.

"Maybe you can ask her everything you want to know," he suggested again.

Kavya shook her head as she walked over and took a seat next to him. "If you know, you can easily tell me."

Something was happening in her stomach. Twinges of grief, the ones she rarely had for Neela.

They sat quietly for a while.

She reviewed in her mind the letter about colorism. She looked down at her arm and rotated it back and forth, from the darker side to her palm up, to the lighter side. She couldn't remember where exactly Neela was on that spectrum.

But she did recall that Ranjeet's mom had once suggested to Kavya that she lighten her own skin. Kavya had replied, "Even if I did that, our children could still be the same skin tone as me. You realize that, right?" And she remembered the look of horror on the woman's face. And how his mom said she would pray that any children would have Kavya's "good genes" from Ajji but with Ranjeet's skin tone. And how his mom still thought she was so progressive for supporting Ranjeet's choice to live with a "darker" woman (gasp!) before marriage (double gasp!).

What was it like for Neela to grow up surrounded by women like that? Skin-lightening ads everywhere. Father dead. Mother at work. Possibly something unspeakable done at home to her by her grandfather.

No, Kavya commanded herself, because her heart was opening. *Remember spaghetti night. Remember it all.*

Mohan looked at her. His breathing grew labored. His turned down eyes almost disappeared into the heavy folds of his eyelids. His entire face sagged.

Finally, he stood up and walked toward the pantry and opened the door. She followed him there. They stared at the shelves of food.

They were both still bouncing around in their moon boots, testing the feeling of no gravity, looking around at the rocks and craters and a big black sky. She half expected Martians, aliens, and otherworldly creatures to come tumbling by.

She wanted to return to Earth. She wanted to go back to knowing nothing. Back to the time before her father's summer visit and the nightmares. She wanted to drink in the oxygen of the world she once knew. She did not want to be out here, in this other world and its naked truthfulness lurking everywhere. But there was no going back now.

DREAM

Kavya suggested they go rest and then have lunch before it was time to go to the airport. She went to her room. Her head felt so heavy. She didn't sleep but wrapped herself in her blanket. She stared at the picture of her boys.

When she got up, she was surprised to see Mohan already at the pantry, eating some of the Indian treats.

"Did you sleep?"

He shook his head. "No, I decided to look at your books instead. Now I'm hungry."

"Should I make us lunch now?"

He gave her a thumbs up.

Kavya chopped the onions and chili peppers for egg bhurji. She turned on the exhaust fan and added a slab of butter to the heated pan. She watched the butter melt. Tiny, frothy bubbles surrounded the silky yellow liquid. She remembered the buttery sauce dripping down Ranjeet's face the last time she had seen him.

It was like how every time she poured boiling water and pasta into a colander, Neela appeared in her mind's eye. And Kavya would thus walk even more carefully, with the pot tight in her hands, determined to be vigilant against any part of her body that may betray her and cause her to repeat history. She wore violence in the banalities of everyday life. Did everyone do that?

She stirred in the onions and peppers, then threw in large pinches of cumin, turmeric, and garam masala. She added a heaping spoonful of ginger-garlic paste. She breathed in the aromas and tried to remember her Ajji cooking for her.

Ajji was always laughing. She told dirty jokes and chatted up the milk walla every day. Sometimes she shed tears while telling a sad story, but then she always wiped them away with the end of her sari and moved on to the next thing.

Kavya searched her memories for any indication that Ajji knew what Neela was really like.

The summer she had turned twelve, Kavya and Neela were visiting India as usual, while Pramod stayed behind.

Kavya pulled Ajji aside in the kitchen and whispered, "I finally got my first bra. My first period will probably come any day."

Ajji hugged her. "Very exciting. Mama gave you the napkins to use when it comes?" She insisted on referring to Neela as "Mama."

"Ajji, she always makes me feel stupid." Kavya pouted. "Yes, she gave me some pads, but I won't even tell her when I get it. She'll just be mean about it for no reason because she's the most miserable woman alive. I hate her."

Kavya looked defiant, expecting Ajji to yell at her to be more respectful.

Instead, her grandmother started shaking. "I know that she has a problem. I know something is very wrong. But she is my daughter, and I love her." She moved away, almost shoving Kavya. And she went to her room and closed the door, which she only did when she was changing or praying. Kavya quietly crept to the door to listen in. She heard heart-wrenching sobs and her Ajji's calls to God to help her.

Kavya stirred the food in the pan as she relived that miserable moment, outside of her grandmother's door.

"Dad?"

"Yes?" Mohan came to stand next to the stove.

"Is Neela okay now, like with her emotional well-being? Does she acknowledge how she treated me?"

He looked at her blankly.

"Does she still have episodes and stuff? Because she sure as hell had them when I was growing up."

"Was it so horrible?" he asked despairingly.

Kavya asked herself this question all the time.

Once, she had gone with Neela to drop off some food for a family friend recovering from surgery. At the house hung a large banner that said, *Get Well Soon, Mommy!*

One of the friend's three children came running out of her room to take Neela's Tupperware container to put it in the fridge. "Mommy, let's have this with the cookies we will bake you!" Then the child grabbed Usha, the mom, and hugged her with her entire body. Kavya watched them intently, hungrily, the way she did whenever she saw a mother and daughter embracing.

And instead of pushing the child away, the way Neela did the few times Kavya tried to hug her, Usha sighed happily and stroked the girl's hair. "My sweetheart. I'm so lucky to have these children and my husband take care of me. God has blessed me so much."

Neela remarked bitterly, "Kavya and my husband would never watch over me like this."

Kavya immediately saw the fleeting grief across Neela's face. Even as a girl, she had memorized every gesture, every imperceptible shift in her aunt. Just to try to anticipate the explosions. To try to do the perfect thing to make Neela okay.

Was it so horrible?

Kavya added the tomatoes and kept stirring the food over a low heat. The slingshot feeling was upon her. She braced herself.

She was back in her childhood room, sitting in her chair, reading. Neela had burst through the door, crying. She wrapped her hands around Kavya's throat and shook her. Kavya calmly watched Neela's face, almost curious about what might happen next. She observed how anger and terror and agony flashed across her aunt's eyes. Neela stopped abruptly and rushed out. Kavya found the phone book, looked up a child abuse prevention number, having just learned about family violence in school, and memorized it. She sometimes recited the number to herself silently, just in case.

Kavya had forgotten about that. Until just now. She could not meet her father's eyes.

She used to hungrily treasure those fleeting moments when Neela did express love. When Neela thought Kavya was asleep and sat on the edge of her bed and rubbed her leg. When Neela stayed up all night to help Kavya redo a huge school project on which she had accidentally spilled milk. When Neela volunteered at the school and brought home extra stickers. When Neela went to three Indian grocery stores to find the exact pickle that Kavya loved the most. When Neela and Pramod watched TV every Friday night with her, as they all laughed together at *Full House.* When Neela and Pramod took her on vacations to Greece, Namibia, and more, and let her buy little souvenirs to display in her room.

Those moments were morsels of goodness. But they were hard to savor when Neela's vicious energy left such an everlasting bitter taste in her mouth.

Kavya finally answered her father, "I'm truly sorry for whatever happened to her. But yes, it was that horrible."

He nodded, as if he knew that would be her answer.

She cleared her throat. "Can you share any stories you remember about Ajji? I just want to learn more about her."

He slowly put his hand over his face, looking defeated. "Kavya, why are you wanting to be in the past?"

"I'm not. But why are you determined to never think about it?" She added the beaten, salted eggs.

"What is the use? Everyone has a tough life."

Kavya slowly scrambled the eggs. "Where is Amma's family now?"

Mohan anxiously rubbed his hands together. He seemed wary of falling into some trap that Kavya had set, the only way out being to bare his soul. He didn't speak.

She turned the flame off and served the bhurji onto two plates. Ugh, she pitied her father. Yes, he had fucked up in more ways than she could count, but he always tried to play by her rules. From interacting with the boys according to the terms she set, to now, flying here and witnessing her anguish, with no room for his own.

Kavya was tired of struggling. She wanted to do something else, not this. Not pressing and prodding her father. After they finished eating, she washed the dishes as he showered.

He brought down his bags.

"We have about an hour. Do you want me to get you some coffee?" she asked.

He nodded.

After a quick trip to the nearby bodega, she returned with a steaming hot cup. "We can go to the park. It's nice outside."

She didn't want to spend one more minute in her house with him hovering around her bookcase and the pantry.

They walked to the park and chose a bench near one of the paths. They watched two older women pushing strollers, interrupting each other with their stories.

Mohan unexpectedly spoke. "You hated the stroller."

Kavya turned to him. "I did?"

"Yes, I had to walk around with you morning and night. So did your Amma. Everyone said, use a stroller, use a car seat, to help with your colic. Nothing worked."

"Huh."

"Maybe you had nightmares as a baby too," he said, slowly. "Maybe after that, I guess my sister gave you bad dreams, when you were growing up."

She looked down. She did not dare look at her father. Her ribs ached. "Yes, she did," she managed to say.

"We all gave you bad dreams."

She let out a dry laugh. "Maybe everyone in our family has bad dreams. You and Neela too."

"Yes. Maybe."

He sipped his coffee. And Kavya wondered if her father's visit last summer did not cause the unraveling of her life. Maybe that visit was actually what broke open, at long last, everything awful and dark inside of her. Maybe it was the only way she could be sitting here, with her father, in the sunshine, together on a bench.

Tell Me the Truth

Kavya slowly walked through the days and weeks after Mohan's visit. She was somewhat intact thanks to visits with Helen, calls with Janet, and brainstorming ideas for her next letter. She stayed alert for panic attacks that didn't come. Instead, she felt the full force of a grief she had never known before.

As soon as Mohan had gone back to Texas, Kavya left messages for her father on his landline when she knew he would be at work. Each one was a variation of seeing if he had any more information about Amma. Almost to her relief, he never called her back. She still wasn't sure what she wanted to know about her mother. But she also ached to find out everything she could.

Once, she decided to call in the evening. He answered on the first ring.

"Kavya, how is the big city?"

She was about to ask him why he never returned her calls. But she was still in that agonizing limbo of wanting/not wanting to know. She decided to ask something else.

"When I was a kid, I heard people say that Neela couldn't have kids. But was caste the reason why she didn't adopt other kids besides me? With me, she knew she was getting a real Brahmin kid. I mean, adoption would challenge the idea of caste purity."

"What caste purity?"

"Dad, c'mon."

After a pause, he said, "I asked Pramod to take care of you for me."

"Then what happened?"

He sounded sheepish. "I only asked him. I don't think he even discussed it with Neela. But she committed to it once Pramod told her about it, because he wanted to do it. Back then, maybe she was just trying to make him happy with her."

"What do you mean? Because they had an infertility issue?"

"No, actually, Ajji had to convince Pramod's family about him marrying her. She was too dark. But Ajji was very clever and said the community could see Pramod's one leg was shorter than the other. Who was going to take him?"

Kavya was startled. Pramod's limp? She had barely ever registered he had one. He complained of an ache sometimes and sort of did this shuffle-walk.

"Well, there's the connection to caste, Dad. Let's match the so-called defective people to each other." She grew angry. "I remember overhearing someone once say something about Pramod having problems. *That* is the problem that made him bad marriage material? Something that makes no difference to someone's worth? Why is every part of our story so screwed up? And then, you two men decided when she should become a parent?"

He didn't say anything.

"She's your sister!" She stopped herself. She wasn't sure if she had a right to lecture him about how he had treated Neela. Instead, she said, "I'll talk to you later, okay?"

* * *

The last time Kavya had seen Neela had been during a meal with Ranjeet, a few months before she moved to Houston.

Neela's thin hair was pulled back with a headband with rhinestones, and she smiled as she ladled food onto Ranjeet's plate.

Neela explained her good grades in school. How she won a singing competition once. How many dishes she could cook. The usual Neela show. When Ranjeet praised the tenderness of the chicken, she glowed. After dinner, she walked him around the house, showing him for the thousandth time the ceramics she had painted. He kindly praised each one. The more he did, the more frantically she found something else to impress him.

Afterward, Ranjeet said to Kavya, "Your aunt is always wanting something."

"Like what?"

"Who knows? She's a bottomless pit of neediness."

And Kavya understood immediately. Because it was something she had known since she was very young.

It was in the way that Neela had once interrupted Kavya's playtime with her dollhouse, when Kavya was about eight, to say, "I need to show you something."

Kavya walked over to the table where Neela was seated. Her aunt showed her the paperwork she was signing for a small surgery she was having, to repair a torn meniscus or something like that. As part of the common protocol for anesthesia, a sentence mentioned the risk of death. An ever-so-slight smile on her face, Neela pointed. "You see that word, right?"

Kavya nodded, so beside herself with fear that she heard words come out of her mouth without being able to control them. "But you won't die, right?"

"Who knows. I don't think so. It would bother you if I died?"

Kavya wanted to wrap her arms around Neela, but they didn't do that in her family, so instead, she softly said, "I don't want that to happen."

Neela stared at her, her jaw moving in its contorted way. "Okay, I hope you're telling me the truth."

Kavya was too young to figure out how to ask, *What do you need from me? What would make it better?*

And now, at close to fifty years old, Kavya was frantically trying to cling to the edges of the present but always dangling down into the living room with Neela, the car with Neela, everywhere with Neela. And somehow, all these years later, she still felt responsible for her aunt.

* * *

Once again, Kavya decided to take her worries to the letter project.

April 14, 2023

Dear Yandelis,

I'm sitting here in my home office thinking about the concept of responsibility. What does it mean to be responsible for our family stories or for the pain our families have inflicted on others? I wanted to throw that question out there as we think through this project.

Prof. Joshi

April 15, 2023

Dear Prof. Joshi,
If I could name any word that is emphasized in your classes, it would be accountability. As an Afro-Dominican woman, I know what it's like to watch my family experience racism in the Dominican Republic and the U.S. But there's more to our story. My grandfather on my mom's side was a white-passing staunch supporter of the dictator Trujillo. Abuelo moved from Puerto Plata to Santo Domingo with a goal to work for the regime. He ended up working for some senior-ranking official. According to the stories my family tells, Abuelo and Abuela were so proud that with barely any education, he could get such an important job. They talked about the Trujillo years as the "good ones" because "crime was under control," even though Trujillo spread a reign of terror, especially against Black people.

I just found out that Trujillo wore makeup to lighten his skin because he didn't want any evidence of his Haitian grandmother in his skin! My mom's side doesn't feel responsible for their anti-Blackness, even with this history, even though most of my father's side is Black Dominican. So then, aren't I part of a line of perpetrators? What's my responsibility?

Yandelis

April 17, 2023

Dear Yandelis,
I remember vividly your brilliant paper about race and the DR. I think you've hit on something very important when it comes to intergenerational trauma. Unless you share your family history openly like you just did, you could easily sit in class and talk about being oppressed as a woman of color, and no one would be the wiser. And unless someone knows my caste, I can get away with

talking about racism and not my family's role in oppression. I'm really glad Dalit work is being more widely read, so that people like me will be held accountable. Being descended from perpetrators of some kind of systemic violence may cause a kind of intergenerational trauma but it doesn't absolve us of our complicities with oppression.

Prof. Joshi

April 18, 2023

Dear Prof. Joshi,

I literally googled "generational responsibility for perpetrator oppression." I found this article by a German woman named Gabriele Schwab. She wrote about how post-war Germans had to confront what their society had done. She said that the fear and anger that made Germans scapegoat Jewish and marginalized communities continued after World War Two, especially because the Soviets and U.S. were all up in Germany to remake that society. It was especially the Russians that Germans feared would take over everything. She says her grandma thought the Russians controlled the sky and weather and she even used to say "Wait until the Russians invade us" to make the kid obey her! And the author's fighting so much to be awake to what Germany did, but she still ends up discovering how she has inherited the habit of silencing and erasing everything bad.

I don't know what else to say because I hate all these stories about my grandfather. The author also says that the narrated memories of our elders feel alive in us a way that other memories don't, and also how both the children of perpetrators and victims go on to "live the ghostly legacies and secrets" of their elders. Since I heard my Abuelo's stories, are they in me somewhere? I feel like all my activism has to make up for what my family did.

Yandelis

April 25, 2023

Dear Yandelis,

Thank you for sharing what you found! I hear you. I think feminist theories of intergenerational trauma should be developed to
grapple with everything you have been raising. But I'm writing to
tell you that we got the grant! Now we can really dive into these
issues!

Prof. J

* * *

Kavya sat in Mark's office, fidgeting. It was so much bigger than every
other office she had seen at the university, with wraparound windows
looking out at the Manhattan skyline. An espresso machine whirred in
the background. The supple brown leather chair she sat in looked new.
Even with shoes on, she could tell she was on an expensive plush rug. His
desk was real wood, not like the splintered, thin particle wood ones in the
faculty offices. The room smelled so clean, but not of the overpowering
bleach and ammonia smell throughout the buildings.

"I asked Debbie to schedule a meeting because I wanted to personally congratulate you on the grant, Kavya." Even when saying kind words,
Mark was gruff and unpleasant.

Kavya smiled politely. "Thank you so much."

He looked her up and down. She subtly readjusted her bag so that it
hid her torso. Finally, he asked, "What made you interested in intergenerational trauma? I asked Jacey what your project is about."

She didn't want to share any of the real reasons, so she instead talked
about what she had written about on her application under "Background."

"When I lived in Houston, I witnessed a lot of advocacy work with
New Orleanian families who had fled Hurricane Katrina. They had to
manage the trauma of the destruction and the racist neglect of the government but also the memories of the same situation in 1965 with Hurricane Betsy." She described some of the studies on intergenerational
trauma that she had cited in the application.

Mark checked his phone as she talked. Unlike her students, he was
not even trying to hide it.

Kavya cleared her throat. "Well, I have taken up enough of your time. Thank you."

"You're a hard worker." He smiled. "That's why I said it would be a good idea to select you even though you're apparently doing some experimental approach and think the rules don't apply to you."

Kavya tried to hide her surprise. "You were on the selection committee?"

"Nope!" He laughed and then smirked.

"Oh, well, I didn't realize the selection committee would discuss it with you," she said nervously. "But, yes, I'll do a reflection paper instead."

"No need to explain. No rubric requirement for you, just like you wanted. Like I said, you're a hard worker, and so I put in a good word. Happy?"

And then she understood that he was showing her who was boss.

She wanted to stand up and say, *I don't want it then.* But she did want it. She needed to see this project through.

"Thank you for your support," she managed to mutter.

Mark stood up, ending the meeting. She rushed down the several flights of stairs before getting outside. Mark was a nobody, but he still managed to leave her with that sensation she used to have as a child, like she had done something wrong. She looked around the front steps of the school, wanting desperately to scream.

She texted Janet, *Need to tell you about something,* and quickly walked around the building in the direction of the Seaport.

She reached the water and watched the waves. Her phone rang. Janet.

"Hey, Kavya. You out with your boy? Need to tell me that y'all are hooking up?"

"Freddy's not my boy or anything else. Stop with all your endless jokes or I'll regret telling you about how we met up."

"Damn. I was just kidding. What did I do?"

Kavya burst into tears.

"Oh no, Kav. What happened?"

And now, as Kavya cried, gasping for air and gagging, she did not even know what to say. After staring out at the water, watching the flags on the boats flap in the wind, the dry heaving finally stopped. She quietly sniffled.

"I'm so sorry, Janet. I'm sorry I'm a jerk. All you've been doing is listening to me cry about my mom."

"Stop. I shouldn't be so childish about the Freddy stuff. Everything's heavy for you right now. It's like your mom has died all over again."

They were quiet.

Janet broke the silence. "I never asked if you told the boys everything about Mohan's visit."

"Not really. I didn't tell them about my mom. I'm going to wait until they get home. They've got the end of their school year and their summer school and all that." Kavya started speaking faster. "But the other day I started to think. Do I come down to Texas and find my mom's death certificate and get the police report? Do I take off for India and try to track down my mom's relatives? Do I find someone from my father's side and force them to tell me about something?"

"About what?"

"All of it! Caste! My mom!"

"You don't have to decide any of this right now," Janet said. "And, uh . . . maybe I shouldn't ask this."

"No, ask. Please."

"Are you even thinking of reaching out to Neela? Maybe weasel some answers out of her?"

That urge rose up inside Kavya. This time, she knew she was going to let it spill right out of her.

"Janet, I don't think I can ever reach out to Neela. It could provoke her. She could ruin everything."

Her voice sounded like it was echoing.

"Janet, Janet, I lied to you. I have to tell you something. It's awful. I have to tell you."

Before Janet could say anything, Kavya continued,

"I can never reach out to Neela because she knows that Ranjeet is the father of my boys."

4

Summer

Monsters

Books and papers littered the floor of Kavya's office. The rest of the faculty had scattered as soon as exams and senior ceremonies ended. But she was regularly coming into school in a futile attempt to organize her office and to avoid the emptiness of her house. The boys celebrated their birthday for the first time without her, and they were still busy with summer school, volunteering, and all kinds of things. So here she was, sorting through stacks of articles.

She unwrapped a chocolate bar and nibbled as she looked around. Sheets of paper, bound as novels or loose with her scribblings, always gave her comfort, for as long as she could remember.

She racked her brain for any memory of her father reading to her as a child. Nothing. Just another one of his failures.

He was the one who could fill in so many gaps about Amma's life and family but just wouldn't.

And yet, Neela was the main monster breathing down her neck. She could almost see her in the office. Sneering through her thick glasses as she looked through the bookshelf. *Stupid girl*, she would say. *What a waste of a life*.

Kavya picked up a pen and drew small circles on a piece of paper.

Mohan was a different kind of monster. A bumbling, mealy-mouthed, hunched-over monster. The kind that would watch or even walk away from someone being sucked into quicksand instead of pulling them out. But not the kind that would pour boiling water on himself. And so, she had let him into her home. And he fumbled around, deceptive in his childishness. And he said things that shattered her, jagged pieces that could never be put back together.

She drew smaller circles to make eyes.

But he gave her the money for that very house. He let her scream at him and order him around. And all that time, he felt responsible for Amma's death and wanted to protect Kavya. She imagined him as a small boy, trembling and crying, while little Neela cowered under the covers, their grandfather towering over her.

She softened, in a way that made her feel human but also terrified. You shouldn't feel sorry for monsters.

* * *

When Kavya was a child, Neela sang at community events. Neela had always looked incandescent when singing, a dulcet voice that couldn't possibly have called her niece a bitch moments before in the car ride. Eyes closed and singing, she emoted an expansiveness that disappeared when she yelled at her husband for being too stupid to know how to pick out the right vegetables.

One time in the car, Neela started singing along to a Hindi cassette tape. She looked over at Kavya briefly. A slight shake of the head, a hint of a smile, a bit of naughtiness as she sang about forbidden love.

Kavya, incapable of bearing the intimacy of the moment, stuck her hands over her ears and said churlishly, "Ugh, you sound awful. Stop it."

Neela stopped singing. Kavya immediately regretted it but didn't know how to say sorry. And when Pramod set up the record player that weekend, Neela walked away to do the dishes instead of singing along as usual. When Kavya peeked around the corner, she saw that her aunt was facing the counter, her back shaking as she cried.

The guilt steadily ate away at Kavya. It was awful of her to take away the one thing that maybe gave Neela some joy.

Kavya tried to make up for it the next time she went to the store with Pramod by buying a plant she found. It was a potted, pale green cactus with tiny golden orange flowers. She set it in the dining room, hoping it would be a happy surprise for her aunt.

"What's this? Why is it on my table?" Neela asked later.

"I bought it for you. Isn't it pretty?" Kavya couldn't make her mouth form an apology.

"Oh, *you* bought it. That makes sense. People choose plants that match their personalities."

"What's my personality?"

"Prickly. Mean. Nasty."

Kavya later hit the cactus off the table, grinding her jaw so forcefully that her teeth audibly slid and scraped against each other. The pot landed on the carpet and cracked. She grabbed it to throw in the trash, and some of the needles poked her. She tightened her grip, driving the sharp ends into her skin. She then tossed it in the garbage and vacuumed up the dirt. Later, she sat in the backyard, staring at her punctured hand.

* * *

Kavya looked at her drawing as she recrossed her legs on her office floor. If Neela and Mohan weren't monsters, what were they? Did they talk with each other about her? She tried to imagine that conversation but could not hear words. Only grunts, growls, moans.

She drew lumpy bodies around the eyes. Added open mouths. Teeth. Now what?

Now that she had told Janet the truth, Ranjeet's paternity was officially real. Her confession rang so loudly in her ears that she didn't know if she could stop herself from telling everyone she knew. She had always planned to tell the truth to her sons but someday far off in the future. A future she kept postponing.

When Kavya had finally told Janet about Ranjeet, her friend wasn't angry, repulsed, or even surprised.

Janet just said, "I figured as much."

"What?" Kavya exclaimed.

"Seriously? How many clues did I need? I went with you to the OB and can do math. You didn't want to go near anyone after you left Ranjeet. Your story about 'Vinay the one-night stand' was just kind of silly. No offense, but you were always wound too tight for casual hook ups. Me, on the other hand."

"Does your family know?"

"No one ever said anything. And who cares if they figured it out? But what about the boys? They're adults now."

What do I tell the boys? When do I tell them? That's all Kavya could think about after that conversation.

She tried to stay present in her office, on the floor. She added webbed feet and tiny claws underneath each creature. She colored in the claws with black ink. When she finished, she crumpled up the sketch and threw it across the room.

Sitting there in the silence, Kavya succumbed to those old fears that Ranjeet would show up one day and take the boys away.

She climbed up on her chair and turned on the computer. She could not stop herself from looking up child custody laws in Texas, compulsively traveling down a rabbit hole of endless horror stories about children being separated from their families and homes.

And then she stumbled across an article about the University of Houston Graduate College of Social Work removing its dean, Alan Dettlaff, for his abolitionist views on the child welfare system. She read his interviews and watched videos about how he wanted to address the systematic causes of poverty instead of pathologizing parents and taking away their children. She learned about how indentured child labor, chattel slavery, and dispossession suffered by Indigenous peoples laid the groundwork for the practice of removing children from "unfit" parents. How family violence and abuse prompted not extensive support and protection for the entire family system but rather children becoming "wards" of the state, subjected to sometimes worse mistreatment in the foster care system.

Kavya remembered the social workers who sometimes showed up at Janet's apartment complex back in Houston. They walked around with clipboards, at times accompanied by the police. She would watch them through the blinds. She would imagine them knocking on her door with Ranjeet in tow loudly declaring, *Hey psycho, they're mine now.*

She shuddered.

She shook off those wretched thoughts and picked up her phone to text Janet. *Hey, in your circles, did you ever hear about the whole thing with Alan Dettlaff at U of H?*

Janet replied soon after. *Nope but googled. The government is always trying to remove children from their homes, when the parents are Black or poor, or now for allowing gender-affirming care. You've got me all riled up!*

And that's how Kavya's next letter idea was born. She worked for several hours as she sketched out ideas and skimmed books and essays. She called a neighbor to get the correct details about an incident that had happened the previous year to a mutual friend.

Hungry and bleary-eyed, she hurried out of her office to catch the last rush hour bus home. She ate dinner in front of her laptop as she toggled between different stories. She pushed aside her plate. Still chewing, she typed out an outline. Those old scenarios she used to imagine of Ranjeet and social workers showing up at her door, popped up again, pecking away at her. She kept working until the fear receded. Until her mind quieted.

When she finally collapsed onto her bed, she grabbed the lotion on the nightstand. She realized with shock that she had not opened her diary since Mohan's visit.

She reached for her pen, her eyes already moist.

Amma, you left me on purpose. I've never thought one negative thing about you. But you left me behind. I know logically that it was a mental health condition that made you think everything would be better if you died. But somewhere, deep inside, didn't you know that Dad and Neela and useless Pramod wouldn't be able to take care of me? I was only able to raise my own children by the skin of my teeth. I'm afraid I've completely screwed them up with my lies and anxiety. But even then, I would never leave them alone in this world. Even Neela didn't die. She crushed her own soul, and mine, but she stuck around. Why did you do it? If you had held on just a bit longer, I would have been old enough to understand. I could have helped you.

Kavya stopped. And then she gripped the pen and pressed down on the paper until it tore.

DEAR PRINCIPAL X

A week later, after a lot more reading and thinking, Kavya was ready to send Yandelis the next letter.

Dear Principal X,

I heard about how you, or someone on your staff, called child protective services because my friend's teenaged son "might have smelled like marijuana" when picking up his little sister from your private school. The social workers showed up at the house and terrified the entire family. I'm sure your phone call had nothing to do with this family being Black, right? I'm sure you were just doing your due diligence, right?

I'm writing this letter to you because I looked up your social media when I heard about what you did (and by the way, even if someone else made the call, you surely would have known about it). You have an old Facebook post saying that you condemn the Trump administration's forced separation of migrant children from their caretakers at the U.S.-Mexico border. Did you know the family policing system (aka, the child welfare system) is also about family separation?

First, let's zoom out to the context of this country's history. Slavery and settler colonialism required regularly dispossessing people of their homes, land, language, culture, and everything that made them feel human, including the ability to take care of and be taken care of by others. White folks took Black babies from enslaved women to sell into chattel slavery and then forced these grieving women to breastfeed their own white children, all for the sake of the plantation economy. The U.S. funded residential schools to assimilate Indigenous children and torture the indigeneity out of them, while simultaneously training them in vocational trades, so they could be "productive" members of society. The residential schools were the solution to the government running out of areas to forcibly relocate Indigenous people and to the growing expenses of fighting Indigenous people's resistance to settler colonialism.

The legacies of these actions are the backdrop to consider today. Just as Indigenous children were harmed in residential schools, so too are Indigenous children currently harmed in foster care due to a child welfare system that contests the ability of Indigenous families to parent their children. This system removes Black children as well, of course, for the smallest "infractions" that are really indicators of living in poverty or not having enough social support services, or due to actions coded as abusive or neglectful (not usually applied in the same way to white families).

Today, child welfare advocates justify their investigations, intrusions, surveillance, and removals as necessary to keep children safe. But are they safe and protected? Read the haunting stories of the abuse children face in the foster care system, and the family trauma that occurs during cycles of removal, reunion, removal, reunion. Learn about the intergenerational trauma of people who are criminalized and dehumanized as bad parents, whose own parents and ancestors suffered the injustices of family separation.

How many times have you heard people talk about their families like this: "They are an extension of me. We are joined at the hip. I would rather chop off my arm than live without them."? Well, stories upon stories illustrate the delight white supremacy has taken in tearing apart kin limb by limb. Feminist scholar Catherine Goetze says that patriarchal, patrimonial governance requires the destruction of families that do not "belong." You decided, because you "suspected" this family, that you would aid and abet the governmental agents that menace the most marginalized families.

Despite my own background in human rights, I haven't adequately wrapped my mind around how family separation is a critical tool of state oppression. Also, another layer here is that Indigenous writers in particular are warning that through the very act of naming intergenerational trauma, academics like me might fuel that racist need to diagnose, pathologize, and fix harmed communities while leaving intact the oppressive systems, like settler colonialism and family policing. My goal isn't to entrench the foul idea that some communities are always, forever broken and defined by trauma. Instead, I write with the fervent hope that you join me in following the lead of Black and Indigenous communities who demand the end of family separation.

Sincerely,
A parent who always did whatever she had to do to keep her children

* * *

Yandelis looked up from her tablet. "Professor, the more I read your letters all together like this, I just feel like there's something powerful here. I mean, you've covered colonialism, casteism, slavery, and settler colonialism, and of course, each letter is only a little snapshot of something bigger, and so now I can imagine how amazing it is when you have several little snapshots from a whole classroom. And I can build on the bibliographies you put together and add even more options for stories the students can read. This is so cool, right? Right?" She looked about ready to burst from excitement, her mouth hanging half-open, like someone waiting to shout *Surprise!* at a birthday party.

"Yeah, the letter project is cool," Kavya said, distracted.

Everything felt wrong. She had always convinced herself that she was protecting her children from Ranjeet. But it was a situation of her own making. She was not a victim of governmental oppression, and maybe she shouldn't have inserted herself into the letter like that.

What kind of mother lied to her own children about where they came from? What kind of mother hid from her own demons? Her sons surely must have picked up on and absorbed her inner turmoil. What were her children grappling with, deep inside their heart of hearts, all because of her?

She noticed that Yandelis was still staring at her. Her hands held at a prayer at her chest, her fingernails loudly tapping against each other.

"I think this project is interesting but also tricky," Kavya started again. "Remember the line in this last letter about how we study and diagnose trauma in other communities. We need to be very mindful of what Indigenous researchers and activists are saying. We have to be careful about how we are witnessing and writing about other people's stories. I am doing this project to create space to talk about intergenerational pain, but I don't want to . . ."

"You don't want us to act like snotty academics who understand trauma when we actually don't understand or even know how to write about other people's trauma, right? Like, you don't want us to be hypocrites?"

Kavya coughed and reached for her water. "Umm. Yeah, hypocrisy."

Just that morning, she had sent the draft of the tenure executive statement that Molly wanted. In it, she included a reference to the grant to work with Yandelis and noted a commitment to "faculty-student collaborative praxis." She thought the tenure committees would eat that up.

She justified it to herself when she wrote the draft. It was just strategic. Tenure would mean continued job stability and health insurance. She didn't want to start over someplace else, with a new therapist, new friends, or even far away from the boys, right? People did this all the time. They said what they needed to for the job or the promotion and then smashed the system. Right?

But now . . .

Kavya wanted to tell Yandelis that she would still pay her the stipend but that academia was a scam. That she was a fraud and couldn't be trusted. *I've been lying to my sons their whole lives.*

"Yandelis, there's something I want to discuss with you."

"Professor? The thing is, and I may be getting ahead of myself, but once we do these letters and talk about it all, how do we solve the problems? How do you create a world without intergenerational trauma?"

"Yeah, the goal is definitely to dismantle and transform systems of oppression." *I don't know. I don't know anything.*

"On the impacted communities' terms, right?"

"Yes." *I have done everything wrong.*

"Then what about that email exchange we had about responsibility? What if our families or communities are the perpetrators of the trauma?"

Kavya pushed aside her howling, accusatory inner thoughts so she could consider Yandelis's question. "I love what you're asking, but I really don't know how to answer it."

She abruptly remembered that Sneha had never responded to her email with the caste letter. Dejected, she stared down at her hands.

Yandelis brightened. "Okay, let's just email each other. That's what you always say, right? If it's too hard to think and discuss, try writing, and see what happens. Let's try to write our answers to this question about what's next."

"Great, I'll send you an email soon to get us started." Kavya tried to sound enthusiastic. Her student deserved that effort from her.

She watched as Yandelis packed up her things, waved goodbye, and left her office.

At least Kavya had a plan for one thing in her life. An email to Yandelis. Poor unsuspecting Yandelis.

She had canceled her therapy appointments after her confession to Janet.

Her conversations with the boys since then seemed dishonest.

She wanted to quit her job and go find out her mother's story.

This was not how her life was supposed to go.

Singapore

As Kavya made her way to the bus stop, she almost collided with a pregnant woman on the phone.

"So sorry!" Kavya exclaimed.

Caressing the bump, the woman mouthed, *It's okay.*

Kavya thought about her own pregnancy. That terrifying and exhilarating feeling of placing her hand on her belly, waiting for the tiny little flutters and the sharp kicks.

As she tracked the bus on her phone app, she could vividly remember that one day when she had been about six months along. During a spell of abject loneliness, she had called her father to tell him about the pregnancy.

Mohan, like always, refrained from asking any questions at all, only saying, "Wow, twins." Kavya knew he would never ask who the father was, but she still told him to keep her pregnancy a secret.

Even as Kavya tried to focus on everything around her in chaotic lower Manhattan, the honking and yelling and revving engines, she floated back there. Back to that time in her life when she was pregnant, starting a journey of motherhood that seemed at once impossible and necessary.

* * *

Houston, Texas. 2004. Kavya held her bulging belly, stretching the limits of her maternity pants, as she made her way through the desolate parking lot to visit the district clerk's office.

A month and a half later, after fingerprints and a court hearing, Kavya Mohan Bendre became Kavya Nalini Joshi. She told Janet's family she wanted to start using her Ajji's first name and her Amma's maiden name so that she could start over with her sons and honor those two women's memories. Thankfully, she did not need to put a father's name on the birth certificates, and no one ever brought up the nonexistent Vinay.

And she had the tiniest bit of relief that maybe Ranjeet would never learn about the kids. Because she would sometimes imagine him finding her and throwing her through the air again, so hard that the amniotic sacs burst.

Kavya called Mohan when she was in labor, but he didn't meet her kids when they were newborns. She put off inviting him over.

Then, when the boys were maybe about four months old, Janet's mother called her.

"Hi honey," Yumiko said slowly. "Your aunt Neela called, wanting to know where you are because she said your father was admitted to the hospital."

Distracted and exhausted, Kavya called Neela. She had enough sense to press *67 so there would be no Caller ID on Neela's end. As the phone rang, she realized she should have maybe just called her father first.

Neela was breathing fire when she learned it was Kavya.

"This is how I had to find out? From my stupid husband? You're walking around with children and no husband? What will people say? Who is the father? What faltu person did you go and sleep with?"

Kavya remained silent, falling into the old familiar pattern of her brain shutting down when her aunt came at her.

She heard nothing at first.

Then Neela shouted, "It's Ranjeet! Ranjeet is the father, isn't he? You never told him!"

Kavya should have known better. She should have anticipated this moment. Thankfully, Janet was out walking the boys in the stroller. But her breath still quickened, as if someone could overhear any minute.

"I will always figure you out," Neela said. "You cannot hide anything from me."

Kavya couldn't speak.

"Where are you now?" Neela asked suspiciously. "Nina Auntie's daughter said she got a postcard about you living in France. What are you doing there for work? How did you block Caller ID with an international call?"

Shit. Shit. Shit.

Kavya managed to utter, "I'm traveling in the U.S. With my . . ."

"With your children?"

Kavya clutched the phone. *Be careful.* "No. With my colleague." Holding her stomach with her other hand, she forced herself to continue. "The children are not with me. I just wanted my dad to know about them. He's the only grandparent anyways."

Neela huffed. "The only grandparent? He is not the only grandparent. Remember Ranjeet's mother? Stupid." And then she said, lowering her voice, "You're doing everyone a favor by keeping yourself and those kids away. Do you know why? Ranjeet has married. He will soon have his own, real children. The wife is so gorgeous. She is so nice to everyone. Really strong and calm. In fact, she's your complete opposite."

Kavya's voice shook. "Stop. Don't say that."

"After everything I have done?" Neela yelled. "Do you know what I went through? Ungrateful girl. Your poor kids. They will be confused their whole lives. They will be living God knows where. Who knows how they will turn out."

Kavya snapped, hissing in a tone even she didn't recognize, "If you or Pramod ever come anywhere near me or my kids, or even talk about us, I will tell everyone what you are. You know everyone already talks about you. I saw Ajji cry about it. But no one knows what I know. I will tell everyone!"

By then, Kavya was in such a state, she was not entirely sure what Neela said in response, but she then heard the dial tone.

Kavya later called Mohan when she was alone in the bathroom, with the shower running. Whispering while crying, she asked furiously, "What the fuck did you say?"

"What?" Mohan was startled.

"Why did Neela ask me to call?"

"She called you?"

"She played a trick and told Yumiko there was some medical situation with you. I called her. And she brought up the kids! She knows Ranjeet is the dad. What if he finds out and takes them from me?" Kavya could barely catch her breath.

"I didn't know he was the father, though."

"Who the fuck did you tell that I have children?"

"I was with Pramod. It was an accident. It was just us, and it came out. I said, 'Now that I'm a grandfather.' I won't do it again."

"How could you do that to me?" Kavya's sobbing grew louder.

"Kavya, listen . . ."

She hung up on him.

* * *

The boys turned one year old. Their first birthday party was unbridled, delightful chaos.

Later that week, Bob delivered several packages of toys Mohan had sent for the kids to Janet's family's house. The note said, *Bob and Yumiko, please send these to Kavya wherever she is. Be happy. Happy Birthday. Dad/ Ajja.*

Against her better judgment, Kavya called Mohan, once again using *67. She said, her voice already wobbly, "Did you bring Pramod along while you shopped for the gifts, since you love sharing my private news with him?"

"I didn't say anything to him."

Kavya refrained from asking how often Mohan kept in touch with his sister and brother-in-law. She didn't want to know the answer.

Instead, she asked, "Do they know where I am? Do *you* know where I am?"

"No. Not at all," Mohan answered.

"If they ever find out ..." She could hear the hysteria in her voice. "What will you say if they ask you about me?"

"We are not talking about such things, Kavya."

"What are you telling people in the community?"

"Nothing. Just Singapore."

"What the hell are you talking about?"

"Kavya, you know, I told my sister, I told the community, that you had to move to Singapore. I made it up. Neela was telling everyone France, and now she's saying Singapore. She bought some things from some store and then told people, 'Look what Kavya sent to me from Singapore.'"

"What in the actual hell?" She paced around her cramped room.

"Yes, see, Kavya? Singapore. No one has asked about any children. I don't think Neela and Pramod told anyone."

"Only because it makes them look bad to be related to some whore with bastard children, right?"

After that phone call, Kavya thought about how Mohan had lied to his own sister. She called him again a few weeks later.

"Dad, you're on probation," she explained to him. "But I want the boys to know you. They deserve to have at least one grandparent. You can stay at a hotel in Houston. You'll give a pseudonym. And we'll meet at Yumiko's store. No pictures. Never tell a soul, not even Pramod, your sister, any coworkers, even a priest, on your deathbed, nothing."

Mohan complied. And they continued like that, so that neither Neela nor Ranjeet could find her and the boys.

Social media then took over everyone's lives. She told the people in her life that they could not post anything about her or her sons online.

She tried to monitor her sons' use and wouldn't let them share pictures of her. She made sure to keep as low a profile of herself as possible, never submitting a picture for the faculty website when she got the New York job or creating any social media accounts. It was easy enough to pretend she was taking a moral stance about digital privacy.

And late at night, after the boys went to bed, Kavya would look online for Ranjeet's latest, keeping track of him. He had two children, a boy and a girl, a little younger than her boys. His family, including his mother, had moved to a small town in Colorado. His wife spent a lot of time on Pinterest posting about children's arts and crafts. Her Instagram featured homemade desserts as well as elaborate scenes of dinosaurs created out of sandwiches and fruits. *Good for her.* An irrational bitterness took over Kavya's thoughts. *She looks like the perfect fucking wife and mother and daughter-in-law of the year.*

Kavya even found a YouTube video with the wife filming Ranjeet and one of the kids. Ranjeet looked the same, maybe a bit grayer. He was kneeling on the ground, nuzzling his head into the girl. The girl was running her fingers through her father's hair. Kavya remembered that Ranjeet loved children. At community parties, you would find him in a corner, surrounded by children laughing at his magic tricks and funny faces. Weren't children supposed to be good judges of character?

She could hear the wife's voice in the background of the video. It was lilting, almost obnoxiously chirpy. What struck Kavya was how light-hearted she sounded. Did she ever sound that relaxed when she was with Ranjeet?

She always cycled through elaborate scenarios, envisioning that her sons ran into Ranjeet's children somewhere, and then somehow became friends. She sometimes tortured herself by imagining her sons voluntarily leaving her to join Ranjeet's family.

That was the thing. You could erase all traces of your past. You could hide yourself from other people. But never from yourself.

DISASSOCIATE

The bus pulled up slowly to avoid hitting the delivery workers and unperturbed pedestrians nimbly weaving their ways through the traffic. Kavya climbed aboard and did not even try to hide the tears rolling down her cheeks. So much lying and pretending her entire life.

On her commute home, she could not bear the guilt and instead focused on what to write to Yandelis. The only thing she had control over. The next day, she was ready.

June 6, 2023

Dear Yandelis,

I admit that your question about the future threw me off. I thought about how so many of us want a future free from generational trauma, which means a future free of oppressive systems. The trauma isn't in the past because the harm keeps happening, right? I was thinking about the promotional material all over campus about students being the changemakers of the future. But what is the future for settlers, dominant caste people, white people, the ones who always assume they/we are entitled to the best future possible? What are we supposed to do in the future?

I remember Eve Tuck and K. Wayne Yang's article, "Decolonization Is Not a Metaphor," about how an Indigenous vision of the future means that the land has been returned to Indigenous stewardship. They also warn that the point of social justice is not to answer "what's next" for settlers, such as where would we go when the land has been returned. The oppressor has to live with that "not knowing" and let the oppressed make the future.

Something else I thought about was when I taught the unit about international criminal law in the human rights class. Do you remember that case where the International Criminal Court judges assessed that they would not offer reparations to Congolese victims claiming intergenerational harm. They ruled that there was allegedly no causal link between the suffering of the claimants and their parents' experiences during the 2003 Bogoro massacre. And I have to say, I know that historic trauma gets passed down, but it is so hard to trace and prove, even with all the studies about trauma transmission.

What worries me is that we can then make intergenerational trauma mean whatever we want for our own agendas. For example, sometimes people want to act like saviors to communities they see as perpetually damaged (by intergenerational trauma, for instance) and in need of fixing (like I referenced in my "Dear

Principal X" letter). Or perpetrators can act like they're the primary victims. Just the other day, I saw this story about some white parents who said that teaching their kids about the U.S.'s history of racism is about "persecuting" white people. They said they shouldn't be made to feel guilty for what their white ancestors did especially when their own families have suffered throughout U.S. history. And that their kids being taught about slavery, white supremacy, and white privilege would make it unbearable and "traumatizing" to be white. What's "next" if we distort the past?

Prof. Joshi

June 6, 2023

Prof. Joshi,
Holy shit. I never thought about any of that. So, what do we do?

Yandelis

June 7, 2023

Dear Yandelis,
I've learned that traumatized people can sometimes lose sensation in entire parts of their bodies. They disassociate; they are not able to connect to their physical and emotional experiences. That's the body "keeping the score" by holding on to trauma. If the world also keeps the score via the ongoing impact of the most oppressive and disruptive political events and systems, then does the world also "cut off feeling" to deal with political trauma? How does the world "disassociate"? Is this widespread belief in "fake news" and conspiracy theories a type of global disassociating? Are the extreme weather events that seem surreal and uncharacteristic a way that the world "cuts off feeling"? (Is that what climate change is?) Should we read sci-fi and speculative fiction to find answers to a future without family and historic trauma? I might be going off on tangents. I'm sorry to say that maybe I can't imagine the future "after" trauma. It's not up to me to imagine, perhaps.

Prof. Joshi

June 7, 2023

Dear Prof. Joshi,

These emails are kind of overwhelming me. And I was thinking that maybe asking about "what's next" was unfair of me. If you can't imagine the future, I definitely can't! I thought you'd be able to because you have kids and might be thinking of the generations after you. I just wanted to find some hope in something. Maybe it's just not possible.

Yandelis

SLOW DOWN

"And then I got my IUD removed, which hurt like hell."

"I just don't understand why you don't freeze your eggs first. You don't even really know if you want to be with this guy."

"Yeah, but . . ."

Kavya tried to pay attention to the conversation. She didn't know why she had agreed to come to this gathering with Mingming and her law school friends. She should have known better. She had felt out of sorts all day.

As she watched Mingming gesture while talking, she took note of what was happening to her own body. The sideways sensation crept up her back. Between her shoulder blades. Now firmly in the base of her skull. Her head heavy and light at the same time. The bar stool unsteady. She leaned forward, placing both hands on the table.

Concentrate. Stop freaking out.

She opened her emails on her phone and reread Yandelis's last message. She started to type an answer. *Not unfair at all. It's just a huge question to answer. We can't give up hope!*

She stared at the screen and erased it all. She started again. *No, let's keep thinking through this. Let's look up essays about . . .*

She erased everything again. She sighed and put the phone down.

"Right, Kavya?"

Upon hearing her name, she looked up. "Umm, yes. Excuse me. I have to run to the bathroom."

She grabbed her purse and slipped off the bar stool, hoping she would be able to walk in a straight line. So far, so good, but when she rushed inside one of the stalls and slammed the door shut, she found herself breathing shallowly. *Stop, stop, stop. Calm the fuck down.*

She opened her purse, opened the pill bottle, and threw a Xanax at the back of her throat. Wavering for a moment, she split another one in half with her nail and downed that piece too.

She waited a few more minutes before exiting the stall. She washed her hands and splashed water on her face as she looked in the mirror. How odd to see that she was all slumped over, just like her father. She straightened up and rolled her shoulders back. Her face looked surprisingly calm even though her thoughts were racing at breakneck speed, lobbing demands at the reflection in the mirror.

You need to find the words so that Yandelis respects you again. Come up with an answer. You have to! It might be too late already. See how she called you out about your kids? You are responsible for what you have done to them. Call Samir and Kabir right now and tell them about Ranjeet. You have to figure out the right thing to say or they'll always hate you. What's wrong with you right now. Why can't you fix anything. Goddamn you.

"No," she said aloud. She stared at herself in the mirror. She did Helen's breathing exercises.

You've been gone for too long. Go back out.

She slowly walked back to the table to find everyone chatting about their jobs. As she sat down, she pretended to be engrossed in something on her phone.

"Oh, sorry, I have to make a quick phone call," Kavya said. Out of the corner of her eye, she saw Mingming watching her as she left the restaurant.

Kavya stood outside, the humidity immediately making her hair curl. She swiped through the apps on her phone. She watched a man try to convince his dog to move. The dog kept its paws affixed to the ground.

And then. The first hint of that delicious drowsiness. She could feel everything slowing down. Like someone was funneling molasses deep inside of her. The sweet, sticky goo coated her tired brain. Calmed her frantically pumping heart.

Her stomach growled. She went back inside, making her way to the table, and poured several chips from the communal bowl onto her plate. She licked the salt off them and listened to herself crunch as she ate. The sleepy feeling deepened. The sharp edges of anxiety finally began to dull.

"Dude, whatever works for you," she heard Mingming say to the friend named Stephanie before turning to Kavya. "All good?"

Kavya nodded.

"Oh hey, how much more do you plan to crank out with Yandelis before we leave for our trip?"

Kavya's mouth moved a split second before her brain kicked in. "We are still trying to figure out what to do. But we're each going to read . . . things." Precise words were out of her reach.

"Like what?"

Oh, she was not in the mood for Mingming's endless questions. "The future, I suppose."

The friend named Tasha leaned in their direction and asked, "What are you talking about?"

Kavya wanted to put her head down on the table and sleep.

"Kavya and her student assistant are researching intergenerational trauma and, apparently, the future," Mingming answered.

"The future? Like policy recommendations?" asked Tasha.

Kavya gripped the edge of the stool. "No." She paused. She found herself saying, "More like how oppressed people can envision their future." Sharper and more concise words. Getting there!

Tasha animatedly described an Afrofuturist exhibit she had seen in Germany. While the others asked Tasha questions, Kavya pretended to listen. *Who is getting the IUD out, Tasha or Stephanie? Why are my thoughts so loud?* She didn't care. She sighed, lazily tracing her finger along the table edge.

A hand was on her shoulder. She turned, her eyelids drooping. She tried to smile so she looked okay. Mingming said, "Kavya. What the hell. Did you have some edibles in the bathroom?"

Kavya shook her head. "Just Xanax," she whispered. She had not yet told Mingming about her father's visit or the aftermath. She quickly added, "You know, just stressed about getting tenure."

Mingming scrunched up her face. "Xanax is supposed to chill you out. Not *chill* you out."

"I react strangely to meds."

"Seriously, with Xanax? I pop that shit at work without thinking. Edibles too, actually."

Kavya giggled and stared at the table. "I'm going to get a car and sleep this off."

Mingming stood up, pulling Kavya along with her. "Good idea. Share your ride so I can follow it and make sure you get home okay."

"Love you."

Kavya waved to Stephanie and Tasha. "It was good to see you both. I'm dead tired and going to head home." They waved back cheerily.

Twenty minutes later, she walked inside her home, tossed her purse on the floor, and flopped onto the couch.

She stared up at the ceiling. *Don't panic. I can live in the gray. I can take my time.* And as if to prove to herself, and in some way to Freddy, that she could, she pulled out her phone to email Yandelis.

She thought for a minute, remembering Tasha's comments about the exhibit.

June 8, 2023

Hi Yandelis!

I'm very glad you asked me about what's next. Have you read any feminist Afrofuturism? There are so many reasons to be hopeful about the future. Let's meet next week. We can talk then. We can co-write a letter. We have all the time in the world.

Prof J

She waited for the *swoosh* of the sent email. And then she fell asleep right there on the couch.

Play

The following Monday, Kavya and Yandelis sat in her office, sipping iced coffees from the lobby kiosk.

Yandelis had done her nails again. Long red talons with little sparkly swirls. *How does she use the restroom with those things? Or do anything?*

"The Smithsonian has an Afrofuturism exhibit right now. I was reading about it online, and maybe that's a place for us to start?" Kavya offered.

"Do you want us to do a letter about feminist futures?"

"Maybe. We'd need to focus on something specific."

Yandelis played with the cup lid, a faraway look in her eyes.

My mother killed herself. Sometimes when she was by herself, Kavya would say the words out loud. She thought about what Neela had threatened, what her mother did, what happened in her community, what happened enough so that every semester, she heard at least one story about a student's loved one, or worse, their own attempts. What if what was "next" wasn't something cool and beautiful at all?

She struggled to figure out what to say to her student. And what to do with herself. She meandered around her small office as she finished her drink. Noticing her peeling posters, she pushed down on them, trying to get the sticky tape to adhere to the white bricks. She ran her fingers across the spines of the books in the metal bookcase. She spotted a stain on the gray carpet tiles and rubbed at it with her foot.

Yandelis pulled out her tablet. "Whenever I'm thinking about the future, I think about climate change. Is there some kind of connection we can make where intergenerational trauma is a part of how oceans, habitats, our air, all of it, are getting destroyed and how it's been impacting us all?"

"Yes, I think that's right." Kavya couldn't focus.

After more silence, Yandelis piped up, "When we're talking about futurism, can we talk about mythological creatures, like centaurs, or spirits, or sea creatures?"

"Umm, okay, but remember the prompt for the project. We're writing to someone who is responsible for or a witness to some event or system. Maybe we look at oil spills and destruction of certain fishing industries, and examine the impact of climate change on communities' livelihoods? I'm sure we could find a lot of generational family stories."

Yandelis ignored everything she said. "I'm just gonna google global politics and, like, every mythological creature I can think of."

Kavya nodded, half-listening.

It was quiet except for the tap-tap of Yandelis's nails for several minutes. "Okay, there's all this stuff about Afrofuturism and mermaids. And like underwater worlds, seas rising, that sort of thing. Let me keep looking."

"Mmm." Kavya flipped through a few books.

"Yes!" Yandelis yelped. "I just found a list of books that are Black mermaid fiction, and, yes, yes! I'm seeing this stuff about mermaids in futurist stories to challenge the destructiveness of human beings, whether that's how human beings participated in the transatlantic slave trade or in destroying the climate and world! Slay! Yes!"

"Huh?"

"Yeah! I mean, Jalondra Davis has this article legit talking about mermaids and what *we* are talking about!" Yandelis practically shouted, as she wriggled excitedly in her chair.

Kavya snapped her fingers. "You know, I do remember that Alexis Gumbs has a story or poem about mermaids and the Middle Passage. I think so at least."

"Hooray!" Yandelis clapped her hands.

"I'm cool with speculative fiction and stuff like that. But is this really where we want to go? Mermaids?"

Yandelis stared, her eyes so wide that Kavya wanted to laugh. "Professor Joshi! First of all, you do realize that the freaking Coney Island Mermaid Parade is *this* weekend. It's meant to be! I just feel like humans have run out of ideas. What if it is something magical that ends up releasing us from all this pain in the world?" Then she sighed dramatically. "Just, the older I get, the more cynical I am about us as human beings."

"You're twenty."

"No, I totally aged during the pandemic. Really. I feel like I've left my youth and optimism behind," Yandelis said woefully.

"I would never have guessed. That's why I was so worried when you emailed me that you had sort of lost hope. I mean, you always look so enthusiastic."

Yandelis said, with a wry laugh, "Resting happy face. Too many years of being a teacher's pet maybe. But not how I have felt on the inside. But I became happy again when you chose me for this project. I thought I had lost my love of learning."

"Yandelis! I didn't know. I'm so sorry." Kavya's face crumpled.

"Don't be! Now think about it. Human beings are screwing it all up, right? Let's see what other kinds of creatures can do. Isn't that the point of futurism, like science fiction and all that?"

Kavya looked at her student, who was sitting there smiling. A pen mark on her chin.

So many surprises when teaching. What would a little dreaming hurt?

* * *

Her sons were about five years old when they went through a phase of *needing* to play "pretend" every single waking hour. Janet and Kavya would run home from work and trade off with each other or with the teenager next door to watch the boys. They hurriedly cooked dinner, threw clothes into the washing machine, and then rushed back down to the laundry room before cranky neighbors tossed their wet clothes onto the dirty tables.

All while Kabir and Samir pulled on their sleeves. "Can you play with us?"

One time, Kavya came home from a particularly exhausting shift at Yumiko's store, right after tutoring an annoying kid, right after teaching an early morning class. A student had yelled at her for not having office hours. Kavya tried to explain that she was an adjunct. She didn't even have office space or a desk to her name!

Her feet were swollen from wearing too-tight shoes and walking around Yumiko's store to help a large sewing club with an endless list of demands. She collapsed onto the couch and waved to Janet, who was quickly throwing together pasta.

Kabir climbed up on her lap. "Mommy, the couch is the cave for the T-Rex so you can't sit here."

"Kabir, honestly, I don't want to do this right now." Kavya groaned.

Then Samir started, "Mama, just play with us, please? Play with us, please? Please?"

Kavya relented because it was easier than arguing. "Fine. I'm the sleepy giant who is hibernating. And if anyone wakes me up, I'll eat them."

With that, she rolled off the couch and onto a rumpled blanket on the floor. She stared at a glob of peanut butter stuck between the floorboards. Both boys started chewing on her legs.

"What are you doing?"

"We're unicorns!" they answered in unison.

"Why are there unicorns in this story? Where's the T-Rex?"

"Mama, did we wake you up? You're hibernating!"

And at that moment, she didn't want to be a grown-up or an instructor or a sales associate. She wanted to be the sleeping giant. She let out a roar so fierce that Janet poked her head out from the kitchen.

Kavya yelled, "Who woke up the giant?" She rolled around on the floor with the boys until they were all laughing so hard they couldn't breathe.

And when Janet called out "Dinner!", Kavya the Giant stomped to the table and shoved the pasta into her mouth with her hands, snorting and growling while the kids laughed hysterically and Janet, calm as ever, poured their milk.

* * *

Kavya looked at Yandelis, this twenty-year-old earnest young woman who maybe wanted to experience a bit of childlike fun. That part of Kavya that said, *No, you can't play with the kids, you have to do the laundry*, or *You can't talk about mermaids, you have to submit your tenure dossier*, also screamed its desires to let loose. If there could be half-women, half-fish in this world, couldn't she be half-responsible grown-up, half-fanciful youngster?

She never got to be young and carefree, did she? Always trying to do the right thing, obeying the rules, pleasing everyone, acting like the good girl. But here she was, keeping secrets, hiding, running. She was never going to be a good girl.

And so she told Yandelis, "Let's do it. Neither of us is going to be cynical anymore. We're going to believe in magical creatures. Go ahead and create a shared document for a new letter. Give me access, and we'll start co-writing it right now."

As Yandelis cheered and then got to work, Kavya found the Gumbs short story, "Bluebellow," she had mentioned. They pored over the words together. In the story, a Black U.S.-based woman named Serena starts seeing and hearing "mirrored mermaids" with "scaling melanated skin" while on a trip to England. These beings communicate with her, asking her for something, but she does not know what. And Serena realizes that the mermaids are "underwater twins," the oceanic counterparts of the living descendants of the slave trade. The mermaids show themselves to Black people who have come "back" across the Atlantic, specifically to Europe.

Yandelis said, "Listen to this," and read a passage:

The history books say that some of us jumped, but now we know it was total. All of us jumped, if not in body th[e]n in spirit. All of us stayed, if not in bone th[e]n in memory. Middle Passage is the name for how we split from ourselves. The surface of the earth a mirror. Or 71% of it. Which is more than 3/5ths. Do you understand? The horrors of that journey baptized us in our twoness, our depth. Never again would we only breathe air. Never again would they only breathe water. Too heavy. Too light. You can see it in the dances. And we weren't looking. Usually we weren't looking at the depth of the ocean like a mirror. We weren't searching for an underwater twin to reconnect to. We had survived so much separation we didn't imagine wholeness, we didn't even dream of reuniting with the part of us that drowned. Until we did.

At the end of the story, Serena is with other Black descendants, all walking into the water. And, hauntingly, her sister Sandra, who is trying to keep abreast of Serena's "ancestral experience," receives a text in which Serena asks to meet her "in the middle."

Yandelis chattered excitedly about the piece, talking about rising ocean temperatures and saving mermaids and what it meant to be Black, and whether Serena became a mermaid or chose to die, or whether it was all a dream.

Kavya drifted away. What did it mean when people chose death to find another future? She tried not to imagine her mother driving with her foot flat on the floor of the car toward a wall. A concrete wall was finite, the end of everything. It was not the same as a vast ocean.

Together, over the week, Yandelis and Kavya made a list of writing about mermaid sightings and rituals in or near every conceivable body of water. They devoured Black feminist tales brimming with mermaid magic and livable futures. They read about the symbolism of sea cows, the creatures that probably inspired mermaid sightings in the first place, in different cultures and communities.

It was an exhilarating time. It should have been the perfect distraction.

But Kavya furtively glanced at her phone during their meetings together. Obsessively so on her commute and at home. She was not sure what she was looking for. Sometimes, she tortured herself and looked up every suicide story from Texas she could find, only to quickly close the browser. Sometimes, she anxiously awaited a message from Neela announcing that she had somehow magically detected that Kavya had finally uttered aloud the truth about Ranjeet. Or an email from her father detailing everything she wanted to know about Amma. Her phone remained silent, but she kept tapping at it, staring at the bright screen.

That Saturday morning, she agreed to go with Yandelis to the mermaid parade for a bit of inspiration. As soon as they found a place to stand, they enjoyed the warm sea air on their backs and cheered on the first marching band. Teenagers in purple-sequined leotards with glitter in their hair held hands as they skipped. The thrilled screams from the nearby roller coaster ebbed in and out in the background. A jalopy bumped by with an extravagant mermaid's tail attached to the back fender. Cadillacs drove past with people in homemade mermaid costumes throwing out plastic bead necklaces at bystanders. Yandelis immediately picked them off the ground and put them around her neck. Kavya handed the bundle she caught to some random kids next to her.

Local drag celebrities shimmied along the path, beers in hand, as their entourages danced around them. Another marching band, Brass Queens, passed them with their all-woman horn section. A couple dressed as an octopus and a crab held a boom box blasting music. Someone in an inflatable shark costume stopped to breakdance for the crowd.

When Kavya and Yandelis eventually wandered over to the boardwalk to stand in line for food, Kavya remarked, "This is only my second time here. I came with my sons once, and then of course there was COVID." *I have been lying to my own children.*

"Oh, I came here almost every year as a child! What was your favorite costume? Mine was the one made from a bunch of tiny balloons. I'm not sure how they didn't pop!"

Kavya focused on the glistening colors in front of her. *Think about what to say to the boys later. Just stay here. Right now.*

"The mother and daughter duo with sea coral!" answered Kavya. A woman had painted her body to look like sea coral and wore an elaborate coral hat and cape. Thanks to her crafty use of wire, her mermaid's tail stayed upright and sturdy as it wrapped around a young girl in a matching outfit.

"For me and my friends, this has been such a queer and trans space, you know?" Yandelis said. "Like, it's just important to be able to do this, especially now."

"For sure. Did you see anything that sparked something for our work?"

Yandelis thought about it. "I think that playing make believe and dressing up feels liberatory to people. And it wasn't just mermaids, right? I think, as we're seeing in our research, people like things that live in the ocean because it's mysterious. And look around here. Like, everyone is trying to imagine something else."

"A better world?"

"A whole ne-ew world!" Yandelis sang.

"Nope, no Disney songs from me! But, yes, a better future. It sounds too simple when I say that phrase."

"Yeah, it's kind of a weird concept. If you can't figure out something now, like what justice looks like, alright, you just put it off in the future. But then, like, what else is there?"

They were finally at the front of the raucous line and shouted their order to a sweaty woman with blue braces. Another line later, they picked up their food. They strolled along the boardwalk until they found a place to sit.

"Thanks for coming with me here, Professor. It's the best kind of field research."

"You're welcome. Thanks for inviting me." Kavya smiled. "After we finish all our research, what kind of letter should we do?"

"Your letters have been addressed to people you don't know or just kinda know," Yandelis said somberly. "I want to write this to my grandma, my father's mom."

Kavya fell into silence. The letter project seemed to have helped her plug along during this wretched year, to navigate the mess and gunk of her body and soul. But she never once thought about writing a letter addressed to anyone in her family.

Yandelis quickly asked, "Is that okay?"

Kavya listened to the laughter rolling throughout the boardwalk. She brushed sand off her shorts. "Yes, it's okay. Let's write to our grandmothers. Both of us. I'll write to my paternal grandmother, too."

"Maybe I'll even show the letter to my abuela. No matter what she's gone through, she looks out for me, in her own way. She is always trying to get me to believe in something big and divine."

"I have the same kinds of thoughts about my grandmother. She would also listen to any kind of wild story I wanted to tell. Maybe our grandmothers were somewhat responsible for that part of us that imagines something better."

Yandelis shot her a grin.

Kavya smiled back and held up her hot dog. "Cheers! To the fall semester, because that's as far ahead as I can look right now."

Yandelis tapped her box of fries to Kavya's hot dog. "Cheers! To the future."

DEAR ABUELA AND AJJI

Dear Abuela and Ajji,

We are writing to you because you silenced yourselves, and sometimes us, and you wouldn't answer the questions or tell the stories that could have helped us. You tried to pass on your prejudices. Abuela, with your homophobia and misogyny, and Ajji, with your casteism. But you were among the very few in our lives who acted like we had a right to be here, on Earth, taking up space. And we are also proud of you. Abuela, for finally starting to claim your Blackness when it probably feels dangerous to do so, and Ajji, for claiming your right to be active in the world when widows weren't supposed to.

We are trying to figure out the future "after" intergenerational trauma. What can happen "after" the pain the two of you inherited, absorbed, created, and then transmitted to us? We need to know that we are not crazy. That we are not alone. That our families and communities can face themselves. That we can stop our violence against each other. That we can enjoy each other and find reconciliation where we always swore that we never would.

Sometimes it is not possible to speak about or understand the horrors around us. Sometimes we get confused. Might something magical arise from the seas to allow stories to be told, to act as a living repository of memories, to warn us of what will happen if we don't take care of our lands, waters, creatures, and each other? We are thinking about mermaids. There is something appealing about these creatures that in their terrifyingly mysterious ways challenge oppression. They live at the borders of human and animal, of queer and straight, of ability and disability, of every other either/or you can think of. We want to share what we came up with, so that you can witness with us the possibly fantastical and magical ways to save our planet and our families.

Ajji, I discovered that mermaid sightings may have actually been encounters with dugongs, a sea cow that emits mournful tunes and has a humanlike habit of lifting its torso out of the water to feed its young. And when I discovered sea cow habitats include the Andaman and Nicobar Islands, I remembered our conversation about a year before you died. You said you wanted to visit those beaches one day. You just wanted to relax. I had never heard you talk about relaxing, ever. And when you died, I even hoped you were resting someplace beautiful. A beach is how I imagined it.

The dugong at the islands are fighting to stay alive against existential threats like hunting and degradation of their habitats. They probably carry the secrets of those islands, which served as a British penal colony, then were owned by the Japanese, and now are Indian union territory. The dugong have been the constant witnesses to the attempted ethnocide against Indigenous peoples and to how India is steadily stripping the islands of environmental protection to increase militarization (one has to keep an eye on China, after all!). Come back to me, Ajji, so we can travel together to the Andaman and Nicobar Islands and help with the efforts to save the dugong habitats. Let's make friends with the dugong, and when you realize that they are the only ones listening, maybe you will answer my questions about our family and Amma's family. Help me protect the future for my sons. I want a healthy Earth for them. I want an ethical lineage for them.

Abuela, I have a different kind of tale for you. Rita Indiana's book *Tentacle* imagines the Dominican Republic's future, after nuclear waste has basically decimated the place. She tells the story of a sea anemone with magical tentacles that allows people to time-travel. A woman, Acilde, undergoes a gender transition operation to serve as Omo Olukun, the "chosen man" who will time-travel back to convince the country's president not to store the nuclear weapons that destroyed everything. But Omo Olukun ultimately decides to forego saving Earth and instead seeks his own power and interests. The book taught me that I can't romanticize sea creatures as our saviors. Sometimes they still embody and enable the worst of us because we humans have agency in the traumas we inflict, and we have to deal with that.

Abuela, I do have to face that while you're at last standing up for yourself as a Black woman here in New York and have always talked about how people treat you, you want to have nothing to do with the Black histories and communities of the Dominican Republic. I know that my mom and her family have been so racist to you. I know my relationship with you is separate from them. But you won't even let me talk about it. You won't let me talk about my father (your son) leaving our home when I was only five. Maybe you and I can never talk with each other, but couldn't we talk through a magical or divine creature? If a sea anemone granted me time-travel power, I wouldn't use it to become rich and powerful. I would use it to make climate activists rule the world. And also to undo Trujillo, to undo anti-Blackness, to undo whatever made you so silent. I used to come with you to church to honor Altagracia, protectoress of the Dominican Republic. But I'm also remembering all of that Santeria paraphernalia from the botanicas and the Afro-magic you put in my life. There's more you want to tell me, right?

Abuela and Ajji, we realize that we cannot make-believe our way out of what's in our bones and flesh. So many anguished people before and around us have experienced whatever trage-dies you've both experienced. That pain has made us who we are, including the hypocrisies and the contradictions. It has made us survivors, and it has made us perpetrators. We can't forget the abuses we've received or inflicted because we have to fight for a better and safer world. And that's why we will always, always, hold onto you. Every single part of you. Even and especially the parts you wouldn't want us to.

With love, Yandelis and Kavya

FINISH LINE

"I think we went off the deep end, no pun intended, with this particular letter," Yandelis pointed out at their next meeting, as they looked at their final draft.

Kavya laughed. "Probably. It's not where I thought we'd go when we first talked about the future. It may not make any sense to anyone else. But it feels right." She played with the scented candle on her desk, flick-ing pieces of wax here and there.

Writing to her grandmother had been wrenching. But it was also a gorgeous thing. She scraped together the wax detritus. She was mainly surprised that she felt a bit hopeful. Most importantly, she was slowly coming to terms with her decision to tell her sons the truth.

"Let's take another look now at the overall letter project assignment."
Kavya opened her laptop.

Letter Project Instructions/Community Workbook

This short guide can be used over a semester by instructors or over
a few months by community organizations or even by a group of
friends or family members. The purpose is to examine historic/
family/intergenerational trauma as a lens to better understand
global politics and to acknowledge the importance of these family stories. Some people may choose to work on the prompts
alongside artistic expression, somatic and trauma therapy, exercise and movement, and/or immersion in nature.

Module 1: Who Is Participating?

Share your journeys to this moment of exploring intergenerational trauma in a circle or in a shared document with names or
anonymously. Three possible prompts include:

- Set a timer for five minutes and complete the phrase, "I am from
  . . .". Use short phrases to describe identities, loved ones, travels,
  homes, hopes, activist causes.
- Read a variety of definitions and critiques of the concept of
  intergenerational trauma and discuss which ideas resonate.
- Describe what you might ask your ancestors, elders, or
  predecessors in your families and communities to prepare you for
  discussing intergenerational trauma. Imagine their responses.

Module 2: Research and Story Time

- As a group, choose a topic (e.g., slavery, specific wars, partitions,
  apartheid, genocides, occupations, migrations, ecological
  changes, oppressive structures, authoritarianism, statelessness, or
  mythologies) that has had generational impact. Some instructors/
  facilitators may designate issues to discuss. Co-create a varied
  and diverse reading list of articles, books, graphic novels, fiction,
  testimonies, journalistic essays, poetry, grassroots newsletters and
  zines, and so on, about families' (however defined) experiences
  with the chosen topic. Participants then sign up for which stories

on the list they will each read. Together, discuss and research the topic and the stories extensively. How do the stories speak to each other, even across time periods, genres, locations, and truths? How might intergenerational trauma be coded or indicated in the stories, such as physical, emotional, or psychological symptoms and experiences; types of interactions/encounters between family members and kinship networks; and, dreams and memories? Participants may bring in personal/family stories where relevant.

Module 3: The Letter Project

- Each participant will individually write a letter to someone who is in some way responsible for, complicit with, or a witness to the topic. Examples could include:
  - o Confronting a relative (or even oneself) about perpetuating a type of oppression
  - o Questioning a professor, organization, medical professionals, or media about how they portray families/communities from certain places/cultures as backwards, dangerous, incompetent, damaged, etc.
  - o Challenging the board of an organization regarding its assumptions about the communities it serves or the politics of a product it markets
  - o Naming how the actions of a historical figure played a role in the topic/event
  - o Praising a social movement that confronted and changed the trajectory of an issue

- When writing, consider what you learned about your chosen topic that you might not have without the focus on historic, family stories. What are you trying to accomplish with your letter (validation of experiences, expression of emotions, naming injustice, calls to action)? What are the ethical dangers of speaking for/representing others' stories and the limits of speaking for oneself?
- After sharing the letters, gather to analyze and debrief.

"It's a little nerdy, but you know, it's good," Yandelis said. "I kind of feel like taking it home to my family and having us do it!"

"I love that. We'll meet up before the semester starts so that we can talk about how we embed the assignment in each of the units. And of course, we'll need to integrate my letters and our co-written letter plus the reading lists."

The sounds of a bullhorn and faint yelling came from the direction of City Hall.

Yandelis peeked out the office window. "Oh, I can't tell what the signs say or what they're shouting. I always like to know who's rallying."

She turned back to Kavya. "You know, the letter project is the main thing I remember from that one class. Before that, I really thought I was too stupid to understand global politics. There were just too many countries and this institution and that institution. I couldn't even spell the word sovereignty."

"You never told me that! You've done so well in all the classes you've taken with me."

"In the classes you've taught for the Gender Studies department, sure. The Dominican Republic and race paper was in one of those, remember? Not to sound cocky, but that's my thing. But you start talking about theories of international relations, and you lose me."

"I wish I had known," Kavya said sadly.

"But that's my point." Yandelis moved over to the desk, tapping her nails across the top. "When I did that letter project, it opened this door, and then I could begin to understand the academic stuff. Now I can really pay attention to what's going on in the world. Now I can even major in political science!"

She paused as she click-clacked her nails back and forth across the desk. "Professor, doing this letter with you made me face some things. But it also validated some of what I've been through. It was good to write to our grandmothers after all."

"I agree with all of that. Oh, I'm so, so happy." Kavya placed her hands over her heart.

And it was true. She doubted this project every other day, but even the wildest idea could become meaningful if she did it with her students. She started to tear up a bit, realizing how much trust her students had in her. To just say yes when she asked them to try something.

And she trusted them too. Even Janet wouldn't have been able to convince her to write to Ajji. Or to get her personally invested in sea cows.

"Listen, I'm so grateful, Yandelis. This project has been a labor of love for me, and you helped me make sense of it all. Thank you for that."

"Aww, Professor! That means so much. You're my role model."

Kavya cleared her throat. "Alright. Enough with all this mush. You're free to go. You get to take the rest of July off, and we'll touch base in August, okay?"

They packed their laptops and papers. As they left her office and Kavya locked the door, Yandelis said, "I'm gonna run to the bathroom, but have fun on your trip. I still don't know why you're going to Canada in the summer."

Kavya laughed. "Where do you think we should go?"

"Santo Domingo, obviously. If you ever go, let me know, and I have some friends who will hook you up."

"In all seriousness, thank you. I can only go on this trip with some peace of mind because you brought us over the finish line."

Yandelis gave her a smile before turning around the corner.

Kavya started in the other direction toward the elevators, lost in thought.

"Kavya!"

She turned to see the colleague she admired the most, Barbara, a professor of history who had been at the university for almost forty years. Barbara was relentlessly, aggressively jovial, wearing a daily costume of a bright top, denim or tulle skirt, and fishnet stockings. She sometimes plopped herself down among a group of faculty arguing in the dining hall. She would tell everyone to lighten up and have some fun.

If someone tried to turn the topic back to whatever very serious matter was previously being discussed, she would place her hand on that person's hand, her large emerald ring glistening against her soft crepe skin. Her fingers would audaciously wrap themselves around the stunned colleague's hand. And she would say something like, *Aren't you bored with this conversation and all the name-dropping? Let's talk about something interesting!*

"Barbara! How are you? I didn't think anyone else was here over the summer."

Barbara motioned for her to come into her office. "This is the only place I can get some peace and quiet," she explained over her shoulder.

Kavya followed and watched Barbara rummage around in a drawer, her bracelets clanking against each other.

"Ah!" Barbara walked up to Kavya with an envelope in her hand. "I've been meaning to email you because this is my letter of support for your tenure application."

Kavya took the envelope. "Thank you so much. This means more than you know." She didn't have the heart to tell her that everything was digitized now, but she would figure that part out later.

She hovered uncertainly until Barbara gestured toward the two chairs in the corner.

Barbara sat down in the chair with a tattered scarf tossed on it. "You don't need to thank me. Your work is interesting to me."

Kavya smiled as she settled into the matching leather armchair. "That's so kind. Now that the letter is done and you don't think I'm trying to kiss up to you, I can tell you that in graduate school, I read your work on histories of Rohingya self-determination. It was so helpful in my thinking about the politics of statelessness."

Barbara nodded as if she had heard this compliment many times. She smiled in an irrepressibly cheery way that reminded Kavya of Yumiko. She sure gravitated toward these happy older women. Can anyone say Mommy issues? Kavya reached for her purse then, and held it close, knowing that the tiny picture of her mother was always in her wallet.

Gripping the purse, something abruptly came to mind. She hesitated. "You heard about what happened with Mark and that whole public fight, right? Will that hurt my tenure case?"

"I don't go to those meetings with the admin anymore, but oh yes, I heard the gossip," Barbara responded casually. "Don't worry. Your dossier is strong, and you'll have the support of our dean. Nothing will happen."

"I really doubt myself sometimes. Why am I trying so hard to get job stability in a place like this? Academia is so messed up."

"Are you that upset over Mark?"

Kavya shook her head. "I just am so naïve sometimes. I know that what we do with our students makes a difference, to them, to us, beyond the university. But the university itself? This place? I go to these meetings and think I can have a positive impact. I shouldn't have gone. There were less than twenty faculty who showed up."

"Kavya, I've been here long enough to know that I can avoid stepping inside a snake pit. Maybe I should have gone to that meeting, though, because it sounds like the tenured faculty didn't push back."

"Snake pit? I've never heard you talk like that."

"Let me give you some advice, even though you didn't ask. Even *after* you get tenure, I want you to be discerning."

"I know. I go in like a bulldozer." Kavya sighed.

"No, you're standing up for what's right. You can do that. But you do have to watch out for the vipers and the Tennessee fainting goats." Barbara chuckled upon seeing Kavya's face. "Vipers have hinged fangs. When they latch on, it's to sink down deep. They will do anything to get their prey. Now, the goats. They call them fainting goats because they get frightened easily and fall over from their muscles contracting and stiffening. They'll leave you hanging and let you take the heat. Figure out which of your colleagues and the administrators are which. Don't let the vipers see your vulnerable spots. Don't let the goats fool you into thinking they're anyone's allies."

"Whew. Wow." Kavya leaned back. "There are a couple of colleagues I refer to with my friends as the White Women Brigade. Maybe they're vipers!"

Barbara laughed. "Oh, you mean Teri and Lynn!"

Kavya gasped.

Barbara laughed even harder. "Those two are such con artists, aren't they? I don't know why everyone buys what they're selling. I'd have to think about this, but are they the invasive pests in the academic taxonomy? Are they something that can camouflage, like lizards or scorpions? I don't know, but don't engage and steer clear."

"Ha! How do I thank you for this incredible advice?"

"Take me out for a nice dinner when I retire, and I'll tell you some stories."

"Ooh. I do love stories," Kavya replied, rubbing her hands together.

Barbara's smile disappeared. "Well," she said slowly. Her bracelets jingled as she brushed her hair out of her eyes. She started and stopped a few times. "I'm telling you this because I'm leaving this place soon, but they certainly went to all kinds of lengths to break the feminist in me."

Kavya stammered, "Oh, I'm sorry, I didn't mean to make light of it."

"And now most of my younger colleagues just see me as this old, silly white woman. Maybe I am. But I was also a witness to so much. For example, you'll notice that no Black female faculty have been retiring recently. They left a long time ago. I saw and tried to fight against how they were treated, but I failed. You'll need to keep your eyes open to what's happening around you, to other people, okay? When you get tenure, you will have to become even more awake."

"I'm so sorry for what you went through." Kavya looked at her colleague with concern. "When the other faculty left, or when things happened to you, did even one person really stand up for you or any of them?"

"Only some goats." Barbara waved her hand, as if to push away any memories clouding the room. She stood up and headed to the door.

Kavya swiftly followed her. "Thank you for sharing so openly with me. Really, it means a lot to me. Thank you for the recommendation letter. And thank you for being a light around here."

"Oh, it's okay." Barbara patted her on the shoulder. "You're an excellent candidate for tenure. I have always told you that you have such a bright future."

Kavya waved goodbye, took the stairs by the elevator bank, and walked outside. She blinked in the bright sun. She watched the summer school students walking about, a few smoking as they leaned against the bike racks.

Did she have a bright future?

STAY

After much hemming and hawing, Kavya finally typed out the text and pressed send. *Okay, Helen, I'm obviously avoiding you. I promise to make an appointment soon. I need to tell you everything, but I need to tell my sons first.*

It had been about three months since Mohan's visit. Two months since telling Janet the truth. Samir and Kabir would be home soon.

Kavya coughed from the fumes of the oven cleaner she had just used. The mid-July heat made it impossible to open the windows. She looked around to see if there was anything else left to clean.

She was wiping down the countertops one more time when Samir let himself in with his key. Kabir soon followed.

Kavya ran to tackle them with hugs.

As they dragged their bags in, she bit her nails. She walked back and forth in the kitchen as she listened to them settling in. Water running for a shower, someone on the phone, the thumping of the suitcases.

She ordered pizza. When it arrived, she asked them to bring the box out to the backyard.

She watched her sons sprinkle hot chili flakes on their slices and talk over each other.

It was like her father's visit all over again. The building pressure. The dry mouth. The clenching stomach. *Spit it out. Now.*

"My loves," Kavya started. "I want to tell you something."

Kabir asked wryly, "Are we going to be burning the Bhagavad Gita now?"

Kavya shot him a look.

"Sorry, Mom. I'm listening," Kabir said sheepishly.

Kavya took a deep breath. She looked out at the backyard and glimpsed the sky peeking through the branches of the London Plane tree, its bark peeling off and scattered throughout the grass like little scrolls.

She exhaled the breath she was holding and looked back at her sons. "I told you that when my dad visited, we talked a lot about caste, right?"

They both nodded.

"More happened. We also ended up talking about Neela and how she mistreated me."

Samir and Kabir looked at each other.

"I always thought my aunt had it in for me. Maybe she did. But I also think she was suffering horribly and needed support and care. I think she probably even frightened herself with the way she acted."

"Oh, shit." Samir almost seemed scared.

"There's more," she added gently. "I called my dad after he got home and learned that after my mom died, my dad only asked Pramod to adopt me. He never even *asked* his own sister."

Samir's mouth dropped open. Kabir shook his head in disbelief.

"And I also found out that . . ." She paused and realized that her body was shaking.

Samir put down his pizza and gently touched her hand. "Are you okay?"

"My mother died by suicide." Her voice cracked.

Within seconds, Samir's eyes welled up. Kabir slowly put his head in his hands.

Kavya started to cry. She couldn't stop. The tears were pouring out of her now. "It's awful. It's so awful."

Samir stroked her hand and then held it. "Mama. Oh, God. That is brutal."

She nodded, wiping her eyes with her other hand. She looked down at Samir's hand. His hand was so much bigger than hers. She remembered holding his curled-up fist while he slept as a baby.

She cleared her throat and tried to steady herself. She sniffled, aware of the pollen that had fallen all over the backyard furniture.

"You know that I have been trying to understand my family history. There is something there that is dark and ugly, something that emerged because of colonialism, because of caste, maybe neither. The real reason I always track your locations on my phone is not just from being an over-protective mom, but because of something that goes back to when I was a kid."

Everything inside of her throbbed with sadness, but she kept talking. "Neela always threatened to kill herself, and it planted this fear that I've never been able to shake. And I only ended up in her care because my dad thought that was the only way to protect me from him, the guy whose wife killed herself. It's all so screwed up, guys."

As Samir winced, wiping away his own tears, a realization hit her.

She spoke slowly. "Maybe everything that I thought was about my dad not wanting me was actually me picking up on his survivor's guilt. I think I absorbed that guilt because I sure as hell grew up feeling like I had done something wrong most of the time. I don't know how much of that was my dad, and how much of that was Neela."

She stopped as she watched Samir train his eyes on her. Kabir still had one hand over his face, head down.

She continued, aware that this was the first time she was saying any of these thoughts aloud, "Last summer, after y'all left for college, he and I met up, but it was the first time for me as an adult that we were alone. It must have stirred up everything, things I can't even remember, like being three and being left by him."

She then smiled at Samir, who was still looking at her. "Honey, I remember you both when you were three years old. You were so aware of everything, especially my place in your life. I was your whole world. Who knows what must have happened to me, to have lost both my mother and my father one fine day."

She looked back and forth between the boys, desperately hoping that they knew that she never wanted to pass on any of that pain to them.

Samir looked ashen, his face almost gray. His grip on his mother's hand had not loosened. Their hands, intertwined, grew clammy.

Kabir finally lifted his head. He was in disbelief, his eyes downcast. He picked at the pizza in front of him, scraping his finger across the crust.

Kavya added, "There was so much silence and covering up, I don't even know what I don't know."

It was time. It was time to tell them.

"So, umm. In my family, it wasn't just silence." She cleared her throat. "It was that you ran away from what was hard. And me too. I ran away from my family. But I've also made you run away."

Kabir jutted his chin forward. "Huh? What does that mean?"

Kavya sat still. She took in the doughy cheesy scent of the pizza. A slight breeze picked up just then, crisp against her skin, slightly cooling her body from the sun's strong rays and the heat rising within her. She wanted to freeze this moment, a family dinner in their little backyard.

It was time.

"I was wondering if you ever wanted to know who your father is." She pushed her legs together. They wouldn't stop trembling. Her entire body weakened, as if she hadn't eaten in days.

Samir let go of his mother's hand.

Kabir slitted his eyes. "The sperm guy?"

"Yes," Kavya said carefully. "I know you both were affected by not really knowing anything about him." She cried yet again. "I'm sorry. I let it affect you, and I led you away from ever even trying to discover the truth. But I was scared."

Samir blinked. "Who is he?"

"Your biological father was someone I knew well. For a long time. Not just some random guy from one night."

"A friend?" Samir asked. Kabir looked away. His jaw slowly clenched. He clasped his hands together.

"Someone I was dating for a few years. And I left him before I discovered I was pregnant. And I was scared the guy would find out and cause problems for me, for the two of you."

Her voice caught as she continued, "And I was embarrassed, so I just told Janet's family it was some guy I met one night instead of the ex-boyfriend, because they knew the ex. And they disapproved of him."

Samir asked, "What was wrong with him?"

Kavya blew air out through her lips. She watched a bee flying around the flowers.

"Mom!" Samir exclaimed.

Kavya was startled by how deep and demanding his voice was.

"Do you two remember how I would have those talks with you about what a respectful relationship looks like? And once I gave you an example of a particularly bad relationship I was in?"

"Yes." Samir dragged the word out, looking baffled.

Kabir's jaw pulsated.

"Ranjeet. His name was . . . is Ranjeet," Kavya said.

The boys traded looks again.

Samir asked incredulously, "That's the guy? The abuser guy? That guy is our *father*?"

Kavya nodded. She grabbed a napkin to blow her nose. She said quickly, "I never told you. But I also never told him, and he even has a wife and kids with her. And I know you might never forgive me. And I'm so sorry. I'm so sorry. I'm sorry."

The boys fell silent. Kavya looked back and forth at their faces. She took another napkin.

Then, Samir stood up and left.

"Samir?" she asked. She quickly turned to Kabir.

Kabir gave her a wounded, enraged look she had never before seen. "What the fuck? What the fuck were you thinking?"

Kavya sat, stunned.

She eventually whispered, "Stop, don't talk to me like that." She had never seen him this angry. She could see the veins in his forehead.

"Oh, I can't be mad?" He bristled.

"Yes, yes, okay? Yes, you can be as angry as you want. Just be careful how you're speaking to me."

"Did you even want us?" Kabir glared at her. "An abusive man got you pregnant. I find it hard to believe you just wanted to keep us."

"You're the best decision I ever made."

"Exactly!" Kabir threw his hands up in the air. "A decision *you* made. It's always you deciding, right? The first time we asked about our dad is when you should have explained who he was."

"You were little kids. I'm supposed to tell you that your father was abusive to me? I'm supposed to tell you after everything I did to protect you from him? To make sure he never found us?"

"But you didn't even tell us when we got older. I think you were actually scared he would find out he had two additional children and that he'd want to meet us. Or maybe even be a father to us."

"Yes, fine! Can't it be all of those reasons? I'm your mother, and I am supposed to protect you from people like that," Kavya cried out.

"You tried to erase the fact that we have a father! You don't get that even if he is bad, we still need to know who he is. Is that where we get our height? Is that why I have a temper? Is that why I punched the hole in the wall after we moved here?" Kabir moved his arms emphatically with each question.

Kavya said frantically, "No, you're nothing like him, never! I screwed up, but don't ever think you're like him. You just punched a wall once. You were angry and moody from all the change from the move. You were a teenager. I'm a hothead too, you know!"

"No! You've been the best mom throughout our whole lives. You can be blunt, and you stand up for others, but you're not a hothead. So, try again." Kabir clenched his fists and shook them near his head. "I have had something so angry inside of me, my entire life. I never knew why! Admit that this anger is from him. It's from him!"

Kavya quietly cried, almost whimpering. She was barely making any sound, but inside, she was desperate, like a wild animal separated from her young. She was terrified as she watched this young man, whose every fold and crevice she had known when he was a baby, transform into something unknown.

Kabir lowered his hands. He was breathing heavily. Kavya tried to meet his eyes, but they were looking well past her.

"I have to find him. I have to see what he is." Kabir erupted, "I have to beat his fucking ass! I have to find out why he did that to you. I have to see if he's sorry. I want to see what he says when he sees me. I have been wondering my *whole* life about him. I fucking researched every Vinay in Texas I could find. I bought one of those DNA tests that I couldn't bear to do. Do you understand? Do you get it?"

Kavya nodded, the tears still flowing down her face. "I do, my love." She desperately added, "Find Neela and Pramod too if you want to. My father will have all the information. Just please, don't cut me off."

Kabir stood up. He walked toward the screen door but stopped to say, "The only one around here who cuts people off is you." And then he disappeared into the house. She heard him scream, "What the fuck!"

A door slammed. She wondered where Samir had gone. But she stayed outside. She looked up at the sky again.

When she had bought this house, she told Janet, "It's such a relaxing backyard with a gorgeous tree!"

But now the tree looked diseased. The scrolls of bark looked like discarded cardboard chewed up by stray animals. There were too many weeds. A crazy lady lived here.

She leaned back in her chair and put her hands over her face. *Please, please, please let it be okay.* Her eyelids were swollen from all the tears.

An hour later, the yard was dark. She swatted at the mosquitoes nibbling on her legs. She saw the light on in the kitchen and stood up. Rubbing her shoulders and neck, she eventually made her way inside, the pizza box and plates balanced on her arm.

The boys were sitting at the table, next to each other, with headphones on. They took them off when they saw her. She left everything on the counter and came over to them.

She knelt on the floor and put her hands on the table. "I'm so sorry. Please believe that I regret how I handled this. I am so sorry." She started to cry again.

Samir leaned forward. "You don't have to keep saying sorry," he said quietly. He sighed and pulled a chair out from the table and pointed it toward her. "Go ahead and sit."

She slid into the chair. For the first time in their lives, she couldn't quite read their expressions. Her stomach sank.

"Where did you both end up going?" she asked.

Samir shrugged. "I just went to the park and walked around."

"Bike ride," Kabir replied curtly.

"Okay." She swallowed. "Well, we're all here now. I'm here. Ask me anything. I'll tell you anything. I'll do anything. If you need Helen to find us a family therapist, I can do that."

Kabir put up his hands. "Mom. Let's just slow down, okay? I think both Samir and I have cooled off for now. But I think we just have to deal with all of this pretty slowly."

For a second, Kavya was relieved to hear Kabir act as "the voice of reason." A bit of what once was.

"It's probably a good thing me and Sam are away for the summer," Kabir continued. "We'll get some time to think, all three of us, on our own. Away from each other."

Samir nodded. "Yeah. I just don't even know what to think. How do I even digest this?"

Kabir looked at his brother. "Sam, I might want to find him. That means that he would find out about you, clearly, if he finds out about me."

"I don't know, man. Let's just talk about it when you decide. And tell Mama when you decide."

Another brief joyous moment as she heard Samir call her "Mama."

"I would tell you both if I decided to contact him," Kabir replied.

"Would it scare you if Kabir did that?" Samir asked his mom. "This guy wouldn't be, like, violent, would he? Like show up with a gun?"

Kavya replied slowly, "No, no weapons." She imagined Ranjeet in front of them right now. What would that be like? "But I will never be alone with him. And I'm not sure how angry he'll be once or if he finds out." She paused. "Right now, the only thing that scares me is that I will lose you both."

"We're nineteen now. No custody battles," Samir offered.

"Yes, that's true. But I can still be afraid of losing you," Kavya said. "Because of how I broke your trust and kept things from you. I have made so many mistakes."

The boys were silent. She was hoping they would say something like, *We still trust you,* or maybe even, *We would never talk to the man who hurt you.* But they were so quiet.

"Maybe we do this together," she finally said. "I want to find out more about my mom's side of the family. And you want to find out about your father. We can do a video call with my dad, and get his help to . . ." She trailed off.

"I have a question," Kabir said quietly. "In all your gender violence research, have you ever found any statistics about the chances that someone will be abusive and violent if their parent was? Like, can it get passed down?"

Kavya's heart leapt right up into her throat. She felt the throbbing move up her neck and into her ears. "Oh, baby, no. I mean, it's complicated. I've been studying intergenerational trauma, actually, and it's related to what you're asking. But whatever happened before you is not your destiny."

"You're not like him." Samir turned to his brother. "I don't know what he was like. But I can tell you that you're not like him. I would tell you if you were, I swear."

Kabir ignored his brother, his face twisted with frustration. "You're using the mom voice. You're trying to make things better. Tell me the truth."

"I get what you're saying. I sometimes get scared that I inherited something from Neela," Kavya said loudly, maybe to make sure Kabir really heard her. Maybe to speak over the pulsing sound rocking her head. "Trust me, I had too many times to count when raising you. Yes, Janet Auntie was there, but I was the parent and ultimately responsible. If I yelled at you or felt overwhelmed, I was scared I might be like my aunt. And that I would make you feel alone, like the way she made me feel."

Seeing Kabir's expression soften, Kavya kept going, "That's not even counting what happened on my mom's side. Her mom died young but how? Why did my dad say my mom didn't really want contact with her family? How would I even begin to guess what traumas got passed down through my mom?"

She thought she saw the slightest frown on Samir's face. She quickly said, "But I'm not suicidal. I'm not."

The boys were silent. Samir's face was strained. Kabir had a faraway look in his eyes. She had been talking *so* much. Why weren't they saying anything?

Needing to make them feel better, Kavya continued, maybe a bit too cheerily, "If there's anything I've learned in all the work I've done, it's that what our relatives did or experienced before us doesn't define our own lives and decisions."

Kabir groaned.

"What's wrong?" Samir asked.

His brother rolled his eyes. "Mom's bullshit therapy talk."

"Well, that therapy talk is exactly what has been helping me make sure I do get to decide who I am," Kavya remarked quietly. She quickly pushed past her shock that she was praising her work with Helen and continued, this time the words rising unmistakably from her gut, "Listen. My whole life with you both, I worried that Neela and Ranjeet would find me. I don't even know what I thought they might do, but the fear took on a life of its own. But now, I've said everything out in the open, to my father and to you. It's this new, simple freedom of not having to hide anymore. I never thought I could do this. Things can change, okay? I believe that."

She raised a finger. "Oh! I just thought of something else. I never inherited Neela's colorism. Truly. I think I must have seen pictures of my mom and realized at some level that we were the same skin tone. And I didn't think about that until now. See? I went on a different path than Neela."

Her revelations did not seem to move Kabir. "I don't think you've told us everything, Mom. What else should we know?"

Kavya thought for a moment. She was so tired. Her brain was slowing down, begging for rest. Had she ever spoken this much about herself in her entire life? "I told you that I changed my name when I was pregnant to give all three of us my mother's maiden name."

Kabir snorted. "That's not true, either?"

"It is! But I also changed it because I didn't want Ranjeet or Neela to find me when I had you. I made it so that they couldn't find me or you."

The boys didn't say anything. Kabir chewed on his lip.

Samir finally responded, "At some point, you do have to tell us everything he did. Our . . . about this Ranjeet guy. What happened that you had to go to these extremes?"

Kavya was on the cusp of promising anything, of apologizing once again. But she needed to own her decisions. "I will tell you everything. But, guys, my choices didn't feel extreme at the time. They felt urgent and necessary, because of the decisions *Ranjeet* made, stuff that scared even Janet Auntie. Got it?" She shifted in the chair, very aware of her old tailbone injury.

And then she turned to Kabir, a little defiant. "And yes. I did consider terminating my pregnancy. But I was in my late twenties. I had finished my schooling. I was in a state of mind where I couldn't possibly imagine entering a relationship ever again. But I also always wanted to be a mother, so why get an abortion and figure out parenthood later when the promise of you was already there? I wanted you so much. I thought I deserved to, at long last, create the kind of family I always wanted to have growing up." Kavya's eyes teared up again, as she said emphatically, "I wanted you, baby."

Kabir raised an eyebrow and kept chewing his lip. Samir looked down at the table. She stopped herself from prodding them. She let it be.

* * *

Over the next two weeks, Kabir, Samir, and Kavya bumped into each other in the hallways, the kitchen, on the way to the bathroom. They were shy and polite with each other. In bits and pieces, she told them about Ranjeet, Neela, her letter project, Mohan, and her Amma. Her sons did not say much.

The three did not talk over each other or joke around as they once did. But every once in a while, when watching a show together or sitting down together for dinner, Kabir would make a wise-ass comment, or Samir would quote lines from his favorite comedians. And then they would all laugh and share a small moment together. And then someone would look away.

And then it was time for Kabir to leave for Albany for a short-term job his suitemate helped him get. And it was time for Samir to move back into the dorms, work as a campus tour guide, and struggle with computer science in a second summer class. Because they were no longer hers.

Kavya stood on the sidewalk as the boys rolled their suitcases out of the house.

"Call me when you get in safely. Both of you," she said.

Samir put his arm around Kabir. "This will be the longest I will have ever been away from you."

Kabir smiled as he leaned his head in. "Remember how Janet Auntie tried to get us to develop telepathic powers? She said at some point we would live apart and all twins should be able to communicate that way?"

Samir laughed and slapped his brother on his back. "Dumbass."

Kabir turned to his mother and hugged her tightly.

"Mom," he whispered. "Take care of yourself for me, okay?" Her tears started before she could say a word. "Oh Jesus, Mom. I was trying to make sure you're good."

"No, no," Kavya said, as she wiped her nose with the back of her hand. "I'm good. It's all good."

Samir hugged her, too. "I love you, Mama. My sweet Mama."

And then she watched them walk away toward the subway station, the suitcases rolling in unison. She wanted them to turn back to wave one more time. Or to run back for one more hug. They didn't. She walked back into the house only when she could no longer see them.

TELL ME ANYTHING

The week after Kavya's sons left, she told Helen the truth about Ranjeet.

Helen only said, "I did wonder." She seemed genuinely thrilled at Kavya's newfound openness. Kavya, on the other hand, was not so sure.

But despite the upheaval of finally telling her children her worst secret, the panic attacks Kavya anticipated didn't come.

She texted Helen one day, perplexed by her sense of calm, even with her relationship with her sons being the tensest it had ever been. *Helen, something bad is coming. I can feel it. When is the other shoe going to drop?*

A couple of hours later, Helen texted back, *Who says it's going to drop? There's a reason I say that the truth will set you free. And if the other shoe drops, you'll be okay. I'm here.*

* * *

A few days later, Kavya sat on the couch, listening to her favorite recording of Chopin's piano concertos. She stared at the phone in her hand. She wanted to be the new Kavya who had promised herself she would stop running.

She called her father.

"Hello? Who's that?"

"Dad, you know it's me. It says so on your cell phone."

"Oh, yes, okay. Hi, Kavya."

And then they had the world's most boring conversation about what they ate. And then hung up. But it was a relief to just talk. Not to push him for details, to make demands, to threaten to cut him off.

Every couple of days, she called. They described what they had eaten for their meals and talked about the weather. A series of non-sequiturs as only her father could deliver them.

The phone calls were brief exchanges of random details about themselves, without acknowledging the emotional weight of what it meant to be in contact, without acknowledging either had any kind of inner life. The small certainty of surface-level vapidities, delivered without any logic or sequence, calmed Kavya instead of infuriating her. It was even kind of nice to free herself from the confines of conventional conversations.

Mohan upped the ante in one call by going into full detail about how his plumber was conspiring with the electrician to swindle him.

One time when she called, he only answered after several rings.

"Hello?"

"Hi, Dad."

She heard silence. Then her father stuttered, "Okay. I am, umm. Yes, so. Okay."

She heard a woman's voice then, and Kavya quickly hung up. She was not sure whether she was more scared that it was a girlfriend—she had never asked him if he dated after Amma's death, and he still wore his wedding ring—or that it was Neela. It happened so quickly she couldn't figure out if she recognized the voice, or that it just sounded familiar because of that particular Mumbai Marathi accent.

After that, Kavya's nightmares, which had dulled in their power and frequency, resurged, threatening to take over once again.

Neela was now a regular visitor at night. Always off to the side, face hidden, as Kavya's dream-mind tried to focus on her.

I see you! Come out! Face me!

But the mornings after, she later realized, she was able to feel well-rested, even steady. She stayed upright. Maybe because she had submitted her tenure dossier and didn't have that hanging over her. Maybe it was a fluke. But Kavya decided to try to be happy that she had possibly reentered Neela's orbit—the Dreaded Bad Thing she had always feared—and she was still here, standing.

The sadness that always lived inside of her had not abated. But the little pieces of joy scattered haphazardly throughout her soul were starting to find each other and connect to each other, until there was a tapestry of delight and happiness, tenuous as it all was, growing and growing. If you pulled at any piece, it might fall apart, like when you poked your finger at a spider's web and watched it disintegrate as the threads wrapped around your nail. But if you left the web alone and just watched it, you could admire that it was beautifully crafted, and you could believe it was the most powerful thing in the world.

And so, that's how, several days later, Kavya gathered the strength to call her father again.

She leaned back on her couch and exhaled. She looked around her home, taking in the slightly scuffed furniture, the just-mopped floors, the stack of mail by the front door, as if to remind herself, *I am an adult now and this is where I live. I'm a grown-up. I can do anything.*

"Hi, Dad."

"Oh, Kavya. We have not talked in some time."

Kavya sighed. "Okay, so I heard a woman's voice the last time. And I kind of freaked out. I told Samir and Kabir about it."

"You did?" Mohan asked.

"Yes, I am being more open with the boys. I told them Ranjeet is their dad. I told them about Neela. I told them about Amma."

Her honesty was rewarded with the sounds of Mohan breathing.

"Okay," Kavya finally said. "I'm not yet ready to ask who that woman was. And whatever, maybe someday you and I will talk about Neela. But maybe never because I'm not yet able to. Oh. And Kabir may try to track down Ranjeet. Not now. I don't know."

Silence.

"Why don't you ever have anything to say?" Kavya asked.

"There's never anything I can say to make things better."

"But even that is sometimes enough. What you just said."

"Okay, Kavya. Can I tell you about the plumber now?"

Swim

Kavya and Mingming hooked arms as they walked toward the Black Loyalist Heritage Centre. The sunlight beamed on them from every direction, bouncing off metal ribbons along the walled entrance.

Written in black on a yellow ribbon were the words, *Is this the place? BIRCHTOWN, haven of freedom?*

The brown ribbon next to it said, *This is the place. Our harbor of hope.*

They followed the ribbons inside, through the doors ensconced in floor-to-ceiling glass walls. That's when they learned that those ribbons were imagined conversations between the people who once lived in Birchtown—the largest settlement upon its founding in 1783 of free Black people in the world outside of Africa—and their descendants.

The ribbons continued to alternate between yellow and brown on a brick wall.

I call to you from this place I built.

I am movement unchained. With my feet unfettered on sun-baked earth.

Kavya leaned against Mingming. "Isn't it wild how this place exists? Are there so many more places like this in the world I don't know about? I'm honestly awestruck."

Mingming gave Kavya's arm a squeeze. "When I found out about this, I knew we had to come here. You always come along to the freezing places I want to visit, so I wanted to do a little something for you."

The next day, they drove to Barrington, marveling at the coves and bays along the way. They checked into their hotel and went to the market to pick up baguettes and cheese for an ocean-view picnic at Sand Hills

Beach. After walking along the pathway, they laid out their blanket in a secluded spot. Rolling green hills and a spruce-fir forest hugged the far edges of the path behind them. An endless patchwork of rocks surrounded the white-sand beach in front of them.

Mingming sighed happily as she bit into a large, gooey mozzarella ball. "This is exactly what I need. I can sit here forever."

Mingming eventually took out her novel. Kavya wandered off. She climbed over the rocks until she reached the shoreline. Turning around, she could still see their picnic blanket and the silhouette of Mingming engrossed in her book.

Kavya dropped her phone and thermos on the sand, untied her shoes, slipped off her socks, and dipped a few toes into the water. It was colder than she expected, but she submerged her foot until she got used to the chill.

She put her other foot in and started wading in. She could feel mud and sharp rocks under her feet. She marveled at the sand dunes as she wiggled her toes.

Her body quivered, perhaps from the temperature, or from the beauty of the endless water. She tried to take a deep breath but unexpectedly moaned. She could feel something traveling through her body, something rumbling. It was that familiar feeling of dread, one that was there for as long as she could remember, that maybe she would do something terrible, or someone would do something terrible to her.

And nestled inside that familiar feeling was a scene that now played back vividly.

* * *

The year Kavya started middle school, she had signed up to join the swim team. She had seen all kinds of people on the team, like jocks, of course, but also a nerd, an orchestra kid, a student government kid, and even a couple of the beautiful perfect kids. Maybe it was time to join a sport, which she had heard would look good on college applications.

With Neela's help, Kavya picked out a swimsuit, swim cap, and goggles with the school logo.

Neela even said, "Good girl! You are taking the initiative."

Kavya was thrilled that she had finally done something that made Neela call her a good girl. She grew unbearably excited about the first team meeting, fantasizing about her aunt cheering her on from the sidelines.

Neela was visibly enthusiastic as well. She told Pramod, "Maybe she will win some medals!"

Kavya went to the first swim practice. She inhaled the warm chlorine smell and looked at the white tiled walls inside the pool, which appeared to be waving to her. Neela sat nearby in a row of pool chairs with parents, siblings, and sitters and took out a book.

The coaches finally gathered all the students. A tall, skinny man spoke first. Kavya blushed as she noticed that he wore the same style of tiny swim briefs as the boys. Couldn't he at least wear shorts?

"Welcome to the first day! I'm Coach Grissom. We're gonna do some laps and look at your form, especially your turns, starts, and finishes, as well as your swimming-lane etiquette. You will demonstrate each of the four strokes. Once we determine your skill level, you'll work with Coach Johnson on submitting your sports physicals."

He pointed to a bony woman in a tight, shiny swimsuit that seemed to have cut off her circulation, as her pale limbs were almost translucent.

Coach Grissom continued, "We are starting with freestyle. Let's go!"

Kavya realized with horror that a swim team was not for *learning* how to swim. She was dumbfounded as she let Coach Grissom move her into a line of five children, parallel with four other lines. When the coach blew the whistle, the people in the front of the line dove into the water, smooth and fast. They swam in a way she had never tried, rolling their heads out of the water to open their mouths, and then doing it again and again. Kavya looked around frantically. She had only ever played in pools where her feet could touch the ground.

Who could she tell? How could she stop this?

In a flash, it was her turn. The coach blew the whistle.

Everyone else in her row dove in. So did Kavya.

She landed on her face and belly. It was such a strange, sharp sensation that she gasped. She swallowed water and kicked as hard as she could. She tried to use her arms to get back to the surface. Water seeped into her goggles and stung her eyes.

At last, someone pulled her out and propped her on the edge of the pool. She gagged and coughed. Someone was hitting her on the back, lifting her arms. She couldn't see anyone around her.

She pulled her goggles off and sobbed.

A person behind her sighed.

A voice said, "Don't worry, Tom, I'll take her over to the parents." The person attached to the voice wrapped a scratchy towel around her, helped her up, and whispered, "It's okay, sweetheart. Let's go." Kavya turned around to see a white woman with permed auburn hair and a faded "Swim Mom" T-shirt.

As Kavya tried to process what had just happened, Swim Mom walked her over to Neela—the only Indian adult in the entire building—and said, "Hi ma'am. Your daughter panicked in the pool. She shouldn't be on a swim team."

Neela stared at her book. She did not look up or acknowledge them.

"Ma'am? Do you speak English? I'm sorry, but your daughter?"

Swim Mom stared at Kavya, perplexed.

Kavya wanted to let this strange, kind woman believe that Neela couldn't understand her words. She leaned forward and said quietly to her aunt, "We have to go."

Neela pressed her lips together and flipped the page so hard that it ripped. Kavya turned and said to Swim Mom, "We'll leave." She handed the towel back.

Swim Mom, who was still holding Kavya's hand, squeezed it before letting go. She said hesitantly, "Well, here she is." She turned to Kavya with that familiar look—that one full of pity and confusion strangers often gave her when they saw how Neela behaved—and backed away.

Another woman came up and asked, "Is that girl okay?"

Swim Mom said, "Yeah, but I don't think the mother can understand English." They walked away quickly, as if it were contagious.

Kavya pleaded to her aunt in a low voice, "I'm sorry. I didn't know I already had to know how to swim to be on the team. It's my fault. I'm sorry."

Without saying a word, Neela slammed her book shut, shoved it into her bag, and left the building. Kavya hurried behind her aunt, quickly grabbing her flip flops and her bag with a towel and dry clothes. She opened the exit door to see that Neela was already at the car. She ran barefoot on the hot pavement, still dripping wet and coughing, and wordlessly got into the back seat.

Neela ignored her completely, even while preparing for and eating dinner. As Kavya brought the dishes to the sink, she tentatively asked, "Maybe I should take swimming lessons? I don't want to panic again in the water."

Neela stared at her, a peculiar, vacant look in her eyes. Her aunt said, "It's not my fault you panicked." And she pushed her arms out, away from her own body, like she was batting down some kind of force. "It's not my fault. It's not my fault." Kavya put down the plate she was holding and ran to her room.

Kavya wore that memory close to her, like a sentimental necklace, to remind her that even if she tried to be good and brave, things could still go bad.

* * *

Kavya stood at the water's edge, sucked back into the memories that would not loosen their grip on her. She rubbed her arms. *Stay here. In the present. Nova Scotia. I'm okay.* Mingming was not too far away. They were going to have a wonderful trip together.

The water swirled around her feet as she moved, mutating into so many shades and tones of blue and green. She turned to wade in the other direction, as she was getting used to the frigid temperature.

And that's when she saw her.

She saw Amma. She saw her mother.

A handful of times in her life, she thought she had glimpsed her mother, only to see that it was some stranger. But this time, it really was her. She had not noticed anyone at all when she first made her way to the shore, but there she was now.

Amma was sitting a mere twenty yards away, on a large rock. The same long face and pointed chin. Thin lips with the slightest underbite. Her hair shorn in a pixie cut. Her brown skin tinged slightly yellow. She was wearing a mahogany blouse and a long matching skirt. A big stack of bangles on each arm. She was with other women, all decadently dressed as well.

Kavya moved toward her, her mind racing. Amma had definitely died in the car crash, right? They had to use dental records, her dad had said. Maybe there had been a mistake.

The water got deeper. The wet sand was bogging Kavya down. Her leggings were soaked up to her thighs, and she grunted as she took each step.

She stopped moving and shouted, "Amma!" But she couldn't hear herself over the water hitting the rocks.

And then Amma turned, but not toward her, but toward a strip of land that extended into the ocean and formed a small rocky mound.

Kavya had not noticed, but there were three women sitting on that little hill as well.

Her mother lifted her head and neck and moved a little. Kavya could now see her entire body. She was not sure what she was seeing at first, but it was a tangle of moss over a shimmering latticework of fabric, and the end of the skirt narrowed and then flared out into a wide triangular shape.

Kavya saw that all the women on the rock were flapping wide triangular sheaths of satiny material into the water. She looked closely at her mother. It wasn't fabric. It was some kind of scaly skin.

It was a tail fin.

Oh no. This was it. This was when Kavya broke apart. This was when she left herself and would never become whole again. Of course. It was that ever-present crackling underneath the surface that always threatened to rip her open, like what had happened to Neela, to her own mother, to too many women across the world. That crackling was so loud and fervent she could no longer hear the waves.

But she did not care. She wanted Amma.

Kavya kept walking, deeper into the wound of wounds. The crackling reached a crescendo, in a way that she knew was going to be catastrophic. But she was gloriously happy amid her madness because she would finally be with Amma.

Then, she heard Amma shout, "Look at me! Look at me! Sing for me!"

She realized she had never heard her own mother's voice. It echoed across the water. She looked at the women on the rocky hill. One had a single braid down her back. That woman shook her head and looked down.

"Please!" Amma shouted to the woman. "I need you to sing for me!"

The woman turned around then. She had burned-out eyes, one corroded ridge for a nose, and a lipless ink-black hole for a mouth that opened and unleashed a smooth low-pitched melody. The other women shouted their praise.

Kavya screamed, terrified. She could hear the women, but they could not hear her. She kept screaming and screaming until her throat tore and burned.

Shining from deep inside the singing woman's hollowed-out sockets and charred, crooked lines seemed to be a white-hot light. Who was this woman? Her fin was undulating.

And because no one noticed Kavya's shouts and howls, she leaned forward all the way in. She kept her head above water and clumsily kicked her legs while her arms pushed through the water. But she was getting nowhere, almost like she was going backward. She gagged on the saltwater. She would not turn back to the shore. But she didn't have the energy to keep kicking.

So, she let herself sink. And then she opened her mouth to see how much water she could let in.

DROWN

Something tickled her arm. Kavya opened her eyes.

"Oops, my bag hit you. I didn't mean to wake you from your nap!"

Kavya bolted upright. She looked around frantically. She didn't see her mother, or the singing woman with the burned face, or anyone else but Mingming. When did she get here?

Before Kavya could speak, Mingming said, "Well, now that you're awake, I think we have enough time to go back to shower, and then synchronize to get to the counter-mapping journeys."

Kavya stared at her.

"Not trying to rush you. I just want to make sure we get lodging before trading our points for the passes."

What the hell? Kavya was speechless as Mingming added, "Oh, and you had wanted to look at the brochure."

They stood up. Kavya took the thin, glossy pamphlet from Mingming's hand. Her friend headed back to the car.

Kavya was trapped deep inside of a fog. She looked back at the water, which was draped in gray clouds with not a person or being in sight. She carefully opened the tri-fold document, which then lit up, triggering a voice recording. The booming voice announced what was written in the pamphlet.

Summer 2073 Update. The Atlantic Settler Mutual Aid Network is the first of its kind on Turtle Island, created in 2060 in the Occupied U.S. and Occupied Canada, not long after the Great

Climate Collapses of the 2040s. We extend our gratitude to the Indigenous feminist networks that bless our efforts and continuously create counter-mapping journeys, which redraw sovereignties, re-envision how we relate to each other, and offer travel as a tool of resistance and solidarity.

You are receiving this brochure after bequeathing your homes, redistributing your resources, and committing to new lives that at first may cause a sense of extreme discomfort and loss but will ultimately lead to wholeness and connection. We release ourselves from the use of violence and oppression to get our needs met. We will help you find places to live communally and work with you on ways to barter for food and necessities, enjoy leisure activities, and complete commitments of labor depending on local ecological, social/emotional, and other needs.

Our points system is straightforward. Synchronize with your avatars to keep track of points earned and spent, and to find the list of counter-mapping journeys and related logistics. We currently recommend Oceanic Feminist Immersion for long-term engagement with communities communing with aquatic ecosystems, multiple species, the spirits of those who died during maritime crossings (the enslaved, the indentured, the refugees), and archives of resistance and "intergenerational intimacies" (gratitude to Black feminist elder Alexis Gumbs and her comrades!). As of now, due to recent acts of terror by the Occupying Forces of the U.S., we are no longer participating in The Occupied Sonoran Desert/ Tohono O'odham Living Memorial to Migrants.

You may earn points if you serve as a test subject for emergent counter-maps around the world, or volunteer for focus groups with Indigenous researchers studying 21st-Century settler mentalities.

Thank you for trusting us, yourselves, and each other with our futures.

"Kavya, coming?"

As Kavya opened and closed the brochure, the voice recording started and stopped.

"You okay?" Mingming called.

Kavya waved the brochure in her hand. "What is this? Is this some joke?"

Then, looking down at her body, she noticed that she looked the same, but it did not feel like her body. She looked at Mingming. The same, but also not at all.

"What year is this? Who made this?" She gasped, "Where are my sons? Why don't I know where they are? This thing says I gave up my home. But where did they go?"

She must have died in the water. She must be transitioning to some other world.

Nausea overpowered her. She dropped to her knees and stuck her hands in the sand.

She could hear Mingming hurrying over.

She folded into herself. She curled smaller and smaller, her back rounding, her elbows and knees pointing toward her stomach, as she bent into herself.

"I didn't mean for this to happen. I just wanted my Amma."

FORGIVE

"Just take a few sips."

Kavya opened her eyes to see a straw come toward her and lurched backward, accidentally knocking the water out of Mingming's hand with her flailing arm.

"Whoa, Kavya! Relax, relax," Mingming said anxiously.

Kavya croaked out, "What happened?"

As she looked around, the fog that had previously enveloped her started to lift. The day was sunny and bright again, her body familiar again. She was on the beach, with a towel wrapped around her. Her feet rested at the edge of the water, her clothes soaked.

"What happened?" she asked again.

"I looked up and happened to see you just drop. You fainted or collapsed right as you were coming out of the water."

Kavya's heart was racing. "My kids. Where's my phone?"

Mingming handed it to her. Kavya quickly checked to see that she could find Kabir's location in Albany, and Samir at Stony Brook. "Oh, thank God!" she exclaimed. She stared at the phone's date. 2023.

Mingming handed her a mango juice box out of the cooler. "It's okay. Calm down, and just get your blood sugar back up."

As Kavya sipped, she looked down to see her hands trembling. "Food?" she asked.

Mingming passed over a chocolate granola bar.

Kavya sipped and chewed, as Mingming carefully watched her.

She looked up at Mingming. "I thought I had died. I thought you and I went on some voyage into the future, or I don't know, something like that. And that we gave all our assets and money to Indigenous peoples. I mean, we should, but we haven't, right?"

Mingming's mouth dropped open. "No . . ." She stopped.

Kavya shook her head. "I had some kind of wild dream. Well, more like a dream inside of a dream. I don't know what to call it if I wasn't sleeping. I fainted?"

Mingming nodded silently. She nervously patted Kavya's back. "Ready to stand up?"

Kavya nodded, rising. She stood up and let out a sigh.

After several moments of silence, Mingming said, "So let me get this straight. Even when you've *passed out*, you're still thinking some academic shit, envisioning reparations to Indigenous folks? Is that what you're telling me?"

"I'm honestly wishing I remembered the details," Kavya said earnestly.

Mingming guffawed.

"I'm sorry. I have been so deep into this stuff about futurism and all kinds of things with Yandelis. And obviously, I've also been all over the place. I didn't mean to ruin the day."

"You didn't ruin anything, Kavya! But let's go back. Take a shower and get some more food in you. And I want to ask the hotel if there's a clinic nearby, just to maybe get you checked out?"

"Okay. Maybe."

Kavya looked out at the water. Was it so far-fetched that she wanted her mother to be a mermaid?

Who was the other woman with the burned face?

She watched the water touch and then recede from the shoreline.

Maybe the other woman was what her mother looked like when she crashed her car. It must have gone up in flames and charred every part of the woman whose absence would shape the whole of Kavya's existence.

Mingming picked up the cooler and placed her other arm around Kavya's waist.

"I'm sorry, Mingming," Kavya said quietly.

"Stop saying sorry," Mingming replied.

"I'm sorry," Kavya said automatically. And then, she unexpectedly laughed. "Oh!" she exclaimed, putting her hand over her mouth. That's when the tears started. She was blubbering and hiccupping and snorting.

Mingming put down the cooler and stared at her.

"I'm sorry!" Kavya said, and then she snickered. "I'm sorry I said sorry!" She started giggling uncontrollably. She had no idea what had come over her, but she could not stop laughing or crying. Finally, bent over wheezing and coughing, she choked out a few words, "Sorry. Ha!"

"Holy hell, Kavya." Mingming was amused.

"I always apologize, don't I? It's how I'm built. It's like how I will always be scared. But I've also always been brave." Kavya smiled widely, tears rolling down her face. "I was brave as hell for inviting my dad to stay with me, wasn't I? I have to tell you about my father's visit and my sons' visit. A thousand things have happened. Do you know how courageous I've been, my entire life, since I was a little three-year-old kid?"

Mingming nodded enthusiastically. "I could never do that with my own father. I agree. I've always thought you're brave."

Still giggling, Kavya threw her arms around her friend. "Who cares if you invite your father or anyone else. You're brave, too!" Mingming laughed and hugged her back.

And then Kavya slowly pulled away from their embrace and took a step toward the ocean. She hoped to see Amma again, even though she knew that none of it had happened. She swallowed. The familiar grief lapped at her feet as she stared.

"Kavya, why do you keep looking out there?"

"When I went into the ocean, I thought I saw someone."

"Someone swimming?"

"No, I saw my ... I thought I saw people on the rocks. Well, not really people ... They had these ... They were ..." Kavya's heavy breathing muffled her words.

Mingming put her arm around Kavya's shoulder and whispered, "Oh, you mean the mermaids. We'll return here tomorrow to wait for them. They'll come back. They always come back."

-The End-

READING LIST

RESOURCES ABOUT INTERGENERATIONAL TRAUMA

Aamir, Dania and Shahzeb Khan. 2021. "Transgenerational Trauma and Postmemorial Atonement: A Case Study of Uzma Aslam Khan's 'The Miraculous True Story of Nomi Ali.'" *Journal of Politics and International Studies* 7 (1): 99–114.

Brave Heart, Maria Yellow Horse. 1998. "The Return to The Sacred Path: Healing the Historical Trauma Response Among the Lakota." *Smith College Studies in Social Work* 68 (3): 287–305.

Burke Harris, Nadine. 2018. *The Deepest Well: Healing the Long-Term Effects of Childhood Adversity*. Boston: Houghton Mifflin Harcourt.

Edkins, Jenny. 2003. *Trauma and the Memory of Politics*. Cambridge: Cambridge University Press.

Felsen, I. 1998. "Transgenerational Transmission of Effects of the Holocaust." In *International Handbook of Multigenerational Legacies of Trauma*, edited by Y. Danieli, 43–68. New York: Plenum.

Foo, Stephanie. 2022. *What My Bones Know: A Memoir of Healing from Complex Trauma*. New York: Ballantine Books.

Helbich, Maria and Samah Jabr. 2022. "A Call for Social Justice and for a Human Rights Approach with Regard to Mental Health in the Occupied Palestinian Territories." *Health and Human Rights Journal* 24 (2): 305–318.

Maxwell, Krista. 2014. "Historicizing Historical Trauma Theory: Troubling the Trans-Generational Transmission Paradigm." *Transcultural Psychiatry* 51 (3): 407–35. https://doi.org/10.1177/1363461514531317.

Menakem, Resmaa. 2017. *My Grandmother's Hands*. Las Vegas, NV: Central Recovery Press.

Million, Dian. 2020. "Trauma's Empty Promise: Indigenous Death, Economics, and Resurgence." In *The Routledge International Handbook of Global Therapeutic Cultures*, edited by Daniel Nehring, Ole Jacob Madsen, Edgar Cabanas, China Mills, and Dylan Kerrigan, 409–420. London: Routledge.

Mullan, Jennifer. 2023. *Decolonizing Therapy: Oppression, Historical Trauma, and Politicizing Your Practice*. New York: W.W. Norton and Company.

Soriano, Jen. 2023. *Nervous: Essays on Heritage and Healing*. New York: Amistad.

Van Der Kolk, Bessel. 2014. *The Body Keeps the Score: Brain, Mind, and Body in the Healing of Trauma*. New York: Penguin Books.

KAVYA'S STORY

Bahadur, Gaiutra. 2014. *Coolie Woman: The Odyssey of Indenture*. Chicago: University of Chicago Press, 63.

Black Loyalist Heritage Centre. n.d. "Black Loyalist Centre and Heritage Site Virtual Tour." https://blackloyalist.com/virtual-tours-offerings/.

Brown, Autumn and Adrienne Maree Brown. 2017. "A Breathing Chorus with Alexis Pauline Gumbs," December 19, 2017. *How to Survive the End of the World*. Podcast, website, 01:11:50. https://podcasters.spotify.com/pod/show/how-to-survive-the-end-of-the-world/episodes/A-Breathing-Chorus-with-Alexis-Pauline-Gumbs-ecs1b7/a-a1uuj67.

Coles, Justin A. 2021. "Black Desire: Black-centric Youthtopias as Critical Race Educational Praxis." *International Journal of Qualitative Studies in Education*: 1–22. https://doi.org/10.1080/09518398.2021.1888163.

Davis, Jalondra. 2021. "Crossing Merfolk, the Human, and the Anthropocene in Nalo Hopkinson's *The New Moon's Arms* and Rivers Solomon's *The Deep*." *Journal of the Fantastic in the Arts* 32 (3): 349–366.

Dutt, Yashica. 2019. *Coming Out as Dalit: A Memoir*. New Delhi: Aleph Book Company.

Feldman, Shelley. 1999. "Feminist Interruptions: The Silence of East Bengal in the Story of Partition." *Interventions* 1 (2): 167–82. https://doi.org/10.1080/13698019900510291.

Flaherty, Colleen. 2023. "Too Far Afield?" *Inside Higher Ed*, January 5, 2023. https://www.insidehighered.com/news/2023/01/06/u-houston-removes-social-justice%E2%80%93focused-dean-social-work.

Ghosh, Amitav. 2005. *The Shadow Lines*. New York: Mariner Books.

Ghosh, Joyjit and Mir Ahammad Ali, eds. 2022. *The Bleeding Border: Stories of Bengal Partition*. New Delhi: Niyogi Books.

Goetze, Catherine. 2022. "When the State Shatters Families. The US Separation Policy of 2018, Cruelty and Patrimonial Sovereignty." *Global Studies Quarterly* 2 (2): 1–10. https://doi.org/10.1093/isagsq/ksab050.

Grinage, Justin. 2019. "Endless Mourning: Racial Melancholia, Black Grief, and the Transformative Possibilities for Racial Justice in Education." *Harvard Educational Review* 89 (2): 227–250. https://doi.org/10.17763/1943-5045-89.2.227.

Gumbs, Alexis Pauline. 2017. "Bluebellow." *Strange Horizons*, January, 16, 2017. http://strangehorizons.com/fiction/bluebellow/.

Gumbs, Alexis Pauline. 2018. *M Archive: After the End of the World*. Durham: Duke University Press.

hooks, bell. 1994. *Teaching to Transgress: Education as the Practice of Freedom*. New York: Routledge, 207.

Lantigua-Williams, Juleyka. 2016. "When a Dictator Becomes Part of Your Family." *The Atlantic*, July 29, 2016. https://www.theatlantic.com/international/archive/2016/07/living-under-a-dictator/623463/.

Nayak, Meghana. 2020. "The Politics of Disinheritance." Special Issue on Inheritance, *Women's Studies Quarterly* 48 (1–2): 236–253.

Resende, Erica and Dovel Budryte. 2014. *Memory and Trauma in International Relations*. New York: Routledge.

Rich, Adrienne. 1972. "When We Dead Re-Awaken: Writing as Re-Vision." *College English* 34 (1): 18–30, 18. https://www.jstor.org/stable/375215.

Schwab, Gabriele. 2004. "Haunting Legacies: Trauma in Children of Perpetrators." *Post-colonial Studies* 7 (2): 177–195, 181, 184.

Soundararajan, Thenmozhi. 2022. *The Trauma of Caste: A Dalit Feminist Meditation on Survivorship, Healing, and Meditation.* Berkeley, CA: North Atlantic Books, 20–21, 61–62, 63–64.

Tapley, Jessica. 2021. "The Memory of Mythmaking: Transgenerational Trauma and Disability As A Collective Experience in Afrofuturist Storytelling." *Master's Theses and Doctoral Dissertations.* 1085. https://commons.emich.edu/theses/1085.

"'These Intergenerational Wounds Continue': How Trauma from Hurricane Katrina and COVID-19 are Affecting Black Orleanians." *The Root.* Video, 4:54. https://www.theroot.com/these-intergenerational-wounds-continue-how-trauma-fro-1844801046.

Tuck, Eve and K. Wayne Yang. 2012. "Decolonization Is Not a Metaphor." *Decolonization: Indigeneity, Education and Society* 1(1): 35.

Tuck, Eve and K. Wayne Yang. 2014. "Unbecoming Claims: Pedagogies of Refusal in Qualitative Research." *Qualitative Inquiry* 20 (6): 811–818. https://doi.org/10.1177/1077800414530265.

PARTITION AND COLORISM

Ahmed, Sara and Jackie Stacey, eds. 2001. *Transformations: Thinking Through the Skin.* London: Routledge.

Butalia, Urvashi. 2000. *The Other Side of Silence: Voices from the Partition of India.* Durham: Duke University Press.

Devi, Jyotirmoyee. 1968. *Epar Ganga, Opar Ganga [The River Churning: A Partition Novel].* Translated by Enakshi Chatterjee. New Delhi: Kali for Women.

Enjeti, Anjali. 2021. *The Parted Earth.* Spartanburg, SC: Hub City Press.

Ghosh, Vishwajyoti. 2013. *This Side, That Side: Restorying Partition, Graphic Narratives from Pakistan, India, Bangladesh.* Delhi: Yoda Press.

Hunter, Margaret. 2011. "Buying Racial Capital: Skin Bleaching and Cosmetic Surgery in a Globalized World." *Journal of Pan African Studies* 4 (4): 142–164. http://www.jpanafrican.org/archive_issues/vol4no4.htm.

Khan, Sorayya. 2003. *Noor.* Islamabad: Alhamra Publishing.

Khan, Yasmin. 2017. *The Great Partition: The Making of India and Pakistan.* New Edition. New Haven: Yale University Press.

Krishna, Sankaran. 1994. "Cartographic Anxiety: Mapping the Body Politic in India." *Alternatives: Global, Local, Political* 19 (4): 507–521.

Majumdar, Monica. 2023. "Colourism." In *Gender-Based Violence: A Comprehensive Guide,* edited by Parveen Ali and Michaela M. Rogers, 239–256. Cham, Switzerland: Springer Nature.

Menon, Madhavi. 2015. "Universalism and Partition: A Queer Theory." *differences* 26 (1): 117–140. https://doi.org/10.1215/10407391-2880627.

Menon, Ritu and Kamla Bhasin. 1998. *Borders and Boundaries: Women in India's Partition.* New Delhi: Kali for Women.

Mookerjea-Leonard, Debali. 2004. "Quarantined: Women and the Partition." *Comparative Studies of South Asia, Africa and the Middle East* 24 (1): 33–46. muse.jhu.edu/article/181217.

Raja, Fozia. 2020. *Daughters of Partition.* Creative Ethnics Publishing.

Roisin, Fariha. 2020. *Like a Bird.* Los Angeles, CA: Unnamed Press.

Rushdie, Salman. 2006. *Midnight's Children.* New York: Random House Trade Paperbacks.

Sah, Hema Gopinathan. 2018. "Kali." *The Aerogram,* May 21, 2018. Accessed February 23, 2023. https://theaerogram.com/read-original-poetry-kali/.

Sidhwa, Bapsi. 2006. *Cracking India.* Minneapolis: Milkweed Editions.

Singh Baldwin, Shauna. 2001. *What the Body Remembers.* New York: Random Books.

Sur, Malini. 2015. "Indelible Lines: Revisiting Borders and Partitions in Modern South Asia." *Mobility in History* 6 (1): 70–78. https://doi.org/10.3167/mih.2015.060108.

Zaminder, Vazira Fazila-Yacoobali. 2007. *The Long Partition and the Making of Modern South Asia: Refugees, Boundaries, Histories.* New York: Columbia University Press.

CASTE

Ayyathurai, Gajendran. 2021. "Emigration Against Caste, Transformation of the Self, and Realization of the Casteless Society in Indian Diaspora." *Essays in Philosophy* 22 (1/2): 45–65.

Claveyrolas, Mathieu. 2018. "From the Indian Ganges to a Mauritian Lake: Hindu Pilgrimage in a 'Diasporic' Context." In *Pilgrimage and Political Economy: Translating the Sacred,* edited by Simon Coleman and John Eade, 21–39. New York: Berghahn Books.

Das Gupta, Monisha, Charu Gupta, and Katerina Martina Teaiwa. 2007. "Rethinking South Asian Diaspora Studies." *Cultural Dynamics* 19 (2/3): 125–140.

Gidla, Sujatha. 2017. *Ants Among Elephants: An Untouchable Family and the Making of Modern India.* Farrar, Straus and Giroux.

Hui, Neha and Uma S. Kambhampati. 2002. "Between Unfreedoms: The Role of Caste in Decisions to Repatriate Among Indentured Workers." *The Economic History Review* 75 (2): 421–446.

Kabir, Ananya Jahanara. 2020. "Beyond Créolité and Coolitude, the Indian on the Plantation Re-creolization in the Transoceanic Frame." *Middle Atlantic Review of Latin American Studies* 4 (2): 174–193.

Lal, Brij V. 2012. *Chalo Jahaj: On a Journey Through Indenture in Fiji.* Canberra: ANU E Press.

Manian, Sabita, and Brad Bullock. 2020. "Indo-Caribbean Diaspora, Foreign Policy, and Iterations of Hindu Identity." *South Asian Diaspora* 13 (1): 81–97. https://doi.org/10.1080/19438192.2020.1773135.

Mehta, Brinda. 2004. *Diasporic (Dis)Locations: Indo-Caribbean Women Writers Negotiate the Kala Pani.* Mona, Jamaica: University of the West Indies Press.

Mootoo, Shani. 1996. *Cereus Blooms at Night.* Vancouver: Press Gang Publishers.

Naidoo, Karen. 2020. *Are You Looking at My Madness? Examining Canadian-Caribbean Youth's Intergenerational Stories of Mental Health.* Dissertation. Toronto: York University. http://hdl.handle.net/10315/37869.

Natarajan, Srividya, S. Anand, Durgabai Vyam, and Subhash Vyam. 2011. *Bhimayana: Experiences of Untouchability.* New Delhi: Navayana.

Natrajan, Balmurli. 2021. "Racialization and Ethnicization: Hindutva Hegemony and Caste." *Ethnic and Racial Studies* 45 (2): 298–318.

Teltumbde, Anand. 2020. *The Republic of Caste: Thinking Equality in the Time of Neoliberal Hindutva.* New Delhi: Navayana Publishing.

Wahab, Amar. 2022. "Introduction: Queering Indentureship." *Journal of Indentureship and Its Legacies* 2 (1): 1–14. https://www.jstor.org/stable/48676206.

FAMILY SEPARATION

Asim, Jabari. 2023. *Yonder.* New York: Simon and Schuster.

Bombay, Amy, Kimberly Matheson, and Hymie Anisman. 2014. "The Intergenerational Effects of Indian Residential Schools: Implications for the Concept of Historical Trauma." *Transcultural Psychiatry.* 51 (3): 320–338. https://doi.org/10.1177/1363461513503380.

Butler, Octavia E. 2018. *Kindred.* London: Headline Book Publishing.

Carlson, Kathryn Blaze. 2015. "Report Links Residential Schools with Missing and Murdered Women." *The Globe and Mail,* June 2. https://www.theglobeandmail.com/news/national/report-links-residential-schools-with-missing-and-murdered-women/article24763624/.

Chase, Yvonne Elder and Jessica Saniguq Ullrich. 2022. "A Connectedness Framework: Breaking the Cycle of Child Removal for Black and Indigenous Children." *International Journal of Child Maltreatment* 5 (1): 181–195. https://doi.org/10.1007/s42448-021-00105-6.

Crosby, Andrew. 2021. "The Racialized Logics of Settler Colonial Policing: Indigenous 'Communities of Concern' and Critical Infrastructure in Canada." *Settler Colonial Studies* 11 (4): 411–430, https://doi.org/10.1080/2201473X.2021.1884426.

Dafnos, Tia. 2019. "The Enduring Settler-Colonial Emergency: Indian Affairs and Contemporary Emergency Management in Canada." *Settler Colonial Studies* 9 (3): 379–395. https://doi.org/10.1080/2201473X.2018.1491157.

Dettlaff, Alan. 2023. *Confronting the Racist Legacy of the American Child Welfare System: The Case for Abolition.* Oxford: Oxford University Press.

Ehrlich, Julie B. 2007. "Breaking the Law by Giving Birth: The War on Drugs, The War on Reproductive Rights, and The War on Women." *N.Y.U. Review of Social Change* 32: 381–421.

Fong, Sarah E.K. 2019. "Racial-Settler Capitalism: Character Building and the Accumulation of Land and Labor in the Late Nineteenth Century." *American Indian Culture and Research Journal* 43 (2): 25–48. https://doi.org/10.17953/aicrj.43.2.fong.

Good, Michelle. 2020. *Five Little Indians.* Toronto: Ontario, Harper Perennial.

Hoosain, Shanaaz. 2013. "The Transmission of Intergenerational Trauma in Displaced Families." PhD Dissertation. Department of Social Work. University of the Western Cape. http://hdl.handle.net/11394/3572.

Jeffers, Honoree Fanonne. 2021. *The Love Songs of W. E. B. Du Bois*. New York: Harper Collins Pub.

Jones, Gayl. 1986. *Corregidora*. Boston: Beacon Press.

Lawther, Cheryl. 2021. "Haunting and Transitional Justice: On Lives, Landscapes and Unresolved Pasts." *International Review of Victimology* 27 (1): 3–22.

Laymon, Kiese. 2013. *Long Division*. New York: Scribner.

Mitchell, Mary Niall. 2008. *Raising Freedom's Child: Black Children and Visions of the Future After Slavery*. New York: New York University Press.

Morrison, Toni. 2007. *Beloved*. London, England: Vintage Classics.

Mosionier, Beatrice. 1983. *In Search of April Raintree*. Winipeg, Manitoba: Pemmican.

Pember, Mary Annette. 2021. "A History Not Yet Laid to Rest." *The Atlantic*, November 24, 2021. https://www.theatlantic.com/ideas/archive/2021/11/native-american -boarding-schools/620760/.

Roberts, Dorothy. 2022. *Torn Apart*. New York: Basic Books.

Sellars, Bev. 2013. *They Called Me Number One: Secrets and Survival at an Indian Residential School*. Vancouver, British Columbia: Talonbooks.

Webstad, Phyllis. 2018. *The Orange Shirt Story*. Victoria, BC: Medicine Wheel Education.

CLIMATE CHANGE AND SEA CREATURES

Anicca, Skye. 2017. "Cripping the Mermaid: A Borderlands Approach to Feminist Disability Studies in Valerie Martin's 'Sea Lovers.'" *Journal of Narrative Theory* 47 (3): 379–402. https://doi.org/10.1353/jnt.2017.0017.

Appanah, Nathacha. 2009. *Blue Bay Palace*. Translated by Alexandra Stanton. Wiltshire: Aflame Books.

Baptiste, Tracey. 2017. *Rise of the Jumbies*. Chapel Hill, North Carolina, Algonquin Young Readers, an imprint of Algonquin Books.

Bowen, Natasha. 2021. *Skin of the Sea*. New York: Random House.

DeLoughrey, Elizabeth and Tatiana Flores. 2020. "Submerged Bodies: The Tidalectics of Representability and the Sea in Caribbean Art." *Environmental Humanities* 12 (1): 132–166. https://doi.org/10.1215/22011919-8142242.

Indiana, Rita. 2018. *Tentacle*. Translated by Achy Obejas. Sheffield: And Other Stories.

Kim, Claudia J. 2021. "Dugong v. Rumsfeld: Social Movements and The Construction of Ecological Security." *European Journal of International Relations* 27 (1): 258–280. https://doi.org/10.1177/1354066120950013.

Palz, Marius. 2020. "A Sea Cow Goes to Court: Extinction and Animal Agency in a Struggle against Militarism." *Relations: Beyond Anthropocentrism* 8: 77–96. https://doi.org/10.7358/rela-2020-0102-palz.

Sen, Uditi. 2017. "Developing Terra Nullius: Colonialism, Nationalism, and Indigeneity in the Andaman Islands." *Comparative Studies in Society and History* 59 (4): 944–973. https://doi.org/10.1017/S0010417517000330.

ACKNOWLEDGMENTS

My nerves were jangling when I submitted my final book manuscript. But just as the book went into production, friends suggested I read Stephanie Foo's brilliant 2022 *What My Bones Know* (New York: Ballantine Books), Jen Soriano's gorgeous 2023 *Nervous* (New York: Amistad), and Jennifer Mullan's urgent 2023 *Decolonizing Therapy* (New York: W.W. Norton and Company). As I read them, I'm realizing my book can be part of this growing, collective journey to share the disjointed and brutal truths too many of us face as we process the aftermath of our ancestors' lives, and seek liberation and joy. As a note, I stitched together Kavya's life and world out of multiple, fragmented narratives, some mine but also those of many others.

I would not have been able to write my first novel without my friend and writing coach, Roohi Choudhry, or Shira Gregory and her stunning vision for the cover. I am also indebted to the people who assisted with information, facilitated key contacts, or read multiple drafts: Andrew Herbert, Catherine Beebe, Jennifer Haydel, Rose Curtin, Anna Gasha, Stephanie Stoddard, Naethra Sreekrishna, Laura Fung-Ross, Neha Charnalia, Miriam Alkon, R. Emilio Fernandez, Megan Milks, Jenny Lobasz, Niraj Nayak, Indigenous feminist activist colleagues who generously shared their thoughts about collective soul wounds, and the facilitators of the Equality Labs Unlearning Caste Supremacy workshop, the Reading Dalit Writers book club, and Academics 4 Black Lives events. Thank you to the Series Editors (Cristina Masters, shine choi, Swati Parashar, Marysia Zalewski), Michael Kerns, Elizabeth Von Buhr, Lynn Zelem, and the entire team at Rowman and Littlefield, three anonymous reviewers, and the Pace University Provost Book Completion Grant. My deepest gratitude goes to my incredibly smart and inspirational students.

And, last of all, but always first of all, I am forever grateful for the little family I created, S, A, and S.

About the Author

Meghana V. Nayak is professor of political science and chair of the Women's and Gender Studies Department at Pace University-NYC. Her previous publications include *Who Is Worthy of Protection: Gender-Based Asylum and U.S. Immigration Politics* (Oxford University Press, 2015) and *Decentering International Relations* (with Eric Selbin, Zed Press, 2010). Her work on gender violence has been published in various journals and edited volumes and has been used by organizations working with asylum seekers. *Tilt* is her first novel.